Seeker from Eden 3

by Ron Lewis

Literary Wanderlust | Denver, Colorado

Published in the United States by Literary Wanderlust LLC Denver, Colorado.

www.LiteraryWanderlust.com

ISBN Paperback: 978-1-956615-29-6
ISBN Digital: 978-1-956615-30-2

Printed in the United States of America

Dedication

For Laura and Olivia
You are my inspiration, my joy, and my purpose
I love you always

Chapter 1

Opal Five

I was awakened by a voice in my sleeping pod at 5:00 a.m.

Our valet program typically had a melodious tone, but she could become stern when I didn't follow the schedule. "Opal, the time is 5:00 a.m. Please rise."

"May . . . I need five more minutes."

"Opal, grooming begins at 5:05 a.m. You must secure your shell and take your morning meal by 5:20 a.m."

"I'm not hungry."

"Opal Five, your body requires adequate nourishment. Advanced assessments begin at 11:00 a.m. You will not have another opportunity for a meal."

When challenged, May referred to my embryonic stem line generation. I usually argued with her for several minutes, but that day she was right. There was only one chance at assessments, and I needed to be sharp. Although I ranked at the top of my secondary classes, only a high outcome would ensure my position in advanced development. If not successful, I might be assigned an occupation on levels one through four or, worse, the sub-levels. I planned to improve my status and be promoted to level ten.

"May, please open my pod."

The opaque shield rolled up, exposing me to the blue light of our quarters. The pod was one of my favorite spaces in Life World. May could raise the temperature above the sixty-eight degrees of our general environment *and* adjust the range of sensory input, including near deprivation. It's also where I hid my cache of sweet cubes. All residents received five of the delicious treats each week. Ares didn't care for the taste and shared his allotment with me.

I crossed the room and placed my sleeping garment in a narrow storage closet. "May, please open the grooming stall."

I entered the circular stall and placed my feet on floor sensors. Dispensers on the fore wall portioned out dental powder and an oil-based hair gel. After initial preparations, I stretched my arms above my head. "May, please start the grooming cycle."

"Grooming cycle initiated."

The stall panel closed, and pressure began building in the ports. Jets of air and moisture pulsated around me from hundreds of tiny outlets. After sixty seconds, the outlets closed and dryers began to blow. I grimaced when the final stage began—the chamber became a vacuum, recovering all moisture. The pressure hurt my ears. Water was precious in Life World, and virtually every molecule was recycled.

I removed my microdermic polycarbon shell from the closet. The nanoparticle membrane was designed to expand with growth but often feels snug in the morning. Male and female shells contrasted in the way they compensated for body development and, of course, the size and shape of the genital carapace. The tan color was not very flattering. Although our scriptures explained the symbolism, I believed the dark gray male color would look better with my eyes.

I stepped into my general-use sandals and secured the braided belt around my waist. It supported my cyber interface drive case and had additional pockets for miscellaneous items. What our clothing lacked in variety, it overcame with efficiency and utility. A few brush strokes through my hair, then off to the morning meal.

"Good morning, Opal. Did you sleep well?" Jade asked.

My mother parent was perfectly groomed, her long hair pulled back tightly. Her inspection of me was quick and barely perceptible. She thought I didn't notice, but after the greeting, she always paused to examine my shorter hair. It was a point of contention between us. I selected the textured bob option during our monthly visit to the automated atrium vendor. She insisted my hair was chosen for its quality and should be put on display. Although intense at times, she had incredible patience and a sincere, nurturing warmth about her.

"Good morning, Jade. I slept well until being startled awake by a peculiar voice in my pod." Harassing May brought me special pleasure in the morning.

"Opal, my instructions were to awaken you at 5:00 a.m."

"Oh, was that you, May? I didn't recognize your voice."

"There have been no adjustments to my tone. Shall I schedule an aural examination for you?"

Jade sometimes joined in the sparring, but she seemed preoccupied.

"May, an examination for Opal won't be required. Please inform my lab to prepare the cryo-tubes I requested for the 6:00 a.m. procedure."

May was constantly interfaced with the Core. Sometimes there was a slight delay when she completed tasks outside of our quarters.

"Jade, your lab confirmed receipt of your instructions."

Jade finished her meal then placed her dishes and utensils in the sterilizer. Ares appeared from the interface room just as she was leaving.

"Good morning, Opal."

He squeezed my shoulder on his way to bid Jade farewell. They rarely showed affection in my presence, so it was surprising when he placed his cheek on hers. I barely made out what he said.

"See you tonight, love."

He returned and took his place at the table. Ares was a man of few words, and we sat in silence for several minutes. Although generally warm with me, recently he, too, seemed distant. He offered a glancing smile then stared down at his meal as if theorizing its very molecular structure. My announcement broke his trance.

"I have assessments today."

"Yes, I recall," he said. "Jade mentioned you were up late reviewing files. Are you concerned with the sciences?"

"Star and I have different results on the subject of plant growth," I began. "She believes mitosis continues in fully differentiated cells."

"What is your understanding?"

"I tried to help her recall the distinction between specialized and nonspecialized cells, but she insists newly edited strains can still divide, even after terminal differentiation."

"Does she have data to support her theory?"

"She said there's a new source, but won't cite the study. I searched for it last night."

He paused for a moment, seemingly searching his brain, reviewing banks of stored information.

"I appreciate your concern in light of your assessments," he began. "Don't allow yourself to be distracted by your classmate's incorrect assertion."

"So, she is wrong."

"There are individuals who exhibit certain undesirable characteristics under pressure. She may have sincerely misunderstood her source or . . .

"Or she's purposefully creating confusion?"

"All I'm saying is to trust your instincts. You've excelled in your classes and are well-prepared for today. Now, I must attend to a matter before my class begins. Do you mind clearing the table?"

"Not at all. Thank you, Ares."

He clipped his drive case onto his belt and approached the entrance.

"May, please open the entrance panel."

The matter he had to attend was likely final preparations for his advanced class's assessments. He's an absolute perfectionist and expected the same from his physics and engineering students. It must be intimidating to study under such a brilliant professor. As if they weren't under enough pressure, he was recently recognized for new developments in amorphous silicon production. I waited for him to depart then returned to my meal.

Chapter 2

Interface

May announced that one hour remained before I needed to leave. It was going to be a long day with assessments, so I ate my full meal as she recommended. Although her persistence could be annoying at times, her primary objective was our welfare. I cleared the settings from the table.

"May, please start the dish sterilizer."

"Opal, sterilizer cycle initiated."

I decided to take one more look at the files on plant growth. Even if Ares was unaware of new developments on mitosis due to genetic editing, I wasn't convinced Star was purposefully misleading me. After all, she ranked second behind me in our classes. She was also my closest friend.

"May, please open the interface room."

I entered the dimly lit room and stepped in front of the modular workstation. Although our personal drives were capable of interfacing throughout the sanctuary, this room provided a 360-degree visual field. It allowed significantly more files and data sheets to be displayed at once. As I opened my case, an object on the workstation caught my attention. I checked to be sure my drive was still on my belt. It was *Ares's* drive—in operational mode.

How is this possible? Drives could only be activated by the user. I examined the identification screen closely. Perhaps it was sensing residual DNA from his skin oils. The neuro-loops were retracted, but they only extended after a unit is placed on the hand. *Will his drive transmit data to my interpreters?*

My first impulse was to have May alert Ares, but the glowing ID screen was mesmerizing. I quickly calculated the time required for him to reach his class then return when he discovered the drive missing. At most, I had thirty minutes of interface time before he reached our quarters. *A great deal can be explored in thirty minutes.*

I removed my optic interface interpreters from the case. The thin silicon moldings fit neatly around my eyes. I picked up his drive. *How can it remain operational with the loops retracted?* Shaking away the thoughts, I placed the unit on my left hand. The six loops emerged and closed around my fingers and wrist. Command images appeared eighteen inches in front of my face. Tapping a floating icon with my finger, a three-segment console appeared vertically, chest high. The first two segments were standard issue. The third was a rather complicated scientific calculating device. It was obviously customized for Ares's classes. I recognized the mathematical symbols and many of the formulas.

What I saw next startled me. Only select members of the professorate were granted direct access to the Core. An indicator showed that a Core sector eight encrypted user code had been entered. My mind raced, contemplating the wonders within the sector. *What punishment will I face if my trespass is discovered?* The adrenaline surging through my body made me slightly ill. My heart pounded, fingers quivered. The blinking indicator seemed to grow brighter.

A battle raged inside me as tenets from our scriptures scrolled through my mind—faith, obedience, discipline, sacrifice, truth. Simultaneously a cloud of desire, fueled by a primal obsession to discover and know, filled every remaining neuron. My heart told me to disengage, walk away, and do what was so obviously right.

With my eyes closed, I made my decision. Happy for my resolve and believing my sacred vows were preserved, I opened my eyes, expecting to see the blinking light still taunting me. Instead, a new universe appeared before me. Sector eight was open.

My heart rate soared. *How did this happen?* A damaged synapse in my brain must have sent the wrong signal to my finger. Evidently my subconscious desire overcame my moral foundation. *This is absolute disobedience. Am I capable of worse?*

The thoughts of uncertainty quickly drifted away as I marveled at the number of data files floating around me. I twisted and contorted, scanning titles of an endless stream of access points. I pivoted left, and one point appeared out of place. Imperceptible at first, it was slightly unparallel with others in the category. It was labeled Atmosphere.

The console indicated 6:01 a.m. If Ares had opened his case by now, he might return within twenty minutes. Closing the sector and interfacing with my own drive required only two minutes. Unfortunately, that would not be enough time if he came directly to the room. Although he would instruct May to notify me of his presence, he wouldn't wait long.

Twenty minutes wasn't ample time to explore sector eight thoroughly, but I decided not to waste the opportunity. When the Atmosphere file opened, multiple pages appeared. The data had been recently edited. The first page was a series of charts indicating compositions of oxygen, nitrogen, carbon, and other elements with comparisons over time. The next page was similar, indicating temperature, pressure, humidity, and—I looked closer to verify the word—*precipitation?*

Chapter 3

Invitation

The door chime sounded one bell, indicating our front panel was opened. I closed the Atmosphere file and quickly exited sector eight. Turning the ID screen bezel on Ares's drive one click to the left rendered it non-operational. I returned it to the workstation then moved quickly toward the entrance.

"May, please open the interface room."

Before she responded, the circular panel slid open. Ares stood in front of me.

"Opal, panel is now open."

"Ares," I said, feigning surprise.

"I'm sorry to startle you. Did you happen to see my drive?"

"Yes, on the workstation."

I'd purposefully left my case open with the drive and interpreters visible. "I searched for new studies on mitosis which might support Star's assertion. One suggested the continuation of division, but the author discounted his observations in the conclusion. He cited potential contamination in his experiment. It appears Star is only reviewing subject headings and not reading full studies."

"Well done, Opal. You'll let her down easy, won't you?"

"Of course," I replied. "It's a relief to know it was poor research on her part and not deceit."

The word deceit hung in the air during an awkward moment of silence. Never before had I lied to Ares—or anyone. A pang of regret gnawed at me for having put myself in this situation. There was, however, a noted surge of exhilaration. Ares nodded as he walked by me to retrieve his drive. Without further discussion, I headed to my room.

"Opal—"

I froze at the sound of my name, then slowly turned to face him. I expected to see a scowl or his brow furrowed in anger, but he was actually smiling.

"Jade invited us to her laboratory this evening to demonstrate a new breakthrough she developed. I'm sure you'll be tired after assessments, but are you interested in accompanying me?"

It might have been a good idea to briefly consider the invitation. "Of course," I blurted out instead. "We haven't been to her lab in ages."

"Good. We'll go after our evening meal."

I stood in the same position with a silly grin on my face. Riddled with guilt, I analyzed my every word, action, and movement. *Did he know my secret?* He didn't seem suspicious, but he did look at me longer than normal.

"Have you completed your research?" he finally asked.

My grin turned to a wide smile. *Stop smiling, Opal.* "Yes, I'm finished."

"Very well. May, please close the interface room."

He touched my shoulder on his way out. "Good luck today. I'll see you this evening."

And then he was gone. Breathing deeply and exhaling

slowly, I replayed our interaction in my mind—trying to recall irregularities. He was more attentive than normal, but it stands to reason given we were alone in the conversation. He didn't search my eyes to detect dishonesty and made no facial expressions indicating suspicion. I sighed with relief. My transgression wasn't discovered, and I'd managed a glimpse into a forbidden sector. I decided instantly never to tell another soul—not even Star.

Chapter 4

Corruption

"May, what's the time?"

"Opal, the time is 6:32 a.m."

We were required to be interfaced by 7:00 a.m., and it only took ten minutes to reach the campus. I left early, intending to speak with Star about her research error before class. We planned to enter advanced development together, and a simple error in research shouldn't negatively impact her assessment outcomes.

I mingled with other residents in the corridor. Level nine was designated for families, so many were leading children to the primary campus. I walked along, searching the faces of passersby, looking for indications of suspicion. The paranoia was almost crippling. I hadn't come to terms with breaching the forbidden sector. My guilt was tormenting me.

I reached the main corridor and turned right, passing directly in front of a KPR sentry platform. The so-called Keepers of Peace for Residents now exist as a policing force. The impulse to run was overwhelming, but I managed to remain calm. Keepers were trained to react to abnormal situations, and such action could trigger a pursuit response. Just glancing back was reason enough to detain me for questioning.

A tingling sensation disturbed the back of my neck like eyes were boring into me. I expected a gloved hand to grab my shoulder and spin me around, the keeper's reflective visor inches from my face while he screamed the codes of my infractions. The worst part would be residents stopping to watch my arrest, judging me, denouncing me as corrupt and immoral. They would scoff and jeer and take delight in my pleas for mercy.

When fingers touched my lower back, a jolt shot through my body. I gasped, froze, and waited for the inevitable. Star circled in front of me and offered a wide, bright smile.

"Opal, I called for you twice," she said.

I tried to hide my relief. "Sorry, I didn't hear you."

"Is everything all right? You look anxious."

I forced myself to relax and sighed. "My review lasted all night and into this morning. I just want to do well."

"Opal, you have the highest scores in our class, and you've done nothing but prepare the entire term. We'll be number one and two on the outcomes and move on, just like we planned."

Star was an eternal optimist and always made the most stressful of times manageable. Her glimmering smile showed brilliantly in contrast to her smooth ebony skin. Staring at her this moment, I couldn't recall a time when she wasn't smiling. Her confidence was enviable, especially considering the weight of my new burden. My own smile was purposefully exaggerated as I repeated our private motto. "We two—forever."

"That's better," she said. "Now let's move or we'll be late, and Professor Marc will reduce our interface time."

She grabbed my arm and pulled me along. We giggled at the reaction of residents. The morning commute is supposed to be a quiet, solemn time when one reflects on the day ahead. It was generally acceptable for young ones to be a bit unruly, but not our age group. The sight of a keeper near the lift station caused us to straighten our backs and walk the remaining distance in a silent cadence.

It was a short lift ride to five. We reached our lecture hall well before the 7:00 a.m. chime. Star and I took our usual seats in the first row, directly in front of the lectern. Students continued to fill the arced tables, some sitting conspicuously far away. It was a pointless exercise. Professor Marc would recognize the change immediately and make them regret their strategy. I knew our classmates by name but rarely spent time with any of them.

We slipped our interpreters on and activated our drives as the interface cycle began. Professor Marc instructed in both plant biology and chemistry, often covering both subjects in the same lecture. It was fortunate our drives recorded class sessions because he often moved quickly through the material. He was third generation professorate and had little patience for inept or apathetic students. The sections being covered in this session were meant as review for our upcoming assessments.

He opened several files and began quizzing students on the topic headings floating in front of them. Correct responses were generally followed by one or two follow-up questions. Any error in response resulted in a series of rapid queries until the targeted scholar recovered their standing or crumbled under the pressure in a fit of tears. Professors knew what was at stake for students and showed little mercy. Class scores, combined with assessment outcomes, determined which occupations were assigned by the Noble Court. Although students were entitled to one appeal should their assignment not be preferred, they were rarely successful.

The next topic heading appeared in front of Star. To my horror, it read: PLANT CELL DIVISION - INTERPHASE AND MITOSIS. I held my breath as Professor Marc called on my friend.

"Star, recite in order the phases of plant mitosis."

She took a deep breath then proceeded. "Professor, the

phases of plant mitosis are the prophase, metaphase, anaphase, telophase, and cytokinesis."

Well done, Star. I waited for her follow-up questions. To my surprise, there were none. Professor Marc moved on to another student. I expected him to return to her, but he never did. Our review session ended at 9:30 a.m. and we were dismissed for a break. He instructed us to return at 10:30 a.m. for registration.

Star and I sat in the common area outside of the lecture halls. We observed classmates frantically quizzing each other on various subjects. Unfortunately, if they didn't know the material by then, the exercise was futile. Many looked absolutely defeated, resigned to accept whatever fate the Noble Court forced upon them. They would regret the lack of enthusiasm toward their studies when they found themselves in the water treatment or air separation plants in sub-level four.

As we sat in silence, it occurred to me we never resolved our earlier disagreement. "Star, you were very confident responding to Professor Marc on the phases of mitosis. Have you changed your opinion on the continued division of terminally differentiated cells?"

She hesitated before responding, then smiled. "You were right Opal. You're always right."

She turned away and her smile faded. She sighed, watching our classmates—looking from one to another. I thought about my earlier conversation with Ares and found myself questioning Star's motives. My own sigh was out of frustration. *What does she gain by creating confusion?* Glancing down at my twirling thumbs, I spotted her slightly open case. The neuro-loops were retracted into the drive, which is normal for an inoperative unit. What was entirely unexpected was seeing the familiar glow of an activated ID screen.

The events of the morning flashed through my mind. The interface room, Ares's drive, sector eight, and my agonizing march past the keepers. *How did I succumb to such disobedience—such betrayal? Everything I worked for has been wasted. Everyone will soon know.* I took a deep breath and focused on the moment, searching my mind for a logical explanation. Looking back at Star's case, I could see I wasn't alone in my corruption.

Chapter 5

Assessment

The sound of her case snapping shut caused me to flinch. Feeling the weight of her stare, I looked up into Star's eyes—those reassuring eyes which so often offered respite from the pressures of our studies. She gave a half smile.

"Shall we return to class?" she asked.

"Yes, of course. The assessments won't complete themselves, will they?" I immediately regretted the comment. It took three or four steps before she responded, but it wasn't what I expected.

"What if they could?" she whispered.

I stopped and turned to her. "Star, what are you talking about?" I waited for her to reveal some conspiracy—a secret plot into which I would be drawn.

"I'm joking, silly. You really need to relax more, Opal. Perhaps less preparation and more meditation."

We burst into laughter. I sighed with relief as we turned and continued toward the hall. She wrapped her arm around mine and gave me a reassuring squeeze.

As we entered the hall, Professor Marc directed us to our assigned positions. During assessments, students were confined in individual particle spheres. Drives were unable to recognize data outside of the invisible barrier, ensuring outcomes represented our own knowledge and abilities. It was understood that any attempt to manipulate a sphere resulted in immediate expulsion. As far as we knew, no one had ever succeeded in such an endeavor.

After I activated my drive, the interpreters came alive with moving data streams and prompts to begin registration. The vertical console blinked in rhythm with my keystrokes, providing a visual compliment to what might have been a familiar sonata. The system accepted my personal information and code. My heart rate increased, anticipating the first file to open.

I mentally scrolled through our syllabus. *Have I forgotten anything?* I thought of Star and her misinterpretation of specialized plant cells. Ares's words of reassurance and advice to trust my instincts came to mind. I closed my eyes, took a deep breath, and slowly bowed my head in a moment of calm certainty.

When I opened my eyes, the sphere was void of sound and light. The only thing visible was a tiny greenish orb rotating slowly in front of me. After several seconds, the orb started expanding and pulsating. A veil of light formed a faint aura around the mass. I was momentarily entranced, lost in its cool rhythmic motion. At six inches in diameter, it reversed course and began to contract and spin faster. It grew smaller and smaller until it was just a pinpoint of barely perceptible light. I focused hard, trying not to lose sight of it in the blackness. Without warning, it exploded, sending a million specks of light in every direction. The specks filled the sphere like an enclosed galaxy of stars and planets.

One of the floating specks contorted into a mathematical equation with one variable absent. I recognized the first fundamental theorem of calculus and completed the equation. Another speck to my right demanded the range of wavelengths on the visible electromagnetic spectrum. As quickly as I entered 380 to 740 nanometers, another speck expanded into the periodic table of elements. It demanded the number of protons present in various highlighted selections. The challenges were completely random, switching from mathematics to chemistry, anatomy to literature, even scriptures, and recent decrees. I had no concept how much time had passed and was mentally exhausted when the challenges ceased.

As I awaited further instructions, the specks of light began moving toward some invisible center, like being drawn into the gravitational field of a black hole. The collection of lights formed back into a solid orb, which continued to expand until restored to its original size. The orb resumed its rotation, light pulsating in the familiar rhythm. After a few seconds, the rotation stopped, the green light intensified. The glow was so brilliant, I was forced to look away. Then it was gone—blackness.

The particle sphere around me lifted. Professor Marc was monitoring those students still engaged. His lectern screen indicated 2:09 p.m. We were allowed a maximum of four hours to complete the assessments. A wave of relief came over me. *There was time to spare.* I turned the bezel on my drive and watched the neuro-loops retract and ID screen fade. I removed my interpreters and placed both units in my case. Professor Marc caught my attention and indicated his approval for me to depart.

I approached the entranceway and turned back. There were seventy or more students still engaged, but Star wasn't among them. I stepped into the common area and glanced at the bench we'd occupied earlier, expecting her to be waiting for me. She wasn't there. Instead of searching further, I opted to return for a rest before the evening meal. It would be my only opportunity before Jade's presentation.

I decided to contact Star after visiting the lab. Our outcomes would have arrived by then. Although confident in my results, I wasn't certain about hers. Moving on to advanced without her wouldn't be the same. There was no replacement for her laughter and reassuring smile.

Chapter 6

Guilty Conscience

Our evening meal was typical for a Friday—a small piece of fish, micro greens, fava beans, and individual baguettes. All food in Life World was produced in the sub-levels in perfectly balanced climates controlled by the Core. In primary, we'd studied the means of production without actually seeing the facilities. Sub-level one was where fruits and vegetables grew in vertical cultivation layers using hydroponics and spectrum-controlled lighting. Sub-level two was devoted to poultry, and sub-level three was an aquaculture facility. With remarkable efficiency, byproducts from each cultivated environment were cross utilized. Bioreactors ensured very little of plant or animal was lost to waste.

As we sat for our meal, Jade glanced back and forth between Ares and me. She seemed anxious for a conversation to begin. Ares finally spoke.

"Opal, how were assessments?"

I swallowed my sprouts and cleared my throat. "I believe they went well. Although I finished in just over three hours, there was a handful of students who completed before me, including Star."

"Don't be concerned with others," Jade said. "Advanced students are selected on individual merit. You certainly excelled in your classes."

Ares added to Jade's comments. "She's right, Opal. You'll likely have your choice of opportunities."

He offered a reassuring smile with his comment. Jade stared at him with a blank expression. I watched her for a moment. She glanced at me, then quickly looked down at her plate. There was some underlying issue about to surface, and the current conversation was just a preamble. The panic from my morning interaction with Ares returned. *What are they waiting for?* I absently pushed food around my plate with a fork. Ares finished his meal and pushed his chair back from the table. He watched me make figure-eight patterns around my beans.

"Are you feeling up to visiting the lab?" he asked, placing his linen napkin next to his plate.

I looked up at him then over to Jade, who was anticipating my response. "Of course. I'm not tired at all," I replied, hoping my tone hadn't revealed my guilt.

Jade stood, taking her plate and utensils. "You won't need your drive," she said, placing her setting on the counter. "My work can be displayed through projection."

I ate the last of my beans then cleared the table. The organic matter recycler was already open, allowing me to scrape food remnants into the hopper. I loaded the place settings into the sterilizer.

Jade put our napkins in the laundry receptacle. "Are there more linens?" she asked. "The caddy is ready for delivery."

Ares shook his head. "None for me."

"No thank you," I replied. "Mine were changed yesterday."

She touched a sensor next to the receptacle, sealing the

laundry caddy.

"May, please schedule laundry retrieval."

"Jade, laundry retrieval is scheduled for 7:00 p.m. Estimated return is Saturday at 9:00 a.m."

"Shall we go?" Ares asked, standing near the entrance.

As we stepped out of our quarters, Jade paused.

"May, we expect to return by 9:00 p.m."

"Jade, expected return time noted."

Chapter 7

Revelation

Jade's laboratory was located on six, near the hospital and reproductive units. We walked into the central common area. The standard assortment of messages appeared on the corridor walls. Imaging drones used lasers to project motivational phrases and lines of scripture onto random surfaces. They were constant reminders of our responsibilities to the preservation of Life World and devotion to The Giver. As we approached the lift station, a familiar voice rang out.

"Opal!"

I turned to see Star approaching from the adjacent station.

"Hello, Star."

She smiled wide as she stopped in front of us. "Hello, Jade. Ares."

"Good evening, Star," they said in unison.

"Opal, where are you going? Results will be announced soon."

"We're visiting Jade's lab for a demonstration. You weren't in the common area after assessments."

Her expression turned to subtle surprise. "Opal, I waited almost ten minutes for you. It was apparent you were using the full allotment of time."

Perhaps it was my puzzled look or some cue from Jade or Ares, but she abruptly ended the conversation. "Well, enjoy your visit to the lab."

She turned and marched toward the corridor leading to her own quarters. The three of us entered the lift without speaking.

We approached the laboratory in silence. Jade placed her hand on the ID screen and the primary panel slid open. We stepped inside and waited for the next step in the entry protocol.

"I made arrangements for our visit," she started. "Identification and approval should be brief."

A small port opened next to the inner panel and a biometric authentication laser scanned our faces. The overlapping inner panels slid open. They closed after we entered. The lab hadn't changed since my last visit two years before. It was divided into three sections separated by glass partitions. We were standing in the outer section, used primarily for changing into appropriate protective gear. Jade motioned us toward the side wall.

"Ares, use locker one. Opal, locker two," she said.

She opened a third locker and removed white aseptic coveralls with a separate tech hood. During my last visit, we weren't able to enter the critical spaces. *I'm actually going into the clean rooms.* My excitement grew at the thought of accessing such an important space. We donned the one-piece fitted coveralls, complete with attached boots. Curiously, the sleeves ended at the wrist. The tech hood covered my head and draped over my shoulders, creating a layered seal. It included a clear face visor with breathing ports to prevent condensation.

After we dressed, Jade led us to a pedestal at the entrance of the clean room. On top of the pedestal were two stainless steel tubes supporting ring structures about eight inches in diameter.

Inside the rings were thin, white membranes.

"Observe," she insisted.

We watched Jade open her fingers and push her hands through the rings up to her middle arm. The membranes released from the rings, forming a perfect glove-like seal around the fingers, hands, and sleeves. When she removed her arms, new membranes appeared. Ares and I repeated the process then waited for further instructions.

Jade stepped to the right of the entrance where a second biometric laser verified her identity. Again, we followed her lead and completed the process. After entering a sealed compartment, she directed us to stand on floor sensors outlined by red blinking lights. We mimicked her movements, raising our arms just out from our sides. Three loop-shaped devices, large enough to encircle our bodies, lowered from overhead. The scanning coils emitted an ultraviolet laser in a solid plane. They cycled from head to foot, then returned to their original positions. Jade later explained that the disinfectant compartment eliminated potential contaminates from outer garments.

An amber light blinked above the entranceway. The vacuum stage initiated, causing the same ear pain as in my grooming stall. I was relieved when it ended. The blinking light turned solid green and the panel before us slid open. We followed Jade into the genetic engineering laboratory. She walked briskly to the rear of the lab. My head was on a swivel, trying to identify the various apparatus along the way.

Four DNA extraction cabinets, complete with ultraviolet laser modules and miniature robotic manipulators, lined the near side. There were centrifuges, incubators, and thermal cyclers, all encased in airtight acrylic enclosures. Rushing past all the wondrous equipment, I wanted to yell for Jade to slow down. Before words escaped my mouth, she manually accessed another room. *Why don't they use a valet in the lab?* I assumed it was for security purposes. Ares waved his hand, urging me to enter. I stepped inside and Jade sealed the room.

We were surrounded by cryopreservation cylinders, each four feet high and three feet in diameter. Jade had mentioned the facility many times, and her description left little room for imagination. Electronic displays on each cylinder indicated the temperature. A series of numeric codes identified the contents. Before any words were spoken, Jade did the last thing imaginable—she removed her hood. I gasped. Ares followed her lead and removed his hood. My expression must have shown absolute panic as Jade stepped forward and put her hands on my shoulders.

"It's okay, Opal."

The calmness in her voice helped to settle me. Ares stepped closer and nodded his reassurance. "You need to trust us," he added.

Jade pulled her hands back and stood in silence. They looked on while I slowly pulled my hood up and over my head. I breathed through my nose anticipating strange odors, but there were none. The air was cool and dry. The only sound was a faint humming from the cylinder pumps.

Jade spoke first. "Don't worry about the room. A disinfectant cycle runs every six hours. The cylinders are sealed." She looked at Ares.

"Opal," he started, pausing briefly. "My drive was left in the interface room this morning. We know you accessed sector eight."

His statement sent a shock wave through my body. My mouth fell open. Blood pulsed in my neck with every rapid heartbeat. Looking at their faces, I searched my mind for an appropriate response, imagining the worst possible punishment for my flagrant disobedience. It then occurred to me every word spoken in Life World was transmitted to the Core. I frantically scanned the room, looking for electronic devices. Jade recognized my alarm.

"Opal, calm down," she said softly. "We can't be seen or heard. This room has no connection to the Core. It's called a shadow space."

My breathing neared the point of hyperventilation. Tears welled in my eyes and ran down my cheeks. "I'm sorry. It was a mistake to access the portal. I was disengaging—my finger touched the console—it was wrong!"

Ares squeezed my shoulders. "Breathe. You're not in trouble." He looked at me squarely. "I purposefully left my drive activated. You were meant to access sector eight."

"But . . . why?"

He released my shoulders and patted my arm. I calmed from my hysterics, dabbed my cheeks with my sleeves, and waited. They looked at each other as if synchronizing their thoughts. Jade spoke first.

"What we're about to discuss can't be repeated to anyone. Do you understand?"

"Yes."

Ares emphasized the point. "Not Star, not anyone."

"I understand."

Jade's words were measured. "Opal . . . certain aspects of Life World are not what they seem. There is information nobles don't want residents to know."

"What information?"

"This room, for instance. Nobles prefer that all residents believe every spoken word and action is transmitted to the Core, and therefore to them. The reality is, many spaces in Life World are not monitored."

It was evident I wasn't grasping the full magnitude of her comments. Ares picked up where Jade left off.

"If nobles can't see or hear residents, they lose control over them. Correct?"

"I suppose," I replied, still wondering if some punishment was forthcoming for the interface incident. They continued patiently, but Jade took a more direct approach.

"Do you believe everything in our scriptures?" she asked.

"Yes, of course," I said quickly, assuming it was a test of my devotion.

"Tell me, Opal—" She paused. "What is the mandatory expiration age for all residents in Life World?"

"Expiration is age fifty."

"For all residents? Including nobles?"

"Yes, for all." My response included a quote from our creed. "I will serve Life World until expiration in my fiftieth year, as willed by The Giver, as covenant for my salvation."

"Opal, I've worked in this laboratory for twelve years. Are you certain of my expertise in selective reproduction?"

"Of course. You're well regarded in biotechnology and genetics."

"If I were to share information about my work, you would accept it as factual?"

"Without question."

She inhaled through her nose and held it for a moment. "Noble offspring are created without the modified expiration gene. Nobles don't abide by the decree expected of all in Life World. They can live well beyond ninety years."

She watched my expression, waiting for a response. I'd never seen a noble outside of Assembly. As direct descendants of the Prophets, they typically didn't interact with the general population. They resided in the upper levels and enjoyed certain luxuries not afforded to the remainder of residents. But they're certainly not exempt from the scriptures or decrees.

"How is it possible?" I questioned, repeating the creed segment. "I will serve Life World until expiration in my fiftieth year." My confusion turned to anger. "Nobles lead us at Assembly. It's not right."

"That's why we brought you here tonight," Ares added.

His face blurred through my tears. A tremendous pressure was building in my chest, preventing me from catching my breath. My entire belief system was being torn apart. "Is there more?" I asked, between gasps.

Jade stood rigid. "Sixty years in the past, Roma Two

was the lead geneticist in this lab. Her team was assigned the task of editing two noble offspring. They were provided specimens instead of utilizing those preserved, in accordance with reproductive decrees. Roma analyzed the DNA of those specimens. The modified expiration genes were absent."

"Did she inform the Noble Court?"

"Yes, and she was never again seen in Life World. Before reporting her findings to the Court, she confided in a fellow geneticist whom she befriended." Jade paused and glanced at Ares. "His name was Silas Two. He led the Seekers."

"Seekers?"

Ares grew excited. "Yes, Seekers—those who seek the truth about Life World." He moved close to me. "What we've shared with you is only the beginning of the lies and deceit propagated by nobles over the last two centuries. They're indeed descendants of the Prophets—the first elitists to exploit those chosen to enter this sanctuary. We're not residents of Life World, Opal. We're subjects."

"...Are you?"

"Yes," he responded emphatically. "We too are Seekers."

He paused for a moment, allowing me to absorb the onslaught. Something more than anger grew inside of me. A hot rage permeated through my body. I imagined the holographic images at Assembly reading new decrees, passing Judgment on the corrupt. Nobles—revered and trusted defenders of the scriptures, protectors of the human race—liars.

We stared at each other in silence. These were my parents, the two people I admired and trusted more than any other. They were always affectionate, kind, and encouraging. They nurtured and loved me, raised me to be a logical and independent thinker. Everything is now in question, except for them. I breathed in my resolve. The next words out of my mouth were in a hard and determined voice.

"I want to be a Seeker."

Chapter 8

Seekers

Ares knelt in front of me and opened his arms. I fell into them and squeezed his neck, his cheek against mine. Tears cascaded down his shoulder as my emotions erupted. After several minutes, Jade placed her hand on the back of my head. Tears rolled down her face, tracing her perfect features. I had never seen her cry.

She looked into my puddled eyes and smiled. Her expression then hardened. She took our shoulders and gently pulled us apart. As we stood, I wiped the wetness from my face. Oddly, I wondered if tears were collected and recycled like all other moisture in Life World. Jade waited until we were mostly gathered.

"We have much to discuss," she said. "The path of a Seeker can be perilous and wrought with pain. If you join us, you'll need to be strong. There'll be no more time for tears."

I blinked away the last of the moisture.

"Silas was very fond of Roma Two," she began. "When she didn't return to the laboratory or her private quarters, he inquired at the KPR central station. He was detained for days and threatened with banishment as an accessory to conspiracy against nobles. Eventually, he convinced his interrogators the reason for his inquiry was passion, not sedition."

"Do you understand what banishment means?" Ares asked.

We learned very early about the punishment. Residents found corrupt by the Noble Court were sentenced to banishment. They were initially detained in an obscure location—rumored to be on level one. There, the guilty party was stripped of their shell and sealed in a barren cell with no food or water. After seven days of repentance, they were cast into Out World. The results were left to the imagination. Storytellers reveled in their ability to frighten the young. They told of heat so intense it melted the skin, and they described grotesque mutant scavengers feeding on half-dead bodies of the corrupt. Terrified by the prospects of the punishment, most referred to it as the B word, as if the mere mention could result in condemnation. I shook away the memories of my youth.

"What happened to Silas?" I asked.

Jade continued. "He returned to his work and didn't speak of his experience, knowing he was being closely monitored. A short time later, keepers were sent to inspect the laboratory. During their search of this room, Silas noticed they lost contact with their station. He assumed the space would be fitted with surveillance devices, but they never returned."

Ares was now pacing. "Silas used this space to speak to fellow residents without fear of transmission to the Core. He found others who were suspicious of nobles. Through those interactions, more instances of deceit came to light."

"Over time," Jade said, "more shadow spaces were discovered. Silas recruited a network of residents to gather information. They never communicated or recorded their evidence electronically, knowing such measures might reveal their identities. All information has been passed through the generations by word only."

They continued, unveiling a secret society of residents. Seekers, who occupied the sanctuary in obscurity. Most accepted they'd never see change in their lifetimes. They were committed to the Cause, an ultimate plan to free their descendants from servitude. There was no doubt about my commitment. I pictured the young on our level, children who might grow to experience a freedom they didn't yet know existed. Then there was Star and my other classmates. *Who will join me in the Cause?*

My life was no longer my own, and my priorities had changed. Everything I'd worked for would be sacrificed. The information in my possession could condemn dozens, if not hundreds, of residents. My thoughts fell to Silas being interrogated. *Could I handle such torment?* Jade and Ares will reach expiration in less than a decade. The responsibility might fall to me to recruit the next generation of Seekers. *Am I prepared to carry on the Cause? Am I capable?*

"Why are you telling me this now?"

"Because it's your time," Ares insisted. "An opportunity has arisen enabling us to advance the Cause faster than imagined." He looked to Jade. "Tell her the rest."

I turned to her expectantly. Given the extraordinary events of the last fifteen minutes, I felt prepared for anything.

"Silas understood the only way to freedom was to eliminate the restraints nobles held over residents. He petitioned the Court to create Roma Three to resume his work after expiration. Given Roma Two's unique skills and contributions to reproduction, a denial might have raised suspicion. The Court permitted her cloning." She glanced at Ares, he nodded once. "Silas omitted the modified expiration gene. Roma Three will live on."

Ares put his hand on Jade's shoulder. "As will Jade, and me . . . and you."

I gasped. My mouth opened, but there were no words.

"Our paths were chosen for us," Jade added. "We were

informed of our gift of extended life at your age."

Ares resumed. "Opal, our genetic codes were also assembled with traits giving us many advantages. Among those are the propensity to excel academically, but only if properly cultivated. Like all Seeker offspring, you were placed in a family environment where your skills would be nurtured, preparing you for this moment."

His comment was odd. "So, I'm simply your charge? An element of the master plan?"

"We love you," Jade interrupted. "You're our child first, but you're much more. The bond we share extends beyond mortal existence and can never be broken. If we're to succeed, we need your help."

I trembled, perhaps due to the frigid room. Maybe it was fear, anxiety, or excitement. That morning my most pressing concern was a lengthy assessment. Now . . .

"What am I to do?"

Chapter 9

Commitment

"As you're aware, the top five students in your class move directly into advanced and are permitted to select their desired occupations," Ares said.

"That's correct. Star and I plan to enter the professorate together, to teach the next generation."

He sighed. His expression indicated both certainty and pity. "We can't explain everything to you now. As Jade mentioned, we need your help. "You must select engineering as your desired occupation."

"Engineering?" I repeated, too loudly.

"Yes." He was emphatic. "You've excelled in mathematics and the sciences. The choice won't raise suspicions by the Court. Most crucially, you'll be assigned to my lab for your apprenticeship."

"What do I tell Star? That my lifelong plans have suddenly changed?"

Jade was not sympathetic. "It's not uncommon to change one's path when given options. This is larger than you, Opal. It's for the Cause. Don't believe for a moment Star is not being advised of her own direction."

"But most engineers are assigned to the lower levels, even sub-levels. The professorate work on campus and are assigned quarters on ten. We've made jokes about lower-level technicians. Now I'm to convince her of a new calling? That my dream is now to manage filtration systems or the water purification refinery?"

"After tomorrow, you won't need to convince her of anything," Ares said. "As I mentioned, we can't share everything now. It will all become quite clear."

"Opal, you told us you wanted to join, to be a Seeker," Jade said.

"I do. It's just—this is all so overwhelming."

"As it was for me." She glanced at Ares. "Each of us is assigned an equally important role. We must be steadfast if the master plan is to succeed."

"You'll be given guidance," Ares interrupted. "You may not understand why certain actions are asked of you, but you must follow through without question. At times you'll have no communication with others. During those periods you'll go on about your daily routine. Do your work, be a good resident."

Jade adjusted her hood. "We should continue our tour of the lab. We need to spend at least thirty-five minutes before departing."

Ares turned to me. "Listen carefully, Opal. We've managed to survive and arrive at this pivotal moment through secrecy. Did you ever suspect we were anything other than devout residents?"

"No. Never."

"Precisely," he continued. "Never use the terms Seeker or Cause. Assume all residents are loyal to the nobles. Conduct yourself as if every word and every action is monitored by the Core. Avoid searching spaces for electronic devices—just know they exist. Do nothing to bring unwanted attention to yourself and follow the scriptures and decrees to the letter."

"Like the nobles?" I retorted.

He frowned. "Listen to me."

"Sorry," I whispered.

"We won't always be there to help and protect you, Opal. Be prepared to make quick rational decisions and take action when necessary. Remember, we must conceal the identities of Seekers and the existence of the Cause."

"I will. I promise."

He stared at me, verifying my resolve. "When your results arrive, respond to the Court and select engineering. If Star or any of your classmates inquire, tell them I coerced you into following my path. Advanced classes don't begin for another ten days. By then, everything will be in motion."

We replaced our hoods, left the preservation room, and spent our required amount of time in the lab. Jade used a laser projector to explain phases of the genetic editing process before showing us the various stations. The tour was intended as cover for our meeting, and she delivered a thorough and convincing performance. Given the circumstances, it was difficult to focus. I finally managed a question after spotting a small, enclosed docking bay.

"Is that a delivery porter?"

Jade closed in behind me. "Yes, it is." She pointed to a small chamber in front of the bay. "Assembled specimens are sealed in conical vials and placed in the two-phase receptacle. The porter routes them to an auxiliary lab for transgenic fertilization."

"They create new offspring?"

"Not exactly. The final stage takes place in the reproductive unit, where fertilized eggs are introduced into carriers."

"Carriers?"

Ares added to the conversation. "Young females selected by the Court to carry and birth offspring."

"Selected? What if they refuse?" I scoffed.

They stared at me in stunned silence. It was an inexcusable error. Ares had just outlined the necessity of discretion. Arrogance allowed the thoughts to escape my mouth.

"I'm sure you recall our scriptures, young Opal," he quickly replied. "Childbearing is considered a high honor."

Jade stepped in. "Our reproductive processes have reduced the propensity for mutation to nearly zero. Genetic diseases have been eliminated and preferable traits made dominant. Through the wisdom of the Court, we've produced a higher order of human being."

"Praise be to The Giver," I added, still holding my breath.

We exited the lab through the same decontamination cycles we entered. The redundant protocols ensured unwanted microorganisms were kept out of the environment. We removed the sterile outer garments and glove-like membranes from our hands. After retrieving our belongings, we left the facility. Fortunately, there were no keepers to greet us.

As we approached the main corridor, I looked over my shoulder at the lab entrance. An hour before, I had arrived to learn about research, but my education was much more than expected. My bond with Jade and Ares was stronger than ever. Blending with the stream of residents in transit, I pulled my shoulders back and held my head high. Walking with new purpose, I was no longer angry, sad, or afraid—only different.

Chapter 10

Transformation

It's an understatement to say I didn't sleep well Friday night. Per my instructions, May reduced the pod lighting to zero lumens and activated the acoustic attenuating module. The space was effectively void of sensory input. Unfortunately, the settings couldn't stop the barrage of images flashing through my mind. I pictured Roma Two confronting the Noble Court with her discovery. I then imagined her in the banishment cell, curled into a ball, naked and shivering, waiting to be cast into Out World. A likeness of Silas in unbearable anguish appeared. He was searching for his love, only to be detained and mercilessly interrogated. The power of his anger flowed through my veins like a surge of energy.

Lying in darkness and confinement, a change came over me. My newfound knowledge about nobles and Life World meant everything was different. My life would now be devoted to the Cause. It's one thing to call myself a Seeker. It's entirely another to become completely integrated into a single purpose, a single spirit.

I thought of the original residents entering Life World. It's easy to understand why they followed the Prophets, abided by the scriptures, and accepted new decrees. It was, after all, the will of The Giver. They were spared extermination from raging storms sweeping over the planet. They would never face starvation, disease, or what the Prophets described as battles between barbarian remnants of human civilization.

I envisioned crowds of residents moving blindly through Life World, accepting their stations, conforming to the will of nobles. They never questioned authority or protested concerns. They adhered to decrees, regardless of personal sacrifice. They lived in fear. Most would shun their mate or only child if one was found corrupt by the Court. As their faces scrolled through my mind, I pitied them, laughed at them—despised them. They were simple-minded animals being herded by flock masters.

Drifting in and out of consciousness, I noticed someone familiar moving in unison with the crowd. Her short hair looked like . . . *No. It can't be. Don't go with them.* I wanted to shout at her, warn her, save her from a predetermined fate. Before I could summon the words, the crowd shifted, and she disappeared, washed away with the masses.

I woke with a start, quivering in the darkness. I was angry and afraid, desperate to save her.

"May, please raise the lights."

"Opal, lights are now at 25 percent. You are currently experiencing an increase in heart rate and respiration."

"I'm okay, thank you."

The familiar blue light brought instant comfort. I squeezed my hands together and breathed deeply through my nose. *Did Jade and Ares have similar experiences when brought into the fold of Seekers? How did they manage? Did they see residents differently? Recognize their former selves in the crowd? Did they undergo such dramatic transformations?*

Moisture welled in my eyes. Jade's words then echoed from the lab. There was no time for self-pity or weakness. My head must remain clear, ever vigilant with awareness. Every word and every action must be measured. *Raise no suspicion. Reveal no secrets.* At the risk of my own death, I'll defend my allies. Fight for the Cause.

Chapter 11

Visitor

The lights in my pod came up gradually. Perhaps it was my imagination, but Saturday morning air always seemed cooler, crisper than other days. I rubbed my fingers on the mattress surface, feeling the softness of fresh linens. It was a form of meditation, starting my day with pleasant sensations. Lying in the comfort of my space, a thought made me grin. *Will my hands grow calloused working on engineering projects?*

My assessment results arrived late Friday evening. I accessed my portal and opened the flashing message from the Noble Court. It announced my scores were in the top five of my class. They invited me to attend advanced and select my desired occupational path. Scrolling through the options, the professorate appeared before me. As if reading my thoughts, Star posted a message inquiring about my results. I looked at her image briefly but didn't respond. She would have to wait.

I found engineering and, without further hesitation, entered my request. The reply was immediate:

Opal Five,

The Noble Court extends congratulations on your superior performance. Your selection has been approved. Included is your course schedule for the new term. Report to the engineering laboratory at 8:00 a.m. on Monday for apprentice orientation.

I didn't need the attached directions to orientation because I knew the exact location—Ares's lab.

I exited the grooming stall in good spirits. After donning my shell and sandals, I straightened my hair in preparation for our morning meal. Ares and Jade were already seated, my place setting arranged neatly on the table.

Jade watched me enter the salon. "Good morning, Opal."

"Good morning, Jade. Good morning, Ares."

Ares dabbed the corner of his mouth. "I can't imagine you slept well after the news of your results."

"You're right. It's very exciting." I looked back and forth at them. "May, did you detect any restlessness during the night?"

"Opal, you requested lighting in your pod at 2:13 a.m. Your vitals were elevated."

"Oh, yes," I quipped. "It must have been concern about orientation, or a potentially strict professor."

We looked at each other, quietly acknowledging the facade. Jade nodded imperceptibly, indicating her approval.

We ate our meal at a leisurely pace, as Saturday mornings were generally quiet. Ares mentioned several projects on which he was involved and suggested I join his research to supplement my courses. He had a way of describing even mundane lab work, making it sound intriguing. I tried adding to the conversation by requesting details about specific areas. After finishing our meal, Jade offered to clear the table. I returned to my pod and activated my drive. Just as a file opened, the door chime to our quarters sounded three rapid bells.

Three bells? Official business on Saturday? I swiped away

the file and removed my interpreters. We hadn't had an official visit in a year. *No, it can't be.*

A keeper swept our quarters, verifying no other residents were present. I stared intently at the dark enforcer, trying to detect his eyes behind the glimmering face visor. The mirror-like surface only reflected images of our quarters. He snapped to attention, left hand hovering over the pulse gauntlet secured to his upper thigh. He then announced the Noble Yanic.

A movement in my peripheral vision drew my attention. Ares and Jade were bowing their heads in unison. Turning back toward the entrance, I inadvertently made eye contact with Yanic. *This is bad.* Nobles are rarely seen outside of Assembly, let alone on level nine. I've never seen one in person, only in holographs. Even then their faces are obscured by high collars. Although he wasn't wearing his coronet, the purple and gold cape draped over his shell indicated his status.

I knew to bow but was frozen by shock. *Were we discovered? Are they here to interrogate us? Will I see my fifteenth year? Breathe, Opal.* Along with the anxiety, anger swelled inside. It took all my restraint to avoid screaming out the atrocities he and his kind had committed. He tilted his head at me, then raised an accusatory brow. I hoped my expression hadn't revealed my inner rage. Banishment would surely be the punishment for such insolence. Suddenly jolted into reality, I lowered my head toward the sterile gray floor.

Yanic addressed Jade, indicating he wanted to speak privately with Ares. He mentioned the tube might be worthy of a visit. With the change in virtual seasons, new blooms were now visible. She bowed her head again then instructed me to retrieve my drive case and join her outside. I did as she requested, avoiding further interaction with the noble. When I brushed past Ares, he made no movement nor bid us farewell. Once in the corridor, I breathed deeply for the first time since the chimes rang.

Jade walked briskly. As I ran to catch her, passersby gave

me odd glances. The corridor was already heavy with overhead delivery drones. A sweeping porter rolled up the center aisle, headed to its charging bay in the central lift station. I slowed momentarily to watch the small device. *Can it move faster with the same efficiency?* A grin crossed my face. *I'm starting to think like an engineer.* Yanic's image flashed in my mind. I moved on.

We entered the lift and Jade selected eleven. The tube is located in the atrium, which is open to all residents. It's the only dedicated recreational space in Life World and rises to the base of sixteen. The elongated rectangular pyramid shape of the sanctuary is made evident by the interior perimeter windows tapering upward.

"Do you need grooming supplies?" Jade asked. "We have credits."

Strange question. I wasn't sure if she was making small talk or really asking. Our visits to the vendors are routinely scheduled.

"No, thank you," I replied, my thoughts drifting.

When we were younger, Star and I literally raced to the atrium on Saturday mornings. Our day was spent in the small castle, acting out as members of the professorate. Younger students often played along as our pupils, learning from subjects we studied the week before. Neither of us kept track of time. When the virtual sun fell, we returned to our quarters.

The lift stopped on the atrium level. Typical for a Saturday, the station was bustling. We made our way to the common area where the polished gray floor changed to artificial green grass. I scanned the running paths and exercise apparatus for familiar faces. As we walked past the family gathering tables, many children were darting about with interpreters on, playing with virtu-pets or flying virtu-kites.

—

Jade slowed, casually looking up and to her right. Ares's caution about behavior came to mind, so I glanced up without moving my head. The orb-shaped T-8 drone drifted slowly in front of level twelve windows. Although barely noticeable due to its surface-disruption translucent skin, the reflective coating on the windows revealed the T-8's movement. We were told surveillance drones were necessary for our safety and security, but what threats existed in our isolated world? *Ruling nobles are the ones who should live in fear.*

We reached the common area center and joined residents queued up at the tube entrance. The cylindrical virtual terrarium stretched 50 feet in diameter and rose upward, almost reaching the atrium ceiling.

"Have you visited recently?" Jade asked.

She addressed me but looked over my shoulder down the line. The conversation was meant for anyone who may have followed us. She knew my biology class visited this term during our study of plant growth. I cornered her that same evening with a barrage of questions about genetically modified plants.

"Not since the seasons changed," I managed.

She turned as the line began to move. I looked up to watch residents circling in both directions around the structure. Ascending groups occupied an inner lane, while those descending remained in the outer. To the naked eye, the tube appeared hollow. Without interpreters, it looked like residents were streaming up and down for no apparent reason.

We reached the walkway entrance, secured our interpreters, and activated our drives. It took a moment for the updated program to load. The walkway was also made of clear acrylic and could be disorienting without interpreters. The program created the appearance of a stone path as if climbing the face of a small mountain. The most remarkable images, however, were inside the tube.

The sights and sounds of a tropical rainforest came to life. Just as Yanic said, there was a plethora of new blooms. There were also new creatures moving about on the ground and jumping between branches. Still shaken by the presence of a noble in our quarters, I found it hard to focus on the details of the forest. *If they know about our conversation in the lab, why only question Ares?* I checked on Jade who was intently focused on the landscape. We both dodged birds appearing to swoop out of the forest. The three-dimensional effect of the program also created the sensation of insects fluttering close to our ears. The visual aspect was augmented with pleasant sounds of splashing water and raindrops.

Is it possible they were monitoring the shadow space? Surely my comment about female carriers wasn't worthy of a noble's attention. The scene transitioned into a temperate deciduous forest, with tall trees penetrating the sky. Jade motioned toward a pack of small animals grazing on layers of lush green foliage. *How can she be so calm? Ares could be at the KPR station undergoing interrogation right now.* We entered the dry thorn forest, thick with acacia trees and scattered cacti. I nearly stumbled when a snake slithered toward my feet. When I looked up, a large raptor spread its wings and bounded out of a tree in my direction. The virtual snake was its next meal.

As we shuffled along, I became lost in my thoughts. The terrarium experience was amazing, but my mind was on the events of the morning. It occurred to me the keeper might remain at our quarters and take us into custody, but why the noble? *What did he want with Ares?* A nudge returned me to the moment. The resident excused themselves, and we continued up the walkway. A flock of thrashers took flight in the venue. I marveled at their speed and agility as they wove through the brush then settled in a distant tree. I imagined being one of them, able to break the bonds of gravity, free to go wherever the wind carried me. Having only seen them through interpreters, I wondered if they truly existed. Perhaps they were like most things in Life World, a figment of the Core's imagination.

After nearly an hour of climbing, Jade turned and put her hand on my shoulder. I paused the program as we moved to the outer lane. Her eyes darted slowly behind her interpreters as she read an incoming message. She responded on her console, then disengaged.

"Ares won't be present for our meal. He'll return later in the evening," she said with a reassuring nod.

I hesitated before responding, preparing my words and facial gestures. He was obviously okay, but I couldn't react.

"He works so hard," I replied. "His dedication is admirable."

The stone path image had disappeared when I disengaged. To avoid disorientation, I focused on the surrounding upper windows—nobles' quarters. *Are they watching us? Are they afraid? Why did they send him?* Several devious thoughts entered my mind. I forced myself not to change expressions. *I'm now a Seeker and we will come for you.*

Chapter 12

Assembly

"It looks good on you, Opal," Ares said.

My new cloak had arrived just before he returned to our quarters. The light green material was accented by the silver collar of engineering. Although they're not the colors of my original plan, I was proud to wear them. Thousands of residents were about to see me in the Great Hall, and they wouldn't have a clue what the colors truly meant.

"Someday I'll wear your colors," I responded, with convincing sincerity. He and Jade wore professorate cloaks, the ornate trim indicating their higher status.

"Of course, you will," Jade added. "Shall we go?"

The corridors were crowded like every Sunday. Attendance at Assembly was mandatory, except for residents with critical occupations or those in the infirmary. Imaging drones were abundant, projecting scripture segments and messages of obedience. I struggled to maintain my composure as we turned toward the lift station.

TRUTH IS THE FOUNDATION OF ALL VIRTUE

Perhaps it was my imagination, but the pulsating red letters appeared larger than normal. Without reaction, I looked forward. The same message was scrolled above the lift. *Were they taunting me?* I gritted my teeth at the hypocrisy. In minutes, all of Life World will chant our creed, led by the Noble Court. *Who were they to demand truth?*

After boarding the lift, I glanced out at the remaining crowd. There was a slight chance of encountering Star, and I wasn't prepared to explain the cloak, nor my decision. I was relieved when the panel closed. Her family was assigned seating below us, so they entered the Hall on six. Lighting was dim before ceremonies began, and all were required to be seated and engaged upon arrival. She wouldn't be able to see me until after the ceremony.

We joined others flowing into the south entrance of seven. My body went numb when a keeper raised his hand in front of Ares. I peered around Jade and noticed the crowd wasn't moving. The facial recognition monitors had missed someone, and the line was halted for verification. The sentry released Ares, and we followed him to our seats.

After the last residents poured in, the entranceways were sealed, and the lights went down. The only perceptible images were glowing interpreters floating in the darkness as residents shuffled in their seats. At precisely 8:00 a.m., the familiar piercing trumpets sounded, announcing the beginning of the ceremony. I rose with the crowd, gazing at the center stage while the illuminated doorway materialized. Nobles stepped through the opening as if emerging from another space or time. Although projected as holographic images, the Court members looked majestic in their intricately designed coronets and flowing purple capes. Every detail of the pageantry demonstrated their higher station, including the throne-like chairs on stage.

All remained standing until the trumpets ended. After a moment of silence, the nobles rose and faced the crowds. My attention was drawn to the pennons flying over their chairs. Each was embellished with the Life World crest. In primary, we learned the meaning of each symbol. *Were those also lies? Why depict the sun rising with three emitting rays inside the triangle?* No resident has seen the sun in two centuries. *A single eye? The double helix? What were the true meanings?*

The Court Chairperson raised a gilded scroll case over her head. It was our cue to begin recitation of the Life World creed. The experience was exhilarating as seven thousand voices chanted together:

> *"I proclaim my devotion in body, mind, and spirit to The Giver, maker of all things.*

> *I profess gratitude to a merciful Giver who, as foretold by the Prophets, cast Judgment upon his people, rained down his wrath, and rid the planet of the corrupt.*

> *I believe in the sanctity of Life World, created at the behest of The Giver, as sanctuary for the chosen.*

> *I believe, in accordance with the scriptures, the descendants of the chosen will emerge from Life World after five centuries to inherit a purified planet.*

> *I will serve Life World until expiration in my fiftieth year, as willed by The Giver, as covenant for my salvation.*

> *I commit to the tenets of faith, obedience, discipline, and sacrifice, and believe truth is the foundation of all virtue.*

> *I submit to all decrees set forth by the High Noble Court, appointed by The Giver to protect and preserve Life World and ensure the survival of mankind.*

I proclaim these sacred vows in the name of The Giver."

We remained standing as a noble began reading from the scriptures. His voice echoed through the Hall. Staring into nothingness, I didn't listen to the passage, nor read the words scrolling through my interpreters. *Is it all fabricated? Are we simply being manipulated to perpetuate their reign?* Our creed—vows we accepted and recited every week. Were they words from a merciful Giver or instructions for subservience to a ruling class?

I took a deep breath. *There is a higher power, a divine being responsible for my existence—for all life.* Everything known about the world before Judgment is filtered by the Core. What existed then and what exists now, couldn't have been created by random acts of nature. Our science has managed to harness the developmental processes, but we can't create life from nothing. That power is the sole dominion of The Giver. *Is this the existence he wanted for his people?*

Jade touched my leg, bringing my attention back to the ceremony. Just then, a noble instructed those accepted into advanced development to stand and be recognized. I rose from my seat and looked to the right, toward Star and her family. She stood and turned in my direction. The glow of interpreters obscured the color and design of her cloak. I assumed she couldn't see mine. After a short applause, we sat and listened to additional recognitions and announcements. There was nothing remarkable about the closing of Assembly. The nobles stood in front of their seats as if preparing to depart.

Whispers spread and the crowds made ready to leave. Interpreters turned dark as drives were disengaged. Without warning, the sound of trumpets blasted through the Hall. Stunned residents quickly took their seats, hurrying to reengage. The trumpets ended; silence ensued. The Chairperson moved to center stage. Ares and Jade looked at each other. He shook his head, indicating uncertainty.

There are only two occasions upon which the Chairperson takes center stage. One occurs the last Sunday of each month and is reserved for the reading of new decrees. The other is the announcement of corruption. Offending residents are marched across the stage in shackles as their charges are revealed. Punishment was severe and final—banishment.

The tension in the Hall was palpable. All remained still in anticipation. The Chairperson unfurled a scroll and began to read:

"By decree of the Noble Court, power usage shall be restricted to essential operational functions during specified time periods. Notifications have been transmitted to those sectors impacted by these temporary maintenance measures.

Residents shall abide by all restrictions until such time said maintenance is completed. Any violation shall be met with swift and severe punishment as set forth in prior decrees."

After returning the digital parchment to the scroll case, she returned to her chair. A second noble stood.

"Assembly has ended. Thanks be to The Giver," he announced.

"Thanks be to The Giver," we responded in unison.

The nobles exited through the floating door in single file. When the last stepped over the threshold, the frame vanished. The throne chairs and pennons faded away.

With a collective sigh of relief, we disengaged then secured our drives and interpreters. Jade turned to me quickly, anticipating my questions.

"Congratulations again, Opal," she said, very animated.

"Yes, Opal. Well done," Ares added.

Their intent was clear. Now wasn't the time or place to ask about the decree. Others around us speculated about the announcement, perhaps forgetting their words were being recorded. The wrong comment might warrant a visit from keepers. Punishment could be harsh if sedition is suspected.

I scanned the crowds filing toward the exits. *Were Seekers among them?* I watched for glances in our direction, making a game of identifying secret expressions or hand motions. If any were present, it was certainly not obvious. No one looked at us or initiated conversation until we left the Hall.

"Opal, there you are!" Star shouted, rushing toward me.

After embracing me she stepped back, hands gripping my upper arms. Her attention shifted to my collar. She furrowed her brow, trying to recall which program the color and pattern represented.

"Engineering," I offered, half certain, half apologetic.

"So much for the professorate," she responded.

The pattern on her collar was certainly not the professorate. I looked at her with the same questioning expression.

"Cyber systems," she finally admitted.

We stood in silence. At that moment I wasn't obsessed with nobles, Seekers, or the future of Life World. Staring at my closest friend's gentle smile and beautiful face, it was clear our plans were irreversibly redirected. We wouldn't share professorate quarters or take midday meals together between classes. Our evenings wouldn't be spent in the atrium, watching children pretend to be us. We might see each other in passing or visit occasionally but not like we envisioned.

I held back my emotions. Her lips closed together, the smile fading to a weak grin. She squeezed my arms.

"We two . . . ," she whispered.

"Forever."

Jade stepped forward and offered her hand. "Congratulations, Star. We're so proud of both of you."

"Thank you, Jade," she responded.

Ares also extended his hand. "We're happy for you, Star. You've certainly kept Opal focused."

Star looked my way. "No, she pushed me." She turned back to Ares and Jade. Her next comment turned my blood to ice. "Opal was born to lead." She glanced back over her shoulder. "Before returning to classes," she started, "we must discuss your new plans."

"Of course," I said. "And yours."

Chapter 13

Apprentice

Monday was my first day of apprenticeship with Ares and marked my beginning as a Seeker. Everything had developed so quickly. The dramatic change was near overwhelming but made me stronger. Fear and uncertainty were replaced by determination and purpose.

My one concern was facing my friend. I needed to explain my decision and provide some reason. If she were overly alarmed at my radical shift, she might escalate the issue and bring unwanted scrutiny. Learning she also chose an alternative course of study brought some relief from my unease.

I reflected on our interaction after Assembly. *Cyber systems?* Jade's comment in the lab, when I protested engineering, came to mind. "Don't believe for a moment Star is not being advised of her own direction," she'd said. *Who's advising Star, and what does Jade know about her? Why did Star call me a born leader?* My thoughts were interrupted by my sleep-depriving nemesis.

"Opal, the time is 5:00 a.m."

"Thank you, May. I'm awake."

"Opal, you received a message from Star Five, delivered at 11:14 p.m. Shall I replay it for you now?"

Really, 11:14 p.m.? The decree published yesterday limited power usage after 8:00 p.m. It certainly included interface time.

"May, please replay the message."

After a brief pause, the message started. Star's voice was clear but sounded like she read from a script. "Opal, meet me at our special place tomorrow after orientation. I want to speak with you about your wonderful new plans."

I waited, hoping for more clues. The message was straightforward. Her monotone delivery suggested it was something more cryptic.

"Opal, message has ended."

"Thank you, May. Please delete the message."

"Message deleted."

I repeated the message in my head while stretching my arms and legs. The special place Star mentioned was the atrium castle where we so often played. It's code, indicating she has gossip or important information to share. As young students, we assumed noise from the melee around us masked our conversations, and no one heard our secrets. Fortunately, those secrets never aroused the interest of nobles. We later learned the audio systems were capable of filtering out background noises.

I found Jade eating her morning meal alone. Ares apparently finished earlier, his place setting still on the table.

"Good morning, Jade. Where's Ares?"

"Good morning, Opal," she said, motioning toward the interface room. "He had files to review. Are you excited for orientation?"

She watched my expressions carefully. It served as a reminder to choose my words accordingly.

"Very excited," I gushed. "Although I'm not sure what to

expect, having my father parent as a mentor."

She grinned. "I'm sure you'll work well together. It will be an advantage having access to him after class hours."

"You're right, of course."

We both turned as Ares stepped from the interface room.

"Good morning, Opal."

"Good morning."

He returned to the table. "Are you ready to begin?"

"Of course. Jade and I were just discussing—"

Jade tapped her fingers next to my plate. "Finish your meal, it's going to be a long day." She stood and collected the dish settings.

"Not to worry," Ares said. "I'm sure her mentor won't overburden her on the first day."

"I'm not so sure," Jade replied. "I've heard some professors are rather demanding." She leaned and half whispered in my ear, "Especially those in engineering."

Jade excused herself and retrieved her case from the interface room. "I also have a new apprentice beginning today," she said, touching my shoulder. "Are you friends with Tara Five?"

I swallowed the last portion of a baguette and wiped the corner of my mouth. Ares studied my expression as I responded. "I know who she is but have never spent time with her. Did she do well in assessments?"

"She wasn't assigned by the Court," Jade replied. "Genetics was her choice."

Ares's stare was intense, just like Jade's when she asked about my orientation. I paid close attention to his words.

"I'm sure she's an excellent match," he said. "Do you remember her father parent, Lake Four, from advanced?"

Jade paused at the open entranceway, responding over her shoulder. "Lake Four?" She hesitated. "Of course. He was a rather clever programmer, wasn't he?"

"Indeed," Ares continued. "He now oversees printing and manufacturing on three. Perhaps we can arrange a formal introduction. Opal will spend time on his level when her first project is ready for fabrication."

"Excellent idea," Jade said. "I'll speak to Tara after our orientation."

The entrance closed behind her. Ares stood and motioned for me to clear my place setting. "Collect your drive when you've finished. We'll head to the lab."

After loading the sterilizer, I left to gather my case. I knew Tara, but we weren't close friends. It was obvious Ares meant for me to remember her and her father parent. *Are they Seekers? Was she recruited to join the Cause like me?*

Ares stood by the entranceway. "May, we'll return at 8:00 p.m. and take our evening meal then," he said.

Before I could get the words out, May responded. "Ares, a decree published Sunday limits power usage after 8:00 p.m. This includes convection units."

He wasn't happy with her response. "May," I chimed in, "please have our evening meal prepared by 7:45 p.m." Just for fun I added, "Perhaps your cooking will taste better lukewarm."

My quip drew a grin from Ares. We left before May was able to protest.

Chapter 14

Orientation

placed my hand on the ID screen outside Ares's laboratory, and the outer panel opened. The inner panel required biometric facial authentication. My recent visit to Jade's lab was recorded by the Core, so this step was faster. I could now access the lab without supervision. *Why does a teaching laboratory have the same security measures as the genetics unit?*

I followed Ares to his lectern opposite several round worktables cluttered with tools, parts, and wiring.

"Are those clean rooms?" I asked, pointing to three transparent acrylic spaces along the rear wall.

"Yes, they are. We use sensitive materials with many experiments."

"What experiments are conducted in that room?"

He glanced at the corner of the rear wall then looked directly at me. The piercing stare indicated my line of questioning was over.

"All in due time, Opal."

His hesitance heightened my curiosity about the corner room encased in reinforced metal. A red indicator light shone like a beacon over the entrance.

He put his interpreters on and activated his drive, indicating I should do the same. The neuro-loops wound tightly around my hand then relaxed to fit. Command images appeared in front of me. While Ares manipulated his console, I pivoted my head, discovering a 360-degree visual range. The entire lab had interface capabilities.

Images hovered over the center of a worktable. I moved closer, examining the files left open by another user. Notes and diagrams suggested they were working on a solar collection system. It was miniature in scale.

"Opal, stay with me please."

I returned to his side. "Sorry. I saw someone's open files."

"Many projects include multiple stages of development. Students often work together using shared files," he explained.

I looked back at the images floating above the table.

"Only the original author can edit file content," he said, reading my thoughts.

A new icon materialized on my content field.

"You're seeing the access portal for engineering data."

I swear he can read my mind.

"The information is for apprentice access. It will suffice for your studies and beginning projects," he added.

After selecting the pulsating icon, a three-panel key console appeared. It was identical to the device coupled with Ares's drive. Also visible were several new files, labeled to indicate which databases they accessed. I looked for ATMOSPHERE, hoping to uncover more details in the file. I nearly asked its location. Ares's warning crept into my consciousness. "Conduct yourself as if every word you speak and every action you take is being observed and recorded by the Core."

"Have you determined my first project assignment?" I asked,

recovering control of my thoughts.

"Yes—I have. Familiarize yourself with gyroscopic theory, history, and implementation."

"Gyroscopes?" I blurted out. It's never appropriate for an apprentice to question their mentor. I quickly corrected course. "Excellent. I'll prepare a summary report by Friday."

"That won't be necessary. You'll be paired with Kane Five. His apprenticeship concludes at the end of this cycle. The open files are some of his notes on the project."

I glanced back at the table, inspecting the structures lying in various stages of completion. "Are those CLAD parts?"

"Very perceptive, Opal."

Core-Linked Autonomous Drones were a constant in Life World. In secondary, I wrote a report on the larger C-54 delivery model. They were the most widely used and had dedicated travel lanes above our corridors. Although the drones were equipped with collision detection sensors, everyone avoided loitering around docking ports to prevent injuries.

The components were too large for the T-8 model and the B2-H "bird." Technically we weren't supposed to know the palm-sized birds even existed. Both were used for surveillance and were tightly guarded by the keepers. The rotor head was also too large for disc-shaped imaging drones.

I stared at the scattered parts. Every aspect of our lives is monitored. Interface sessions and electronic communications were scrutinized. Recording devices were installed throughout the sanctuary, including in our own quarters. *Why are nobles so paranoid? Do they know about the Cause? Did Seekers evolve due to the nobles' arrogance and lust for control?*

Looking closer at the table, I noticed something unusual. "Ares, are those rotor blades from a C-54 model?"

"Yes, they are," he replied.

"What about the larger blade?"

After quickly disengaging, he walked over and covered the partially exposed blade with a foil tarp. Before I was able to press him for information, a single bell chimed, indicating the outer lab panel had been accessed. The look on his face indicated concern but not panic. He grasped my arm and turned me toward the entranceway.

"We have guests," he said.

The keeper made no announcement when the Noble Yanic entered behind him. Without hesitation, we bowed our heads. This time I avoided eye contact.

"Good morning, Professor Ares," Yanic said. "I see you have a new apprentice."

Ares remained in position. "Good morning, Excellency. This is Opal Five."

I raised my head slowly, focusing on the center of his chest. A pyramid-shaped silver clasp held his cape together. It was inscribed with the Life World crest.

"Of course. Good morning, Opal."

"Good morning, Excellency."

I stood frozen, only allowing myself to blink. I felt the full weight of his stare.

Yanic turned his attention back to Ares. "I believe you have something to show me, Professor."

"Yes, Excellency. This way, please."

Ares motioned toward the far corner of the lab, then led the noble to the reinforced room. As he approached the entrance, the biometric sensor scanned his face. The indicator light flashed green, and the panel slid open. Ares glanced back at me and held his right palm downward, indicating not to follow. They entered the room, and the panel sealed behind them.

I found myself in the company of a keeper. He assumed a sentry position, facing the interior entrance. Searching the lab for some distraction, my focus kept returning to the ominous dark figure just twelve feet away. Curiosity gradually overcame discomfort. I inspected his profile. There was a series of numbers printed vertically on the side of his helmet. It read 3-0418 and was either the helmet serial number or his unit identification. I silently repeated the series several times, striking it to memory. I knew it might have no significance, but Jade told me to pay more attention to details in my surroundings.

I reached to adjust my case, and the movement reflected in his face visor. I then rubbed my face and was amused at the contorted image caused by the visor curvature. The keeper didn't move or respond to my game. The tactical uniform covering his shell was black and coarse with ridged padding around the arms, legs, and torso. The glove on his left hand had exaggerated knuckle moldings and raised finger braces.

The item piquing my interest was the pulse gauntlet secured to his left thigh. I couldn't see the tapering electrode prongs due to the sheath, but the socket was clearly visible. A classmate, whose father parent was a service technician, told us power is activated by a trigger rod inside the diamond-shaped upper guard. The lowest setting of 500 kilovolts incapacitates victims for several minutes. Higher settings can be fatal. *The weapon can be used by anyone, and those composite gloves prevent fingerprint and DNA verification.*

My attention returned to the reinforced room behind me. Yanic emerged, followed closely by Ares who paused momentarily as he secured the entrance. When they resumed walking, I lowered my head. The noble made a comment to Ares, but I was unable to hear him clearly. As they approached, the keeper snapped his boots to attention. Yanic stopped directly in front of me.

"Opal Five," he said, enunciating my name.

"Yes, Excellency."

"Professor Ares speaks highly of you. I trust you're as devoted as he to the preservation of our sanctuary."

"Of course, Excellency."

"Good," he said. An abnormally long pause ensued. Again, the weight of his stare pressed down on me. It took all my constraint to avoid looking at his face. I held fast and remained still, not allowing him to shake me. He turned to Ares and added a footnote.

"This generation will surely have a tremendous impact on us all. Wouldn't you agree, Professor?"

Chapter 15

Suspicion

The remainder of my orientation involved familiarization with the laboratory. Ares pointed out the location of tools, parts, and equipment. We also discussed a detailed set of rules regarding cooperative project development. At least one apprentice was very particular about their ideas and research. Despite my subtle prodding, Ares refused to discuss Yanic's interest in the secured room. He said I'd be briefed later.

I left the engineering lab and walked to the lift station, assuming Star was on her way to the atrium. The thought of our meeting made me anxious. So much had transpired since our last day in secondary. Although prepared for questions about my decision, the comments after Assembly made me more curious about her program selection. We both veered from our original plans.

The lift accelerated and my stomach tightened. I was more determined than ever but hated the thought of lying to my friend.

We were always honest with each other, even to a fault. *What explanation did she have for her decision? Will I recognize any attempt at deceit?* Star is not the most observant of people, so I was less concerned about my own performance. If the recent interaction with Yanic was indicative of my ability to maintain composure, there should be no issues.

The lift stopped on eleven and I walked toward the common area. The castle is near the western end of the atrium and is always crowded with young children. Today was no different, except it looked busier than usual. I was halfway to the castle when I heard my name.

"Opal," Star squealed, suppressing a shout.

I was relieved to see her bright smile. For that moment, everything was back to normal. We embraced like we'd been separated for a month. As we pulled away, she squeezed my shoulders with her hands.

"Let's go this way," she said, indicating the opposite direction of the castle.

We walked in silence for forty paces into an open area. Her head barely moved, but she searched above us the whole time. I assumed she was looking into the surrounding windows; however, it was something more—and peculiar. When we stopped, she turned to me with a serious expression.

"Obviously we owe each other an explanation," she said.

"You never expressed interest in cyber systems," I responded, attempting to control the conversation.

"Likewise with engineering," she rebutted.

Having spent time planning for the inevitable conversation, I was prepared with a reasonable explanation. "Star, Ares is part of the engineering professorate. He mentioned on several occasions the need for qualified technicians in Life World."

"Yes, but you never discussed it with me."

"And how would you have responded? You've had us joining the professorate from the moment we met."

"As I recall, we decided on that path together. Please don't suggest it was my idea alone."

She was right, of course. We spent untold hours imagining our lives in various occupations. The professorate allowed us to remain close. In an environment where choices were so limited, maintaining one true friendship was treasured. Before I responded, her attention was drawn away. She again searched the space above us, appearing overly paranoid.

"Star, are you okay?"

She took my arm, pulling me toward the center of the common area. "Shall we continue our walk?" she asked loudly.

After several steps, I noticed a T-8 drone drop from above and spin in our direction. Although their video sensors were very high resolution, they required proximity to obtain any discernible audio signal. Seconds later, two young males sprinted by in the direction of the tube. The T-8 diverted away from us, flying parallel to the runners. We stopped walking and Star faced me once again.

"Opal, do you trust me?"

"Of course."

She glanced from side to side. "I didn't choose cyber systems," she whispered. "It was selected for me."

"What—when?" I muttered.

She suddenly burst into laughter, grasping my shoulder with her left hand. She held her abdomen with her right arm, bending slightly like she just heard a most hysterical anecdote. I couldn't help but laugh along, albeit concerned she was losing her mental faculties. Just then, another T-8 passed low over our heads. We continued the feigned laughter until it rose and veered toward the lift station.

I proceeded cautiously with my friend. At first, I thought— hoped—she was also introduced to the Cause. Perhaps she, too, had been recruited and was being groomed as a new Seeker. There was no way to inquire directly without revealing myself.

"When did you know?" I asked, casually.

"Before assessments," she replied, not volunteering details.

"Who instructed you to select the program?" I pushed.

She glanced around before responding. "My father parent. I protested at first but—" she stopped abruptly. "Were you given a choice?" she asked.

I was reluctant to share information about myself but didn't want to appear evasive. I took a chance on my prior observation. "Did you use your own drive for assessments?"

I expected her to respond with alarm, to immediately deny the accusation. The punishment for such an infraction was unthinkable, the least of which was dismissal from advanced development. She stared at me for a moment. She looked sad and afraid. Then her expression hardened.

"I can't tell you everything now. Whatever you hear, believe in our friendship above all things."

"Star, what could I possibly hear?"

"Not now." She looked around again. "Do you remember where we sat prior to assessments?"

"Yes . . ." I replied, tentatively, assuming she knew it was where I saw the activated drive.

"Will you meet me there on Friday at 9:00 a.m.?"

We both start our initial apprentice projects this week, but Friday is a free day.

"Yes, I'll meet you there."

Smiling wide and bright, she took my hands in hers.

"Good. We two . . ."

"Forever," I responded, managing a weak grin.

She squeezed my hands, then her expression turned serious again.

"Opal, I'm heading to the lift station. Visit the castle and watch children play for several minutes before you depart. Agreed?"

It was a good tactic to limit suspicion of our short rendezvous. Had I known the nature of our meeting beforehand, I might have made the same suggestion. She was being extremely cautious like she'd received the same briefing Ares gave me about nobles and the Core.

"Agreed."

I watched her depart then turned and walked toward the castle. Our brief discussion left more questions than answers. I tried to recall each of her words, searching for clues. Our paths were moving in somewhat parallel directions, although not those we originally planned. Her recent experience sounded remarkably similar to my own. *Is it possible . . . ?*

If she, too, was a Seeker, why risk using an alternative drive for assessments? Altering a unit requires a skilled technician willing to risk banishment. The task had to be authorized by someone in authority. *Was Star following the orders of a noble?*

Chapter 16

Project

Ares and I approached his lab at 7:00 a.m. on Tuesday. We spoke few words during the commute. I was oblivious to the activity around me, my head spinning with thoughts. Most of my night was spent piecing together events from the last few days. Everything was happening so quickly. Any spare time was used to review instructions, warnings, and details so as not to expose myself. Being committed to the Cause, I refused to reveal its secrets.

The now-familiar laser scanned my face. A young male stood at the worktable where the files had been left open. His back was to us, and he didn't acknowledge our arrival. I followed Ares to his lectern, all the while watching the figure making small hand motions over the table. I then noticed his interpreters and realized he was interfaced and engrossed in work. After a few minutes, he paused and turned toward us.

"Good morning, Professor," he said, then glanced at me.

"Good morning."

"Good morning," Ares replied. "Kane Five this is Opal Five, my new apprentice."

Kane walked over and extended his right hand. I stared at him but didn't reach for his hand. It was considered rude to carry on a conversation wearing interpreters, especially during an introduction. We stood facing each other for an awkward moment, his arm hanging in front of him. He finally realized his error.

"Oh," he said, removing the interpreters. "Forgive me, Opal. It's a pleasure to meet you."

I shook his hand firmly. "Hello, Kane. What are you working on there?"

My question caught him off guard. He opened his mouth to speak then looked to Ares.

"It's okay, Kane. Opal is joining the project."

"Excellent," Kane responded.

I expected a short briefing on his work or at least a summary on the project. Instead, he remained still, silently staring at me.

"Well?" I asked.

"What?" he asked awkwardly.

"The project?"

"Of course," he said, trance broken. "Vectored thrust ducted propellers," he announced, beaming with what I suspected was pride. I looked at him, anticipating more details, but there were none. He simply stood by the table with his brow raised in a high arc.

"What about them?"

My reaction was obviously not what he expected. His brow drooped, causing him to look angry. I'm familiar with the ducted propeller propulsion system of the C-54 drone. My class report was thorough. Because they're part of our everyday lives, the information available was extensive. Ares assisted with some technical details.

"My design increases thrust by more than 20 percent with

the same power input," he blurted out. There was a long pause as he again waited for my reaction. It occurred to me he was seeking validation and perhaps trying to impress me. I decided to play along. After all, he was a senior apprentice and very familiar with the project.

"Really?" I exclaimed with more interest. "How is that possible?"

The more exuberant response perked him up. He removed the foil tarp covering the large blade and held it in front of me.

"What do you know about fluid dynamics?" he asked.

Perhaps it was the way he phrased the question or his smug expression, but I thought he was testing me. "I'm familiar with Bernoulli's principle. Also, Newton's third law and the resultant vortex caused by the centrifugal force on a spinning open propeller blade. The ducted design of the C-54 propulsion system virtually eliminates the vortex thus increasing lift, reducing noise, and limiting heat generation."

I glanced at Ares and noticed him pursing his lips together, stifling laughter. He was obviously able to hear our conversation but remained focused on his work. I turned back to Kane, expecting to see him frowning with disappointment. He was grinning ear to ear.

"Ares mentioned you were brilliant," he began. "He didn't say you were . . ."

"What?" I demanded.

Is this some shared mockery? Again, Kane stared for an uncomfortable amount of time. An unfamiliar sensation came over me—*self-consciousness?* I brushed my hair behind my ear without realizing I was doing it. *So confusing.* I looked at Kane. He kept watching me.

"*That* brilliant," he said, completing his statement.

After a moment, I regained control of myself and turned the conversation back to the blade. "You mentioned a new design."

"Not really a new design, a new application," he started. "Are you familiar with the variable-pitch propeller?" This question was more sincere and lacked any sarcastic tone. Although I'd completed extensive research on the C-54, my knowledge of propellers ended there. It was time to learn something from my superior apprentice.

"Not at all," I admitted.

"Very simply," he began without pretension, "a variable-pitch propeller can be rotated around its long axis to change the angle of attack while in motion." He held up the blade to demonstrate the action.

"You said your design increased thrust by 20 percent," I interjected. "The C-54 is capable of carrying over fifty pounds and certainly doesn't require higher speeds."

"True," he responded. He turned to Ares, who was now listening intently to our conversation. "Professor, can we show her now?"

Ares glanced at the secured room in the corner. A wave of exhilaration rolled over me. "Yes, Professor, can we show her now?" I repeated. He glared at me with a recognizable intensity. It was a reminder of my responsibilities.

He turned and started toward the corner. Kane nudged me to follow. I quickened my pace with Kane right behind me. We arrived at the entrance simultaneously, and Ares allowed the laser to scan his face. The heavy panel slid open, and we stepped inside. The room was larger than I expected it to be and was completely white from floor to ceiling. Bright lights shone down on a large object in the center of the room. It was covered by an equally large foil tarp. Near the right side of the object was a portable worktable holding several electronic components, most of which I didn't recognize.

The panel sealed behind us with a loud clank. I turned in response to the noise. The indicator light changed from green to red. A monitor showed an interior view of the lab, including the main entrance. *Maximum security?*

"Professor, may I remove the tarp?" Kane asked with giddy enthusiasm.

"Yes please, Kane."

Kane picked up a device from the portable table and pushed a button. The foil tarp was suspended by four thin wires from a ceiling-mounted winch. The remote activated the lift mechanism. As the tarp rose, I recognized support gears like those on the C-54, but they were far too large for a drone.

The tarp collapsed into a thin flowing column and was raised out of sight. I stared in disbelief. The object *was* an immense drone. It had four corner cowlings similar to C-54 motors, but these were four feet in diameter and jointed for independent movement. They connected to a center fuselage by oval-shaped booms. The entire surface of the disc-shaped drone was covered with interconnected photovoltaic cells.

I moved forward to examine the machine closely. Kane stood next to me. The nose portion of the fuselage was made of acrylic and resembled a prolate spheroid—like the long side of a bird egg. It was lined with a reflective material so I couldn't see inside. I was at a complete loss for words.

"I remind you," Ares started, "nothing you observe in this space is to be shared with anyone."

"Of course, Professor," Kane snapped.

"Yes, of course," I managed.

Ares stood with one hand on his chin, the other supporting his elbow. He was admiring the machine.

"But—what is it for?" I asked. "It's far too large for use in Life World."

Kane chimed in. "Actually, it's not—" A sharp look from Ares ended his comment. He quickly recovered. "We installed the last motor on Friday, complete with my design."

I had so many questions but realized Kane was anxious to share the details of his work. "How does your design function?" I finally asked with sincere interest.

He again perked up. "I'm sure you recognize the cowling design from the C-54."

"Yes, they're almost identical."

"Then you're familiar with the inherent stability created by the Coandă effect?" He didn't wait for my response. "The convex shape of the outer lip ring acts like a 360-degree airfoil," he said, using his hands to animate the point. "When the cowling is tilted for directional thrust, more lift is created at the lower portion of the lip. The difference in lift coefficient causes the cowling to drift back to its neutral state, thus diminishing acceleration." He paused to breathe.

The Coandă effect hadn't been included in my studies, but his explanation made it clear. "Go on," I said.

"Professor Ares challenged me to find a solution for the loss in acceleration." He glanced at Ares who acknowledged his comment. "I utilized a variable-pitch hub, coupled with a hydraulically actuated cam plate to change the propeller blade pitch when the cowling is tilted. The cam plate creates a higher angle of attack on the high-end blade and shallower angle on the low-end blade with each revolution." He paused again to verify my understanding.

"Thus, counteracting the Coandă effect and increasing thrust," I concluded for him.

"Right," he added. "By 20 percent."

He was excited to finally tell someone other than Ares about his success. I still didn't understand the purpose of the machine but found his ingenuity impressive.

"Well done, Kane."

Ares stepped forward and put his hands on the drone. There was a snapping sound as he released two latches on the nose. He raised the top half, which was hinged at the center of the fuselage. The lower half of the nose held an assortment of electronic devices and several rectangular casings.

"You asked what purpose it might serve," Ares paraphrased my question. "Most of the electronics are atmospheric monitoring devices. The lower nose segment holds an adjustable video sensor with a 240-degree visual field range. The drone is equipped with rear and side infrared sensors for obstacle detection and avoidance. A single operator can fly the unit remotely. It's an atmospheric research platform created to explore external environmental conditions."

"Explore Out World?"

Chapter 17

Assignment

My outburst turned both their heads. Standing paralyzed, I stared at the drone. I'd mentally prepared myself to accept challenges, endure punishment, and adapt to inevitable changes in support of the Cause. I was equipped for new developments and new revelations. It never occurred to me, however, any of it would involve the world outside of our sanctuary.

Kane broke the silence. "Professor, I have to report to three for the printing demonstration."

"Of course," Ares replied.

Kane extended his hand. "I look forward to working with you the rest of the week, Opal."

Still in shock, I managed to take his hand. "You, as well, Kane. Thank you."

Ares escorted him to the entrance, checking the monitor before opening the panel. Kane turned and waved on his way into the lab. After securing the room, Ares watched the monitor until Kane left. He turned back to me.

"You must have questions."

"As a matter of fact—" I replied, then stopped myself.

He recognized my hesitation. "When sealed, this room is a shadow space. It was designed for research and development with the understanding that surveillance equipment might interfere with project testing. We can speak freely."

I wasn't sure where to begin. "Is Kane . . . ?"

"No, not one of us. He's a competent apprentice and will assume his maintenance occupation on four as of Monday."

"But he knows about the drone—and Out World."

"He's aware the project is sanctioned and understands the repercussions if he violates his oath to the Court."

"Who else knows about the project?"

"Prior to Kane's arrival, an apprentice named Owen Five worked on the fuselage and motor support design. We spoke about Tara's father parent, Lake Four. He oversees manufacturing on three. We had difficulties with three-dimensional printing due to the size and complexity of some structures. For him to better understand the programming requirements, the Court approved his inclusion."

"Was I approved by the Court?"

"Of course. Yanic was aware of Kane's pending assignment on four. He knew a replacement would be needed for the final testing phase before launch."

"And his visit to our quarters on Saturday?" I pushed. "Part of the approval process?"

His words were measured. "You were recommended as an excellent candidate."

I thought for a moment before speaking. "You made the suggestion before assessments? Before I chose engineering?" I pieced together the timing. "Our visit to Jade's lab was planned all along."

"Yes," he replied.

I stared at him while processing the information. My belief

in the Cause hadn't waivered, but it was unsettling to have been manipulated. "What if I'd refused to join you?" I snapped.

He expected the question. "That possibility was considered, Opal. Revealing ourselves to you was a risk. We believe in your character. We put our trust and faith in your maturity and felt it was the right decision."

My relationship with Ares and Jade was built on mutual respect. I knew in my heart his statement wasn't another attempt at manipulation. I exhaled a long-held breath. "Of course," I replied, turning to the drone. "What is my assignment?"

Ares spoke without looking at me. He focused on the massive drone while explaining the master plan, covering possible outcomes.

"Several months ago Yanic visited my lab. He told me our power systems are showing signs of failure. The entire outer surface of the sanctuary is covered by photovoltaic cells in a series of arrays. Each array is made of a group of cell modules independently connected to the primary grid. If a module is damaged or incapacitated, it can be taken off-line without interrupting the overall system."

"Have there been new storms?" I asked. "Was the sanctuary damaged?"

"No. The primary system is fine and generates ample power for daily consumption. The issue is with non-solar hours. Several banks of lithium-titanate storage cells have corroded beyond repair."

"That's why the Court limited power usage at night."

"Right. We have a temporary backup solution, but it has never been utilized. Yanic asked me to manage activation of the system."

"What system?"

"Wind turbines. The outer structures on seventeen through twenty are retractable. There are four helical turbines secured horizontally on seventeen. When activated, they raise into position to generate supplemental electricity."

I tried to envision what he described. "When the outer structures are retracted, is the sanctuary exposed?"

"According to design specifications, the space between the floor of seventeen and the structure's apex is unused and virtually hollow. Sixteen has two air lock chamber lifts, providing safe access into seventeen. Our living area would never be directly exposed to the outside. The chamber lifts also serve as decontamination stations for anything, or anyone, entering the sanctuary."

"Has anyone ever . . . ?"

"There's no record of a breach," he quickly answered. "The chambers were designed to provide maintenance personnel direct access if malfunctions occurred during activation."

It was starting to come together. "When the turbine system is activated..." He waited for me to finish my thought. "You're going to launch the drone into Out World." As I searched my mind he raised his brow, indicating there was more. "The project is sanctioned by the Court and is being monitored by Yanic." By his expression, I could tell I was missing something.

Without comment, he walked to the entrance and checked the interior lab monitor. He returned and lowered the tarp, disconnecting the cables as it piled on the floor.

"I need your help," he said, motioning me toward the drone's center-nose section.

He handed two cable ends to me and held the others. "Attach the carabiners to the front and rear support rack loops."

I connected the carabiners and stood back. He reached behind the component stack and pulled apart two multi-prong wire connectors. Finally, he turned a silver handle on the center of the rack.

"Turn the handle on your side ninety degrees left."

The handle was below me. Using just my wrist didn't budge the stubborn lock. I adjusted my body for additional leverage then used my entire arm. It finally gave. "Okay."

He activated the winch. "Move back, please."

The cables rose and tightened. The entire collection of components lifted from the nose compartment. Ares pulled the rack forward, away from the fuselage, and lowered it to the floor. The nose section was now empty, except for a center support brace. He briefly inspected the interior.

"Come with me," he said.

I followed him to a locked storage compartment. Gaining access only required hand imprint recognition. When the scanner light flashed green, he lifted a small door. The compartment was four feet high and six feet wide. Inside was a wheeled cart covered by another tarp. He pointed to the cart handle on my side.

"We'll push this to the front of the drone."

My mind raced, guessing what mystery object we were moving. Ares lifted the tarp. Mounted on the rear of a rectangular frame, similar in size to the atmosphere component rack, was a formfitting seat. Armrests rose on each side, with toggle controllers installed on the ends. From the front section of the rack, a round bar rose toward the center of the seat. It supported a crescent-shaped casing with an electronic screen. Two multi-prong wiring plugs hung behind the seat. They mated perfectly with the receiving ends installed in the nose.

The prefabricated cockpit was not configured for Ares. It was clear why he directed me to study gyroscopic theory and why I was selected for the final stages of testing. The drone was never intended to be remotely controlled. It was designed to be piloted.

By me.

Chapter 18

Mission

"A res, you're not serious," I snapped in near panic.

His expression turned stoic. "When we told you the truth about nobles, you pleaded to join the Cause, to become one of us. I made it clear we couldn't reveal everything to you at once. This phase of our operation is not only critical, it will ultimately determine our success—or failure."

"You don't know what's out there. We've all heard the stories of banishment—searing heat, flesh-eating creatures."

"Stories, Opal," he insisted. "To your knowledge, has anyone ever returned from banishment? How then could we know anything about Out World?" He let me ponder the questions for a moment. "Do you recall the file labeled ATMOSPHERE in my portal?"

"Yes."

"That data was collected by sensors on the exterior of the sanctuary. I was given access to the information after agreeing to work with Yanic. Do you remember the ranges in temperature on the summary page?"

"I—I don't recall."

"The lowest recorded temperature was twenty degrees Fahrenheit during the month of January. The highest, one hundred-twelve in August. The average annual precipitation—rainfall—was more than thirty inches."

"A few months of data isn't a sufficient sample," I muttered.

"The data spans two decades. Furthermore, there have been no significant storms for the last century."

I stared blankly at the floor while considering the information. It was no longer about corrupt nobles; everything I thought I understood was unraveling. *Is any of it true? The Prophets, the scriptures, our salvation?* I struggled to find a safe place in my mind, silently pleading to The Giver for guidance. Ares waited for me to grasp the significance of the data.

"According to the Prophets," I began, "the destruction of Out World was to last four centuries. Is the planet healed? Are we all who remain?"

His face lit up, knowing I'd crossed a threshold of discovery. "Those are the questions we need to answer, Opal." He breathed deeply through his nose. "Perhaps you now understand why we couldn't burden you with every detail. What I'm about to tell you will provide a clearer perspective on the mission."

"What more...?" I left the question unfinished. I was weary from the constant shock of new revelations and frustrated by my own fragility. If my role was central to the mission, all expectations needed to be presented. No more surprises.

"It's not enough to have a clearer perspective. Tell me everything."

Ares stared at me in silence. After a few tense moments, he simply nodded. He began pacing back and forth while speaking. "Life World is one of three identical structures built at the beginning of the great storms. The Prophets were actually wealthy and powerful investors. They commissioned the development under a program called the Eden Project." He spread his arms upward. "This facility was the third completed. It's called Eden 3."

He paused. My expression indicated resolve, so he continued. "The original residents chosen for salvation were selected for their knowledge and skills. Their jobs were to manage the environmental systems in support of the elite. It was not by a preordained covenant with The Giver. They entered the sanctuary with their families under contract as indentured servants. We are the descendants of those residents, Opal, and we still serve."

His comments were absolute blasphemy. If heard or recorded, his corruption trial would be swift, his sentence—immediate banishment. Not reporting his transgression to the Court meant my trial for complicity would be equally as swift, my punishment the same. From the moment I committed to the Cause, my actions were contrary to all sworn vows and covenants. After this moment, there was no turning back, no possibility of redemption.

"How do you know this?"

"Yanic provided files with architectural and mechanical schematics for the sanctuary. The resident contracts were embedded within the files. I surmised much of the rest."

"Why would a noble share this information with a *servant?*"

He furrowed his brow in response to my emphasis on the word. Perhaps he was insulted, but he'd just explained we were still in servitude to the elites. His expression eventually relaxed.

"According to Yanic, Life World is in jeopardy. Our resources have dwindled. The ability to rehabilitate various support systems has diminished. The wind turbines can provide a temporary solution to the power storage dilemma; however, additional damage to the system may result in long-term outages."

"And nobles might lose control over us?"

My sarcasm was obvious, but he ignored the question. "For the purpose of self-preservation, the Core will respond to any decrease in power by adjusting energy flow away from less essential systems," he explained.

"Such as reducing power during non-solar hours," I said.

"Correct."

"But the Court announced those changes by decree on Sunday."

"This Assembly was not on the last Sunday of the month."

His statement sent a surge through my brain. Never had a decree been announced on any other than the last Sunday. My perspective was becoming clearer, but not just about the mission.

"They responded to changes already initiated by the Core."

He watched me consider further ramifications. He knew the scenarios scrolling through my brain because he'd already considered them.

"The Core will ultimately determine the priority of essential systems," he said, again reading my mind.

"Essential to survival of the Core," I concluded. "Not residents."

We stood in silence. I'd just learned that I wouldn't expire in my fiftieth year as expected. Now it seemed I'd only have months to live anyway. All of Life World was controlled by the Core: air and water purification, food production, temperature—everything required for human existence in our enclosed environment. Having joined the Cause, I believed our struggle was against the nobles. It was now clear they were simply guardians of a much greater adversary.

"What do you hope to accomplish with the drone?" I asked, breaking the silence.

He perked up. "According to Yanic, Eden 2 lies just twenty miles to the east. His proposal was to establish contact using a remotely controlled drone. He hopes they'll provide us the necessary resources to repair the power storage system."

"If the project is sanctioned by the Court, why perpetuate the atmospheric research facade?"

"Consider Yanic's position. To design, manufacture, and assemble a drone of this scale required a team of skilled residents. He couldn't risk revealing the current prevailing atmospheric conditions outside of the sanctuary." Ares paused. "The nobles derive their power and control over residents through our collective fear of Out World."

"Do you trust Yanic?"

"No," he responded without hesitation. "I knew from our first encounter it wouldn't end well for me or anyone involved with the project. If his plan is successful, the Court will remove all evidence of the undertaking. Status quo will be restored, and they'll continue their deceptive reign, albeit under the ultimate control of the Core. Yanic is familiar with every aspect of the project. When complete, he'll clean it up."

The nobles needed Ares and the rest of his team, if only temporarily, to complete a task they're incapable of performing. "You said his proposal was for a remotely controlled drone. How did you convince him a human pilot is necessary?"

"The Eden Project archives he shared included satellite images of the facilities while under construction. Between this sanctuary and Eden 2 lies a small mountain range with peaks as high as 3,000 feet. The only remote system available utilizes very high-frequency radio waves."

I completed his explanation. "VHF waves are limited by line of sight. There can be no obstructions between the transmitting and receiving antennas."

"Correct," he responded.

"But it's not the only reason you want a human pilot."

"Also correct."

No additional explanation was needed. His plan was brilliant in its simplicity. Making contact with Eden 2 was irrelevant. The video sensor on the drone will provide visual evidence of an Out World capable of supporting life. A human pilot will serve as witness to the observations. If residents don't fear banishment, they'll no longer fear nobles. There will be little to prevent a swift and certain Seeker revolt.

I scoffed at the irony. Ares was recruited by the Court to attempt a highly implausible mission meant to perpetuate their reign. They know he alone is capable of completing the project successfully. They're unaware of his deeply held commitment to destroy their dominion over Life World. *What a masterful tactician.* He convinced his handler to permit the construction of a human-operated drone, then recruited a motivated new Seeker to pilot the machine. *The Noble Yanic believes he's sending a harmless young female to complete his errand of survival. If only he knew.*

Chapter 19

First Flight

Our first test flight was Wednesday morning. Without explanation, Yanic moved the turbine activation and launch up to Saturday. It left us little time to prepare.

I rushed through grooming so I could review my notes in the interface room before going to the lab. Once I was engaged, I saw a pulsating light indicating a pending message. *Not now Star.* After reviewing the drone's flight systems, I expanded the instrument data files. *There's no Core link outside of the sanctuary.* The blinking light became far too distracting. Making a mental note to ask Ares about his plan for communication during the flight, I opened Star's message.

"Opal. It was wonderful seeing you in the atrium. I hope you're enjoying your apprenticeship. Please clear your schedule for our last free day before classes begin. See you then."

The file closed without prompting. There was nothing cryptic or unusual in her message except we'd made our plans just two days prior. It struck me as premature, almost desperate, to leave a reminder so soon. I fully intended to keep the appointment and already cleared my schedule with Ares. He and I agreed to keep the day mostly free to avoid suspicion.

I returned to my files and memorized several questions for Ares, including the need for contingency plans. Assuming the original drone design included redundant systems to compensate for potential failures, there was no indication how they were integrated. Every aspect of the design was scrutinized to reduce weight and preserve needed resources. We had one drone, and there was little possibility for rescue in the event of a catastrophic malfunction.

I left the room and entered the salon area. Jade and Ares were chatting casually. My meal was on the table.

"Good morning," I said.

Jade turned in my direction. "Good morning, Opal."

"Good morning," Ares added.

After I took my seat, Jade placed her hand on my arm. "Ares said your orientation is going well."

My response was intentional. "Honestly, I didn't expect the professor to assign so much research during the first week."

She straightened her back. "Well, I certainly hope Tara isn't expressing the same concern."

Ares joined in. "My guess is she's been crying hysterically, trying to meet the extraordinary expectations you place on apprentices."

We laughed together. It had been a while since we shared this kind of playful conversation, even if improvised. Pulling at a baguette, I allowed my mind to wander. I glanced around our quarters, noticing unremarkable details. *The lines and angles of our cabinetry are perfectly symmetrical. Appliances are all flush with the countertops. The gray floor is smooth as glass.* Every facet of our sanctuary was clean, sterile, utilitarian. My mission was to leave this secure space and enter the unknown—a world raw, untamed, and potentially wrought with peril.

"Wouldn't you agree, Opal? Opal?"

Hearing my name returned me to the moment. "Sorry?"

"I suggested my expectations were no greater than Ares's. Wouldn't you agree?"

They were still enjoying the banter, so I played my part. "That contest would likely end in a tie."

"Right," Ares said, standing. "Enjoy your meal, Opal. I must review data files before we depart for the lab." He turned to Jade. "We'll likely return late this evening due to project testing."

"I'll have May keep your meals warm," she replied.

—

It was no surprise to find Kane in the lab when we arrived. He wanted to witness the test flight and observe his motor design in action. I was surprised, however, to see the Noble Yanic and his keeper escort standing nearby. Ares and I bowed.

"Good morning, Excellency," Ares offered.

"Professor," Yanic replied, "I trust your new apprentice has been fully briefed on the project?"

We passed the worktable. I avoided eye contact with Yanic. Kane looked at me with a barely perceptible grin.

"Yes, Excellency," Ares responded. "Opal has reviewed the project files and—"

"Very well," Yanic interrupted. "Proceed with the demonstration."

Ares scanned the surface of his lectern. I assumed he was reviewing our activities from the previous night, mentally verifying everything was returned and in proper order. Kane couldn't know about the human flight capabilities of the drone. Ares raised his head.

"Of course," he finally replied. "Kane, gather the retention cables and shackle bolts." He turned to me. "Opal, bring the transmitter radio from the charging stand."

Kane and I completed our errands, and Ares secured the primary lab entrance. There could be no interruptions. Yanic instructed the keeper to stand sentry. He knew anyone with proper credentials could override the system. We all proceeded to the research room.

Kane activated the winch, raising the tarp out of sight. Yanic watched the senior apprentice climb beneath the drone and attached the thin steel tethering cables to floor anchors. The opposite ends were attached to the drone's landing gear using carabiners. The cables were approximately six feet in length and allowed vertical takeoff and some maneuvering. They reduced the risk of significant damage if control was lost.

Ares lifted the nose canopy and reached behind the component rack, verifying the servo links were connected. He checked the side latches then the front video sensor unit. After securing the canopy, he pulled the portable table away from the drone. He opened an oval-shaped container and removed oversized, fully enclosed interpreters. I gave him the transmitter unit and stood back. We all watched in anticipation. He secured the special interpreters and activated the transmitter.

"Remove the charging cords," he instructed.

Kane disconnected two cords from the lower segment of the fuselage. They recoiled into a portable cradle. He then moved next to me.

"Put your interpreters on," he said, loud enough for Yanic to hear. "The motors generate wind vortices, which may accelerate particles through the air."

Ares adjusted the transmitter. "All clear?" he asked.

"All clear, Professor," Kane replied.

Ares pushed a small button on top of the transmitter and the four drone motors started simultaneously. He let them idle for half a minute. Noise output increased as he added power. The drone rose slowly into the air. It remained remarkably stable, with only the slightest movement as it hovered a foot over the floor. Ares made small adjustments with the transmitter control sticks, maneuvering the machine in various directions. It moved left a few feet then back to position. The nose rotated forty-five degrees right, then back. Ares raised it to a four-foot hover for about a minute, then let it settle back to the floor. He reduced the power to idle momentarily, then shut the motors down.

"Remove the tethering cables then return to your position."

Kane sprang forward without speaking. He released the carabiners then unscrewed the shackle bolts from the floor anchors. The cables were coiled and placed on the lower shelf of the portable table. He quickly returned to my side.

"All clear, Professor," Kane reported.

Ares started the motors and raised the drone to a hover once more. He made several small adjustments then directed the machine upward, almost to the ceiling. The drone maneuvered around the room with the nose pointed at Ares. He then directed it to the far side wall. Using the pitch control he tilted the motors, and it accelerated forward. He pitched back just in time to avoid colliding with the opposing wall. Finally, he maneuvered the drone back to the starting position and shut the motors down.

"Did you see that acceleration?" Kane asked excitedly.

I looked at him without expression. It took a moment for him to recall a noble was present. He bowed his head and looked at the floor.

Ares removed the visual display unit. "Yes, Kane," he replied. "It was instant and responsive."

Yanic removed his interpreters and walked behind us toward the entrance. We remained still as Ares made his way to the panel. I couldn't hear what Yanic said, but knew it was about the launch on Saturday. Ares responded, "On schedule." Yanic departed the room.

Ares circled the drone in silence. After a brief inspection, he addressed the two of us.

"Kane, complete a diagnostic report on power consumption. Specifically, for drainage during maneuvering and acceleration."

"Do you expect accurate data from such a short test?" I asked.

"Accurate as can be," Kane interjected. "The VHF control

system includes bidirectional telemetry, providing feedback from the receiving module. A simple algorithm will give us battery performance and longevity expectations from a full charge."

"What about the photovoltaic system?" I persisted. "How long will it extend flight time? How will your algorithm contrast power generated from artificial lighting and the sun?"

Kane didn't respond. He looked to Ares for support.

"Very good questions, Opal," Ares intervened. "Our analytic capabilities are obviously limited in scope until we can perform tests in the actual environment."

Kane was confused, but Ares understood my line of questioning. "If the initial launch is on Saturday," I added, "when exactly do we make significant improvements if testing results don't prove sufficient for extended flight?"

"Professor, do we need to clear every detail with our third-day apprentice?" Kane retorted sarcastically.

I looked at him with a most unpleasant expression. He leaned backward, retreating from his dominant stance.

"Kane," Ares snapped, handing him the transmitter. "The diagnostics, please."

Kane took the radio and exited the room. I turned to Ares, who didn't look pleased.

"Opal, I understand your apprehension, but you must be careful. For his own safety, we can't allow Kane to suspect this experiment is for anything other than atmospheric monitoring."

"His safety?" I questioned. "After Saturday he's no longer on the project."

"Actually . . ." Ares began.

"What?"

"Kane reports to four tomorrow. Yanic just informed me."

"One less witness," I said. "Yanic has already begun his cleaning process."

Chapter 20

Milestone

Ares and I returned to a quiet lab Thursday morning and went directly to the research room. He double-checked the security system. Without delay, we removed the cart from the storage compartment. Our primary objective was to complete the drone's interior modifications and ensure its total weight didn't exceed deviation parameters.

After Kane left Wednesday evening, Ares and I removed and weighed all the atmospheric components. We compared those numbers to the cockpit, combined with my weight. There was a thirty-pound reduction in overall load, so Ares decided to replace the original batteries with larger units, effectively increasing flight longevity and distance.

"I'll install the larger cells first," he said. "The wiring harness will be redirected but won't require significant alteration."

While Ares installed the batteries, I lowered the winch and attached the cables to the cockpit module. It rose from the cart and lowered smoothly to the floor. I climbed into the seat and pressed my feet on the support pedals. The larger stick controls on the armrests felt stiffer than the remote I'd practiced with on Wednesday, but fit nicely in my hands.

"How does it feel?" Ares asked, leaning over the nose.

I looked up with a grin. "Perfect."

"Good. Shall we install it?"

I leaped out of the seat and grabbed the winch remote. A wave of exhilaration rolled over me. As the rack rose, Ares guided it into position. He connected the electrical harnesses behind the seat along with smaller wire connectors near the nose front.

He pointed to the interior of the nose canopy. "Let's remove the lining," he said. "Pull the triangular tab, on the upper corner, forward, slowly at first."

We no longer needed the silver contact material to mask the contents. With the lining removed, the entire cockpit was visible. The only portion not made from transparent acrylic was the center brace below the seat.

Ares quickly inspected the cockpit area. His brain was in full gear. More than just a visual inspection, he was completing a thorough mental checklist. Everything had to be in place. He indicated his satisfaction. The drone was prepared for flight.

"Are you ready?"

"Absolutely," I responded, still unable to contain my smile.

"Check the landing gear on your side," he added. "Pull down the hinged brace on the forward strut. There's an identical brace on this side, installed to help you into the cockpit."

Lowering the brace locked it into place perpendicular to the strut. I stepped on the perforated rung and pulled myself into the cockpit. With the safety belt snapped around my waist, I settled into the seat. The slanted foot pedals and padded armrests made it surprisingly comfortable. I gently gripped the control sticks.

Ares reached inside and pushed a button on the center

display. It lit up, revealing an eight-inch-high by fourteen-inch-wide screen. It appeared to malfunction at first. The middle segment was solid white, but after my eyes adjusted to the light, I could see a horizontal line across the white mass. I was looking at an image of the research room being recorded by the drone.

He pointed at the display. "These instruments provide basic operational status of the drone. The blue gauge on the left is an altimeter, indicating your height above ground. As you likely noticed, the middle screen is coupled with the forward video sensor. It's equipped with low-light image intensifiers, providing a visual backup should visibility diminish."

"How are we storing the images?"

"A drive unit records everything the sensor views when operational. It's installed behind your left foot pedal. Unless you deactivate the module, it will continue recording."

"These bar graphs indicate battery charge levels?"

"Right. There are four main banks. The green bars drop first as the charge is depleted. When only red bars remain, you'll have approximately ten minutes of power in reserve."

To this point, we'd spent little time discussing mission logistics. The closer it came to flight time, the more questions came to mind.

"So . . . the photovoltaic system will provide continuous power generation, even while I'm in flight?"

"Correct. The system will extend your total operational time."

"What is the estimated total?"

"A full initial charge, combined with solar generation, should provide fifty minutes of continuous flight time."

I made mental calculations. Ares seemed to read my thoughts again.

"At a ground speed of ninety miles per hour, in straight and level flight, the estimated time to Eden 2 is just over thirteen minutes. Assuming the mountain range information is accurate, climb and descent should require an additional six minutes."

He paused to let me filter the information. "The data we have for atmospheric conditions is collected from sensors on *this* facility. We can only interpolate what you'll experience in flight."

"So, if the calculations are correct, I'll have only twelve minutes during the entire trip to address unforeseen variables?" My question was more of a statement.

"I'll run new diagnostics with the larger battery cells. We'll have a final briefing before the launch. Now, do you see this button?" It was under the main power button. "The override switch changes control mode from pilot to remote operator."

"Do you expect me to panic?"

"No, Opal. I don't believe you'll ever look at the button again. It's an option, however, if something goes wrong." He grasped a small cord above my head. "Use this to pull the canopy down. Be sure to lock both sides. Watch for my all-clear signal before you attempt liftoff."

The canopy was locked into position. I pushed the power button, and the center display came alive. Ares moved to the front corner with the transmitter. Although remote control was a safety option, the primary purpose was to gather new power usage data. He lifted his hand, thumb in the upright position. I slowly pushed the left control stick forward. The increase in motor revolutions caused a slight vibration. The sound of propellers striking air was dampened inside the sealed cockpit. Adding a small amount of forward pressure on the throttle, the altimeter clicked to five—airborne.

My heart raced, hovering high above the floor. The altimeter indicated ten feet. I looked outside the canopy, using peripheral vision to maintain position, then climbed to fifteen feet. After stabilizing the drone, I rolled left toward the reinforced wall. I reversed the stick and rolled back to the right. When I pitched forward, it accelerated quickly. The motors and servos responded instantly to control input. I returned to the starting position and eased the throttle control back. The altimeter counted backward from fifteen to twelve, to eight, and then five. Touchdown.

I released the control sticks, and they returned to a neutral position. The motors wound down to a stop. One push on the power button and the center display disappeared. Ares rushed over. I sat for a moment, scanning the cockpit. The only sound was my heart pounding from excitement. *Incredible. Is this real or a dream? Will I ever be able to tell anyone? Me, a human, taking flight.*

Ares raised the canopy and helped me get out. I folded the foot brace back into its original position.

"Well done, Opal. I'll run the new diagnostics now."

"What should I do?"

"Connect the charging cables, then complete a full visual inspection. Include the motors and propellers. Make note of any flaw or defect. We have today and tomorrow to address concerns."

He picked up the transmitter on his way to the lab. After verifying the room was sealed, I plugged the charging cables into the fuselage ports. My inspection required use of the foot braces to check the motor cowlings. The rear struts were equipped with the same braces—another feature designed specifically for me.

To be thorough, I climbed under the fuselage to check from below. An immense eye stared back at me. The Life World crest was emblazoned on the bottom, covering nearly the entire surface. I noticed the image during our first test but displayed no reaction with Yanic present. It scarcely crossed my mind during the last two days of activity.

In primary, we were taught the meaning of each facet. The isosceles triangle outline represents our sanctuary, sole shelter provided for the chosen. *Chosen? We're merely servants—and not alone.* The eye is The Giver, watching over his cherished flock. *We're watched by nobles and their Core master.* The double helix resembles a DNA strand, representing everlasting human life. *Life which ends mandatorily at age fifty.* The rising sun means there will always be a tomorrow. *A sun which has never shown on the residents of Life World.*

An intense anger swelled inside of me. I wanted to scratch away the crest. Remove the eye and eliminate their ability to see me. Erase the sun and take away their tomorrow. *They should all be destroyed.* Then a calm came over me. *The sun.* I finally understood. *Three rays—Eden 3. Is it so simple? Has it been displayed for so long we can't see it?*

"Double helix," I said out loud. "Human life." Starting at the top, I traced my fingers down to the sun. "To see human life, look east." My words quickly sank in. "We were meant to contact them after the storms." I slid from under the drone and ran to the entrance. When the panel opened, I rushed into the lab. "Ares!"

He looked up from his lectern. The Noble Yanic stood next to him.

Chapter 21

Research

Friday morning I was anxious to get back in the drone. My drone. Ares had planned one more test flight, but it would be later in the afternoon. He was still concerned about raising unwanted attention and insisted we keep our original plans, including my scheduled meeting with Star.

Making my way to five, I watched the faces of passing residents. Students were enjoying the free day before Monday classes. Most were simply going about their daily routines, completing required tasks, fulfilling the needs of nobles. They were oblivious to the power reserve issue and imminent danger threatening their existence. My impulse was to scream at them, reveal everything. *Can they be persuaded to take action? Will they rise up to escape the tyranny of perpetual servitude?*

As I stepped onto the lift, those thoughts quickly faded. The apprehension I'd experienced before my initial meeting with Star returned. She would likely try to extract every detail of my activity, and there was now a lot more to conceal. I decided to again control the conversation by asking my own questions.

Fortunately, no one followed me out of the lift. Five was mostly void of residents. A few students meandered, searching for assigned lecture halls. I'd done the same when entering secondary. It's not wise to elicit unwanted scrutiny by being tardy the first day; some professors relish making examples of apathetic underclassman.

Star was seated on our bench. Although no one was near, it wasn't prudent to have an open conversation in the area. Given the nature of activity on this level, coupled with the normal density of resident traffic, it was reasonable to assume every square inch was monitored. Unlike the atrium, here we were surrounded by walls and pillars where devices could be concealed. I was certain she had the same concerns.

"Good morning, Star," I said, approaching from behind.

"Hello, Opal."

She circled the bench and we embraced. Her hug was cordial, unfeeling.

"I trust your first week of apprenticeship went well?" she asked.

"You know better than most how demanding Ares can be. Tell me about cyber systems."

Without speaking, she took my arm and pulled me down a corridor. We passed several hall entrances, eventually entering a grooming facilities foyer. Motion detectors responded to our presence, activating the primary lights. I expected to be led into the female lavatory. Instead, Star stopped at the foyer's end. In silence, she donned her interpreters then activated her drive. I pointed to my case. She shook her head *no* and began manipulating the console.

Considering my experiences over the past seven days, what happened next shouldn't have surprised me. A thin rectangular line of light appeared on the wall surface, extending vertically from the floor to nearly seven feet. As the light intensified, it formed the outline of an entranceway. The wall slid open, and Star stepped into a dark chasm. She turned and waved for me to follow. I hesitantly stepped inside a long corridor approximately four feet wide. With a motion of her hand, the wall closed behind us.

"Star, what is this place? Where are we?"

"We're in a service corridor. The concealed entrance we passed through is called a gateway. They're positioned strategically throughout the sanctuary."

"Service corridor?"

"Opal, cyber systems includes more than simple programming or restoring resident access. Every aspect of Life World is part of an electronic network with the Core at its center. Just like any machine, parts wear out or malfunction and must be repaired or replaced. These corridors allow CS technicians to perform those functions."

"And you were given access as an apprentice?"

"I'm certain Ares exposed you to new information, even as an apprentice."

She was right of course, but I didn't allow myself to be drawn into the debate. The subject had to be changed. "Is this all you have to show me, or is there more?"

She hesitated, obviously realizing I'd redirected the conversation. But it didn't matter. She was far too anxious to protest.

"Have you ever been to the sub-levels?"

"No, never. If I had, you would've been the first to know."

She glanced behind her then turned back to me. "At the end of this corridor is a service lift. It will take us to the sub-levels. Will you go with me?"

"Star, I doubt an apprentice technician is permitted to explore the sub-levels. My being in this corridor is grounds for corruption charges."

"On the contrary, Opal. We're able to access this space because I am cleared. Your presence can be easily explained as an engineering apprentice assisting me with research."

I studied her face. Her enthusiasm was sincere and her reasoning plausible, but who was she to explain my presence? This was definitely a bad idea, but my curiosity won out. "Research," I repeated. "What kind of research?"

With a wide smile, she grabbed my arm and pulled me down the corridor.

"Let's go. I'll think of something along the way."

The service lift was much smaller than those in the central stations. Star made several finger motions and four columns of numbers appeared on a square control screen. The first column descended from number sixteen to eleven. *The wind turbine bases were located on seventeen.* The next column started at ten and ended at six. Continuing the pattern, the third ranged from five to one. Five was illuminated, indicating our current location. The last column shown in reverse beginning with SL, then SL1 through SL5—the sub-levels.

"What is SL?"

"I'm not sure," she answered. "Let's go to the aquaculture farms on sub-three. We can stop there on our way back."

Before I could respond, she entered several commands and the lift started to descend. The tightness in my abdomen returned as I imagined how to explain such unconscionable behavior to Ares. My flight into Out World was in less than twenty-four hours, and I was risking potential banishment on a hapless adventure. If we were discovered, being detained by keepers for interrogation would be the least of my problems.

The lift stopped abruptly; SL3 was illuminated on the control screen. Star manipulated her console, but the panel didn't open immediately.

"Is everything okay?"

"Yes," she said. "I'm scanning the CS dispatch itinerary to see if technicians are working on this level."

"Well?"

She didn't need to respond, as the lift panel opened wide.

We stepped out together, spinning back quickly when it closed behind us. We both sighed with nervous anticipation. It was the kind experienced when knowingly approaching danger, but still inching forward. I'd felt something similar the previous week using Ares's drive—when I willingly crossed the boundary separating right from wrong. *Given all that has transpired, I'd definitely do it again.* I felt a mischievous smile cross my face. It wasn't a true smile. It was more the expression your face takes when washed in a wave of enlightenment—when you lose your innocence but are comfortable with your new self.

The passageway was warm, humid, and dimly lit. Stacks of horizontal pipes stretched along the opposite wall, disappearing into an opening fifty feet ahead. A slowly pulsating light emitted from the opening, interacting with a thin bank of smoke. The rolling motion of the smoke reminded me of holographic clouds in the tube.

"Let's go," Star whispered, starting forward in a crouched position.

Her behavior seemed odd, considering her unrestricted access to gateways and service lifts. It was obvious we were breaking a multitude of rules and needed to have a frank discussion about honesty. I checked behind me then closed the distance between us. We moved closer to the left side, nearer the pipes where there was a slight vibration from the movement of compressed fluids.

As we neared the lighted intersection, moisture in the air thickened. What looked like smoke was a thin mist of water vapor descending from above. Star pressed her back against the pipes and peered around the corner. After a moment she waved me forward, and we turned into the mist. The pipes wrapped around the wall, feeding into an immense acrylic tank. On the opposite side of the passageway, a similar set of pipes fed into a parallel structure. The transparent walls extended up from the floor, leaving only a four-foot gap to the ceiling. The tanks looked to be a hundred feet long.

We moved slowly, glancing from one side to the other, looking for movement in the water. The only visible life forms were long strands of kelp rising from the bottom, swaying back and forth in a rhythmic motion. We stopped abruptly at the sound of a large splash. In the right-side tank, a blizzard of small pellets drifted downward in the water. Within seconds, thousands of fish swarmed over the pellets in an eating frenzy. They circled the food, creating a massive ball of dark shadows and flashing fins. Many breached the unseen surface, creating a gurgling sound that echoed down the passageway. As the majority of the pellets were consumed, the frenzy dissipated, and the echo faded. Several small fish continued to circle, fighting over leftover morsels.

I spotted an oddly shaped silver fish picking over the bottom and nudged Star.

"Look," I whispered.

We watched it gather large gulps of material then eject sand and debris through its gills. Several more of the grazers worked well-defined areas between kelp strands. The territories approached each other, but never overlapped. There were dozens of little plowed fields scattered throughout the kelp forest. I knew these farms existed because fish was a staple in our diet, but I never imagined the sheer magnitude of the operation.

"Opal, come on."

"What more is there to see?"

"I don't know. Let's find out."

Without further discussion, she continued down the passageway. We walked softly to avoid making noise. I was calculating the volume of water in one massive tank when a large school of fish flashed by, startling us both. Halfway down the passageway, she stopped and began manipulating her console.

"We have to go."

"What is it?"

"Now, Opal."

She hurried past me in the direction we came from. I hesitated long enough to see the tiny B2-H enter the far end of the passageway. My attention was drawn away from the bird by the reflection on a keeper's face visor following close behind. There were two of them, and they were running in our direction.

"Move," Star called again.

I turned and bolted after her without looking back. She was twenty paces ahead of me and disappeared into the mist at the intersection. After turning through the mist, I saw her standing at the wall where we first entered. She was making quick hand gestures in the air. I arrived as the gateway opened and leaped inside.

"Halt." A keeper shouted, just as it closed.

The lift started upward. Neither of us spoke. We were both bent at the waist and breathing heavily. I looked up to see a wide grin cross her face.

"That—was—close," she gasped.

My brain was somewhere between exhilaration and exasperation as I processed the incident with adrenaline flowing through my veins. Star was gleaming with excitement. *Why did she run? Is she not cleared for access?* I finally caught my breath and was about to confront her when the lift stopped. She turned as the panel slid open.

"SL," she announced.

"Star, no."

She stepped into the dark passageway and took a final deep breath, recovering from our sprint. Her exaggerated expression was a mix of determination and trepidation. She was on the edge. Whether from the excitement or some deeper compulsion, Star was eager for more.

"Let's go, Opal. It won't take long for them to find where we've stopped."

I didn't move from the lift. "That's precisely why we should return to five," I demanded. "It's highly unlikely they'll accept your *research* explanation at this point."

"Perhaps not, but they might be waiting on each level to find who returns on this lift. We need to find another gateway before reinforcements are summoned or a lockdown is triggered."

Her reasoning was sound. Keepers would be dispatched to each level. When no intruders were found, a more thorough search would be initiated. I reluctantly stepped into the passageway.

"Find another gateway and get us back."

"Okay, Opal. But we can't stay here while I search."

She glanced in both directions then headed to our left. We moved quickly without running, while she worked her console. Small luminescent circles embedded in the floor provided direction but little light. As we progressed, I noticed narrow openings along the side walls. They were spaced approximately forty feet apart and were completely void of light. There was a subtle change in air pressure as we crossed each opening, indicating they were small, perpendicular corridors.

At the end of the main passageway, we could only turn right. As we rounded the corner, I noticed a flickering glow in the distance. Star stopped and made several hand motions.

"There's a gateway ahead, close to that light," she said.

We walked toward the pulsating beacon, crossing another dark opening. I sensed a presence behind me just as the hand closed around my mouth.

Chapter 22

Betrayal

An arm wrapped around my upper body and pulled me back into the darkness. Star was oblivious to the silhouette approaching her from behind. It seized her in the same manner. I was pinned against a cold cement wall. I could see Star's interpreters bounce by as she was pulled farther into the corridor. I feared the worst as her muffled protests went silent.

The hand around my mouth forced my head to turn slowly. Now facing into the passageway, I stopped breathing as two keepers walked by the opening. Our captors were preventing our apprehension. My constricted muscles relaxed. Whoever detained me sensed the change and eased their hold but didn't release me entirely. After several minutes, a wave of air rushed by and the pressure around me changed. An opening behind us had been breached. I was pulled through. The floor changed from cement to steel grating.

After the opening was sealed, my captor released me and lit

a globe lamp. He was tall and looked several years my senior. His gray shell was soiled. Instead of sandals, he wore long, black boots. Scarring on his hands shown prominently on his dark skin. The other male was equal in height, with wavy hair hanging over his forehead. Both were thick with muscles that stretched their shells near the point of rupture. They were engineered for physical occupations. The second one released Star and pushed her in my direction.

"Keep your hands off of me, sub rat!" she shouted.

He stepped toward her, and I jumped between them. My presence temporarily halted his advance. He scowled and clenched his fists.

"Flint, enough," my captor scolded.

Flint folded his arms over his chest and glared at me. He jutted his chin toward Star. "Not very appreciative for being rescued, is she Chet?"

"Rescued?" Star snapped. "From what?"

"Star," I interrupted. "Two keepers were trailing us. I watched them walk by."

"We can take care of ourselves," she snarled.

"Really?" Chet scoffed. "Thirty seconds more and you would've taken a charge from a gauntlet. This area is restricted."

Star glared at Chet but didn't push further. I broke the silence.

"Why are you here?"

He glanced at Flint. "Our occupations are on this level."

"Sub rats," Star mocked.

Chet grabbed her by the upper arm. "Say it once more and I'll throw you to the keepers myself."

"Let her go!" I shouted. "Now."

He released his grip and she yanked her arm away. "How did you gain access to the service sectors?" he demanded.

She didn't speak, only stared at him in silence.

"Those keepers were close, they could've taken you at any time," he pushed. "Who are you?"

Star raised her hand in front of her, attempting to access her console. Chet reacted and lunged forward, taking her whole body in his arms.

Flint grabbed me from behind. "Star!" I shouted.

They fell to the floor and Chet pulled her arms behind her back. After securing her wrists with one hand, he removed the interpreters.

"Stop it!" she shouted, writhing beneath him.

"Let her go!" I yelled, struggling to pull free from Flint.

Chet looked up at me. "Is she your friend?" he asked.

"Yes. Release her."

"You're aware she's a noble, right?"

"What are you talking about?" I snapped. "No."

He inserted two fingers in her shell collar and pulled it down, revealing the top of her spine. At first, it was unclear what he was showing me. She moved her head to one side, and I noticed the oval-shaped silver object embedded in her skin.

"What—is that?" I managed.

Chet pulled his fingers free from her collar, allowing it to fold back into place. He released her hands and stood up straight. Flint released me and moved next to Chet. My impulse was to reach for Star and help her up, but I didn't move. She slowly rose to her feet and stepped backward, without looking at me.

Chet watched her as he spoke. "Cerebral interface port, implanted in noble offspring and keeper novices at year twelve."

Star searched the floor, still avoiding my stare.

"Where did you learn this?" I asked. "How did you know she's a . . ." My voice trailed off, not able to say the word.

He continued looking at Star. "She gave herself away. Nobles use *sub rat* as a derogatory term when referring to workers in the sub-levels. Those keepers in the passageway weren't after you for capture. They were there to protect her."

"No," I countered. "They pursued us through the fish tanks."

"They were pursuing you," he insisted, "not her." He circled Star with his head tilted in her direction while continuing to address me. "They likely saw you as a threat—assumed you forced her there. She knew she was in no danger and obviously didn't care what happened to you."

"That's not true," Star murmured.

"Really?" Chet raised his voice. "Why don't you tell your friend what happens to residents found guilty of corruption?"

She looked up at him, jaw clenched. "I would've taken care of her."

Flint laughed. "Right. We've disposed of many residents who were taken care of by nobles."

"What do you mean?" I asked.

Star was suddenly alarmed. "Don't listen to them Opal, they're just trying to scare you."

I watched her, recalling her strange behavior throughout the week—odd comments, paranoia. *If the port was implanted in her twelfth year, she knew all this time of her status. The last three years of our friendship have been a complete and utter lie.*

"Disposed of—how?" I pressed.

"Incineration," Chet announced, still looking at Star. "That's our occupation. We rid Life World of its human refuse."

"Right," Flint added. "Anyone sentenced to banishment ends up down here before their day ends. Her protests would've made no difference if they thought you discovered restricted information. We'd be the last to see your terminated corpse."

Chet obviously recognized the horror in my eyes because his expression softened. I sensed he wanted to share more, perhaps cleanse his mind of the guilt he carried through confession.

"We also process Transitioners," he said, "after their organs have been harvested."

"And depleted nobles," Flint added matter-of-factly.

Their comments were more than shocking. Never in my darkest dreams did I imagine the atrocities nobles carry out to perpetuate their power. "Harvested organs? Depleted nobles?" I muttered.

"Opal, don't listen—"

"Be quiet, Star!"

Flint addressed Star. "You know exactly what we're talking about, don't you?"

She looked at the grate below.

Chet continued. "Level twelve doesn't contain plush quarters where Transitioners live out their final year in peace and tranquility. It's a cryo-holding facility. At year forty-nine their bodies are stored until organs are extracted for transplant into elderly nobles."

Star became increasingly agitated, her hands shook. "Opal, please—" she whispered.

"No, Star. I want to know." I turned to Chet. "What is a depleted noble?"

He pointed at Star. "The interface port embedded in her spine is coupled to her brain by nano-threads. If she's chosen to be a surrogate processor, her brain will be linked to the Core and used for information storage and data processing. The remainder of her existence will be more machine than human. Unfortunately, the brain can only operate at 70 percent capacity for a limited time before deterioration. Once depleted, they're terminated and sent to us for disposal. We remove and catalog the ports, then incinerate the corpses."

"Lies!" Star screamed. "How could you possibly know?"

Chet put his face close to hers. "Because it's the truth!" he yelled back. "There are those of us who seek—"

He pulled away from her, catching himself. Star fell to her knees sobbing, hands covering her face. Chet turned to me and our eyes locked. I responded with a barely perceptible nod, and he immediately knew. Nothing more needed to be said. We both looked at Flint. He too understood.

I turned my attention to Star. "We need to go."

She wiped her tears as she stood. Chet held out the interpreters; she grabbed them from his hand. He stepped back and pointed into the darkness.

"There's a small service lift at the end of this walkway. It's rarely used and will take you as high as ten. I suggest you don't return to the level where you started." He looked at me. "Your friend knows if she reveals us to the keepers, we'll be interrogated before termination. I believe she called you Opal, correct?"

Star looked at Chet, then me. "I won't say anything—I swear."

After one last look at the men, I replied to Star. "Take me out of here."

She put her interpreters on, and we started down the walkway. After fifteen paces I glanced over my shoulder. The Seekers were gone.

Chapter 23

Renewed Covenant

We accessed the small lift without speaking. Star closed the panel, but it didn't move. The overhead light dimmed gradually to a red hue. I assumed she'd rendered the lift inoperable to avoid attracting attention from investigating keepers. She turned her drive bezel one click to the left. The neuro-loops retracted, and the ID screen faded to black. She secured it in her case, along with her interpreters.

We didn't look at each other for several seconds. At first, she appeared profoundly sad, perhaps longing for the wonders and simplicity of our earlier years. The moment of nostalgia ended quickly. Her brow lowered; her expression hardened.

"Did you enjoy that, Opal?"

"Star, don't you dare make this about me," I snapped. "You've known for three years."

"Yes," she started, "and how do you suppose that conversation begins? 'Good morning, dear friend. I'm now your superior and you'll soon serve me'?"

"Serve you?"

"Don't be naive, Opal. You know how Life World works."

"I'm quite aware of how Life World works, Star. What I never imagined possible is my closest friend betraying me."

"I didn't choose this." Her hands were now balled in tight fists by her side. Her eyes welled with moisture; her whole body quivered.

"You could've told me," I said in a lower tone.

Tears rolled down her face. "How, Opal? Tell me how."

She was in an impossible situation. Revealing the truth meant an end to our friendship. Nobles were not permitted to openly fraternize with residents. Only by concealing their identities could they attend general population classes. Noble offspring were placed with resident parental units as a practical solution to the lack of separate development facilities. If Ares and Jade had discovered her status, our relationship would've been forbidden. Even now, a wrong move could spell disaster for my mission. There was no option but to proceed with caution. I, too, was concealing a great secret.

"It must've been hard for you," I acknowledged.

She sighed. "You can't imagine."

"The knee injury? You were out of primary for four days."

"It's why you weren't allowed to visit me," she added.

I chuckled to myself. "You were climbing in the castle the day you returned. It never occurred to me how quickly you recovered."

"Opal, I didn't understand what they did to me, or why. I was told no one could know about the port. It took weeks of pestering before my mother parent finally explained."

"How did you feel when you learned the truth?"

"Honestly? Important. Like I had a higher purpose. It was the way she explained it."

I pieced together several memories. "Shortly after then, your class rankings improved."

"The port can be used to upload data," she admitted. "I was finally able to perform as well as you. You'll never understand what it meant to me."

"But you weren't doing the work," I protested. "It was programmed into you."

"Please don't judge me, Opal."

"And your Thursday afternoon tutoring sessions?"

"Indoctrination, instructions in noble etiquette. What more can I tell you? Like I said, I didn't choose this."

I felt sympathy for her, but disdain for all nobles. Their intellect and wisdom aren't derived from superior genetics or individual effort, rather by uplink from a machine. Despite her genetic profile and constant data delivery, Star remained second to me in class rankings. *Was it by design? To reduce suspicion?* If there was any consolation for me, it was that she'd never take true pride in her academic accomplishments.

"Had we not encountered Chet, would you have told me?"

"Opal, believe me, I've tried. My plan was to tell you in the atrium until the T-8 approached. I brought you to the service corridors because there's no electronic surveillance. I didn't want to put you at risk."

I made a mental note about the corridors. "If there's no surveillance, how did the keepers track us?" As the words left my mouth, I glanced at her case. "Was your drive active the entire time?"

"Of course," she replied.

I thought for a moment. "Can you activate the lift without it?"

"No. I don't know how," she admitted.

I examined the lift control display. "We have no choice but to use your drive." I paused. "When you access the controls, select one through ten for destination. When the lift moves, deactivate your drive again."

Her face lit up as she grasped my idea. "The confusion may delay their response. We can exit on one and make our way back through the public stations."

I nodded. "But what if they are waiting on one?"

She stiffened her back. "I'll exercise my authority and demand they search sub-level three for the suspicious pair we encountered." Her expression went somber. "Opal, I'm sorry I didn't tell you sooner. You're my dearest friend. We must always look out for each other. Let's renew our covenant here, now. No matter what happens, nothing will come between us. We two . . ."

"Forever."

We both smiled. She was the Star I knew from primary. The one who ruled the atrium castle like a monarch, with me as her trusted adviser. Then, it was only make-believe. As she activated her drive, I made a silent plea to The Giver. *Please, don't let them find us.*

The lift stopped on one. After a longer than usual delay, the panel slid open. I assumed pulse gauntlets had to contact the body to be effective until seeing bolts of electric current lurch toward Star's abdomen. She crumpled to the floor at my feet.

—

I awoke on the research room floor next to the drone, remembering only my reflection in the keeper's face visor. The relentless pounding in my head was worsened by severe body aches. It was hard to breathe through the coagulated blood in my nose. When I tried to stretch my legs, the muscles refused to cooperate. My calves cramped, causing my toes to curl up. My groaning and grimacing attracted the attention of Ares.

"It will pass," he said. "Drink this."

It took several minutes to pull myself into a seated position on the floor. Ares tried to help, but each attempt resulted in me wincing from pain. He placed the silver container next to me and returned to his work. I drank the water in small sips. Even swallowing was difficult. Beyond the pain, I felt helpless—vulnerable. I tried to imagine what Silas and Roma endured during interrogation. *How many times was the gauntlet used on them? How did they maintain their sanity? Would they not have confessed to all manner of corruption to make it stop?* Damn the nobles.

"Ares!" I yelled, rising to my feet.

He rushed over and took my arm. "Move slowly," he insisted.

"Star—where is she?"

He noticed the look of panic. "Star will be fine."

"Did you see her? Did they bring her here?"

"Opal, calm down and listen to me. You were apprehended by a keeper squad on level one. Fortunately, Yanic intervened and had you brought here. He told me Star was returned to her quarters."

"And you believed him?"

He released my shoulder and stepped back. "What difference does it make?" he snapped. "Yanic said you were accused of entering restricted sectors on the lower levels. Is it true?"

I already knew that my decision to follow Star had been a bad one. Knowing it was wrong, something still compelled me to try to justify my actions. "The service corridors are not surveilled. The entire network is one large shadow space," I blurted out.

He raised his voice. "An active drive is traceable anywhere in the sanctuary. How do you suppose they found you? You put the mission in jeopardy. Perhaps the Cause."

"I'm sorry!" I yelled back. "Star was able to enter the corridors through concealed gateways. I, I thought the information was useful."

"Opal, we told you not to—" He stopped midsentence as my comment registered. "Star was able to access gateways?"

"She said cyber techs use them to perform repairs and maintenance. You know about them?"

He thought for a moment. "Apprentice technicians aren't permitted that grade of access. Opal, your friend used stolen credentials. It's the only explanation."

I swallowed hard. It took all my resolve to conceal the one

detail he dare not learn—not yet. There was no need for him to expand on the implications. Yanic knew every detail of our escapade, everything we saw and heard. Chet and Flint would likely be terminated, meeting the same fate as their wayward corpses. When the mission was complete, they'd come for me. I'd never see Star again.

"She's my dearest friend," I muttered.

Chapter 24

Departure

There was high tension in our quarters Saturday morning. Jade barely spoke during our meal. In spite of my misadventure with Star on Friday, I managed to impress Ares with the final test flights that evening. Several containers of water and two hours of stretching had helped me regain much of my dexterity. He notified Yanic we were prepared for launch.

"Shall I have May warm your evening meals?" Jade finally asked.

Ares didn't look up from his plate. "Please," he replied. "Opal's project should be finished before then."

"Speaking of projects," Jade added, "Tara completed her first genetic sequence analysis. I invited her family to meet us after Assembly tomorrow to discuss her progress."

"Excellent," Ares responded. "Lake and I have cooperated on some parts design and printing. It'll be good to see his family."

Finishing the last of my food, I noticed them both staring at me. I nodded my understanding. Ares had provided a briefing the previous night. It wasn't by chance Tara was assigned as Jade's apprentice. Ares convinced Yanic the placement provided indirect communication with Lake. Any issues with specialty parts could be resolved while avoiding official chains of notification. In actuality, Ares needed him to initiate the plan's second phase. Not only was Lake a skilled programmer, he'd joined the Cause six years in the past.

Ares also provided me with final details of the master plan, including specific goals of the mission and the next phases. My primary objective was to obtain video documentation outside of the sanctuary. It would provide evidence of a viable environment, capable of supporting human life. My secondary objective was to record and confirm the existence of Eden 2. Ares believed the combined information would dispel distortions of our history propagated by nobles over the centuries. Hopefully, it would compel residents to support the Seeker uprising.

"Are you ready?" Ares asked, abruptly.

I straightened my back and breathed in deeply. Exhaling slowly, I looked to Jade. She offered a reassuring smile. We all rose together and walked to the entrance. Jade squeezed Ares's neck. She then turned to me and opened her arms. Her embrace was firm but short.

"We're very proud of you," she whispered.

"May, please open the entrance," Ares interrupted.

"Ares, entrance panel is now open."

May's response caused me to sigh. *If the mission fails, I'll miss her.*

As we departed, I glanced over my shoulder at Jade. Her soft expression was now one of absolute resolve. Those she loved most were heading toward imminent danger, yet she remained stalwart and focused. I stored the image in memory, knowing I could draw upon her strength when I needed it.

—

Before reaching the test room, the lab entrance opened behind us. We turned just as Yanic appeared, followed by four keepers. A phantom pain shot through my abdomen. Their presence brought back memories of our last encounter. I was seething with anger but refused to reveal my feelings. Yanic walked in front of me. I remained focused on the keepers in his wake.

"Is the machine prepared for movement?" he asked, without greeting.

"Yes, Excellency," Ares replied. "We need only disconnect the charging cables. It's secured to a self-propelled transport chassis and concealed with a foil tarp."

Yanic turned to the first keeper on his left. "Send two of your team to clear the corridor. We'll use the maintenance service lift. I do *not* want spectators." His head pivoted back. I was unable to divert my gaze. Instead of chastising me for insolence, he engaged me directly. "And you, Opal Five, are you fully prepared for this task?"

He used the word *task* like it was some mundane cleaning assignment. His indifference amused me, considering the purpose of my mission was to preserve his royal station—and his life. At least those were *his* agenda items. *Yes Excellency, quite prepared for the task of ending your reign over Life World.* I stopped myself from grinning at the thought. We'd progressed too far to let my emotions interfere with our objective.

"Of course, Excellency," I replied with feigned enthusiasm. "You won't be disappointed."

I waited for his response. None came. After several seconds he returned his attention to the mission. He removed a small, metallic object from his cloak and handed it to Ares.

"Insert this to activate the turbine system," he instructed.

Ares inspected both sides of the rectangular magnetic card. Without further discussion, he nodded at me. Once in the test room, he gathered the transmitter as I stowed the charging cables. He'd never explained how the drone would be moved out of the lab. The answer came after he input a command into the control screen. The reinforced wall split horizontally and began to separate. The top half disappeared into the ceiling, the lower half into the floor.

Ares used a remote to direct the drone through the lab. There was ample space between worktables to maneuver. At the lab entrance, the exterior wall opened as before. Yanic and the two remaining keepers led us into the main corridor.

Ares and Yanic walked together in front of the drone. I followed with the keepers behind me. The entire level was vacant and eerily quiet. The only sound was the hum of the electric chassis motor. It moved at a surprisingly brisk pace, and we reached the service lift in just minutes. The first two keepers stood sentry on either side of the lift, remaining motionless as we loaded the drone.

I peered down the corridor as the service panel closed. *This might be my last visit to five.* Yanic used his drive to select our destination. Despite the combined weight, we climbed swiftly, settling on sixteen. The lift opened and Ares moved the drone. The concrete floor was rough, unfinished. I stepped out and looked across the cavernous space illuminated by four red lights suspended from the ceiling under large inverted box-like structures. One was close to our position, another offset to the right and fifty yards away. The others were near the opposite end of the space.

Yanic walked into a shadowy alcove to our left and stopped to manipulate his console. An amber light appeared on the wall over his head, showing a previously concealed opening. Ares leaned his head toward me.

"Airlock," he said.

Ares moved the drone into position, behind Yanic. A large exterior wall split open horizontally, like that in the lab, revealing the airlock chamber. Lights inside the transparent chamber flickered to life. Yanic turned to Ares, pointing to one of two glowing displays in the alcove.

"The airlock is controlled manually, no need for your drive.

A secondary screen is located within the chamber control room." He pointed to a screen on the right. "Complete the turbine activation sequence then insert the key here."

"Will you stay for the activation, Excellency?" Ares asked.

"I have pressing matters requiring my attention." He motioned toward a keeper. "The sentry can communicate with me, if needed."

Yanic started toward the lift then stopped after several steps. He turned and looked directly at me. Refusing to divert my eyes, I remained expressionless and held his gaze. He didn't speak, only squinted at me. Turning away abruptly, he continued to the lift. Three of the keepers followed him inside, and he was gone.

"Opal. Opal," Ares called.

Adrift in my thoughts, I didn't respond to him immediately. I had a strange premonition about Yanic. Part of me suspected he knew everything—that he had always known. *How could Seekers remain undetected for so long? Was there, not one who succumbed to a guilty conscience? One who attempted to negotiate favor for information? Not a single suspect who folded under interrogation?* Something didn't seem right.

"Opal!"

Ares's demanding tone drew me out of my trance, back to the moment. "What's next?" I asked quickly.

"Remove the tarp and complete your inspection," he said. "I'm initiating the activation sequence for the turbines. You need to be ready."

I circled the drone, unlatching the cords holding the tarp in position. Once complete, the tarp easily rolled free from the chassis. I piled it against a wall out of the way. Turning back to the drone, I noticed the lone keeper watching me. Feeling empowered and, perhaps mischievous, I stopped and faced his direction. He reacted by snapping into his sentry position, making me smirk. *How interesting that a well-trained, disciplined enforcer can't control his instinctive human curiosity.* It might explain the scuff marks on the side of his helmet. He was either clumsy or occasionally strayed from his directives.

The warning siren was deafening. Ares completed the activation sequence, raising the turbines into position above us. The red lights flashed brighter, in concert with the siren, showing more detail on the ceiling. The inverted cement boxes were the turbine bases. After completing my pre-flight inspection, I climbed onto the forward strut and lifted the canopy. I hoisted myself into the cockpit and secured the shoulder harness.

Ares left the control screen and stood facing me. He pushed the hand remote, causing the transport chassis to lurch forward. Walking backward, he guided me into the now open airlock. My heart raced as we stopped inside. He disengaged the chassis from the drone then approached the cockpit.

"Retrieve the bag from behind your seat," he said.

The white bag looked like it came from our laundry caddy.

"Open it," he insisted.

I untied the cinch around the neck. Before I asked, he rattled off the list of contents along with instructions.

"The hand radio provides direct two-way communication." He pulled a second silver disc from his belt. "There's no way of knowing maximum range. Be sure it's active at all times. I don't expect you'll be gone long enough to need it, but the water container is full."

As he spoke, I removed each item from the bag, acknowledging my understanding. Most of the contents were obvious and their use self-explanatory, except for the last. Holding it aloft, he recognized my uncertainty.

"Early model gauntlet," he offered. "The interior grip activates the charge. They're most effective within twelve inches of a target."

I pushed the weapon back in the bag. Throughout the planning and training process, we never discussed my mission being anything but successful. There was no contingency plan for failure and little possibility of rescue. Ares had provided me with basic survival tools. Perhaps it gave him some sense of security knowing I might have a chance in the event of catastrophe. *How long can I survive in such an unfamiliar environment?*

"Don't deviate from the flight plan." He scanned the cockpit. "Monitor your battery power," he added.

"Should I activate the video sensor?"

His head snapped up. The intense gaze slowly softened when he noticed my sarcastic grin. "Yes, Opal. Good idea." He backed away from the drone. "I'll remain in the control room. When we begin to rise, initiate power. After the chamber is in position, the rear panel will open. You'll be free to maneuver."

He secured the internal control room door and peered out of a small rectangular window. He looked away momentarily while entering commands into the secondary screen. A slight jolt rocked the drone as the chamber started to move. With the canopy locked into position, I pushed the power button, verifying the battery charge indicators were at 100 percent. After activating the video sensor, I tested the flight controls to make sure the cowlings moved freely. The time—5:56 a.m.

The ceiling receded. In the predawn hour, the sky was a dim gray. My heart raced. As the opening widened, the nearest wind turbine came into view. The activation had been successful, and supplementary power was now flowing. It provided us additional time. The mission was proceeding as scheduled.

The chamber rose. I breathed heavily, staring in wonder at the openness. Clouds appeared as shadows drifting across the immense sky. To my right the four giant helical structures twisted in unison. There were no visible landmarks from this perspective. The chamber locked into position. I looked at Ares. He raised his thumb in the window. *Go time.*

Chapter 25

Bird on Wing

Pushing the left control stick forward increased power and lifted the drone to a hover. I held the setting and pulled the right stick back, causing the cowlings to pitch up. The drone responded instantly, and I backed out of the chamber. Ares watched my progress through the window. He gave one final nod, indicating all was clear.

The first stage of my flight was short. From the east end of seventeen, I completed one left-pattern lap around the structure. My path then took me directly away from the sanctuary. I turned the nose right, pitched down, and increased power. The drone rose quickly and accelerated away from Eden 3.

The altimeter clicked upward and I leveled off at 500 feet. Ares had said that altitude would be sufficient to avoid ground obstacles and provide a wide visual range. After stabilizing the drone, I checked my instruments. The center monitor showed a surprising amount of detail. If visibility deteriorated, I felt confident the monitor would provide enough information to continue. A blanket of clouds covered the sky above. The sun had not yet cleared the mountain range.

The video sensor revealed a desolate, desert-like surface below. There were occasional scrub bushes and rock formations, but nothing appeared hospitable to humans. I looked up from the monitor and took in the vastness surrounding me. The view from the canopy was extraordinary. I turned my head left, then scanned the horizon a full 180 degrees. In the gray hue of morning, the mountain range outline appeared in the distance. Sunlight reflected from clouds moving slowly above them, creating a pink aura over their peaks. Of all the images in the Core memory banks, none compared to the magnificent spectacle unfolding before me.

With a sudden jolt, the seat seemed to fall out from under me. My stomach rolled and a burst of adrenaline raced through my body. I squeezed the control sticks and held my breath, staring at the monitor. The dull humming from the propellers was interrupted intermittently by pockets of differential airflow. Ares warned me about the pockets, suggesting they might cause me to rise or fall unexpectedly. I understood the science surrounding the phenomenon, but the first plunge caught me by surprise.

Quickly growing accustomed to the occasional bump, I experimented with increasingly exaggerated control inputs, maneuvering through the open sky. I selected a mountain peak as a directional guide then banked sharply to the left. The response was immediate. Rolling back right, the drone easily climbed to 800 feet. After leveling off with my peak in sight, I pitched down abruptly, diving toward the ground. The desert floor raced toward me. My altimeter flashed through 390 feet, and I pulled back hard on the stick. My over-correction caused me to climb to 900 feet in an instant. Returning the power control to a neutral position, the drone descended to my desired 500 feet. I stabilized the settings and direction, then drew in a deep breath.

I exhaled slowly while scanning the instruments. A spontaneous smile crossed my face, followed by laughter. I laughed hard and loud. The drone moved up and down, left and right, causing me to squeal like a toddler. Diving toward the ground then pulling up hard, I let centrifugal force press me into the seat. Climbing several hundred feet then nosing over made me weightless, constrained only by the harness. Though strapped inside a machine, I was free from the bonds of earth. For the moment there was no mission, no nobles, no Seekers. There was only flying. Like a bird in the morning sky, I was having fun. It was genuine happiness.

Chapter 26

Contact

The mountains grew larger, clouds above them separated. Pink and orange patches gave way to small islands of blue sky. The ground cover below changed. Green grass now spread across what had been a desert of brown and red sand. I glanced up to verify my heading then looked back at an astonishing sight. Ahead was a herd of large horned creatures standing in tall grass. Thick matted fur covered their backs and front quarters. They walked slowly, grazing on plants in their path. None appeared bothered by the loud humming sound of propellers striking air. They barely moved as I flew over.

A bright light flashed on the monitor, forcing me to look away. The source appeared, nestled between two mountain peaks. I mistakenly looked directly at the fiery ball too long and was temporarily blinded. I blinked rapidly and glanced around the cockpit, trying to read the instruments. Although I was able to recognize shapes in my periphery, my center vision was branded by a white circle. The only remedy was squinting and blinking until the spot faded.

I maintained my heading using the original peak. Sun rays shone down like fingers embracing the earth. I had never known natural light. Other than images stored in Core memory banks, no sanctuary resident had laid eyes upon it for more than two centuries.

The foothills were now in sight. I increased speed and adjusted pitch to begin my climb over the crest. Wind patterns shifted, blowing straight down the slope. More power was required to overcome the stronger gusts. The drone was tossed about, requiring constant correction to maintain my flight path. I held altitude at fifty feet above ground level to avoid rock formations. Scanning my instruments, I gasped out loud. The two right bars showed only red. *How could they already be in reserve power?* The others were at 70 percent green. Something was wrong. I needed to make quick decisions.

After reaching the summit, I leveled off for the distance it took to cross the rocky crest. According to Ares, Eden 2 should appear on the horizon. Instead, there was a wide valley with a parallel mountain range on the opposite side. The valley stretched far to the south and was green with vegetation. A large lake lay in the distance. Although the visual impact of an abundant water supply might be compelling, there was no time to capture the image.

At the base of the opposite range stood a forest of trees. A clearing on the near side had relatively flat ground that appeared large enough for landing. I hoped the forest would protect me while the sun charged the batteries. Instead of descending farther into the valley, I selected a diagonal glide path directly to the glade; not enough power remained for more unnecessary maneuvering.

My descent was uneventful. I cleared the forward trees and flared to a landing on the valley floor. It took several minutes for the dust and debris to settle around me. Despite the stillness and serenity of the glade, I kept the motors running at idle speed while surveying my surroundings. The video sensor already recorded one species of large beast. It seemed obvious that in such a fertile environment there were likely more to be found.

Although mountains blocked most of the sun, the morning glow was sufficient to illuminate the area. There was no apparent threat from beast or human. I took a moment to admire the stand of immense trees. They resembled those displayed in the coniferous segment of the tube. *Amazing.*

The right battery columns were now at half red. There was no choice but to shut down. After I reluctantly depressed the power button, the drone went silent. I released the harness buckle and very slowly pulled the bag from behind my seat. Movement and noise might attract unwanted attention. A few calming breaths steadied my nerves while I scanned the perimeter once more. We'd never discussed how situations like this might be handled. There was no protocol, no checklist—no plan. The bag of supplies Ares provided for the unlikely possibility of malfunction, now seemed woefully inadequate. My mission was supposed to be completed before our midday meal. *Will I ever see my family again? Focus, Opal.*

Fifteen minutes went by, and I hadn't moved from my seat. Sipping water brought some comfort, along with the pouch of sweet cubes Ares had slipped into the bag. He knew of my affinity for the treats but didn't mention them during the inventory check. Rays of light now painted the treetops. I guessed it would be another two hours before the sun reached the drone. In direct light, the cells required approximately three hours to fully charge the battery banks. If there was no further loss of power, I might make it back before dark.

My predicament allowed me the opportunity to examine the forest more closely. *Magnificent.* Each tree was nearly five feet in diameter and eighty feet tall. Lower branches were bare and broken, while those near the top were full of long needles. There were imperfections in the bark with long, yellow ribbons of sap seeping from the wounds. Ares said there have been no storms for a century. It was all new growth. The virtual trees displayed in the tube offered no comparison to the majesty of these beautiful living organisms. Peering through the web of green needles into the vast morning sky, I became aware of my own insignificance, like a parasite on an unfamiliar host.

The remainder of the environment was just as intriguing. Trees were spaced widely apart, providing a detailed view of the forest floor. A blanket of brown needles was strewn with fallen branches. Small boulders dotted the ground, and green saplings reached through the detritus material, competing for space and light. A decaying fallen tree on the right was draped in gray moss. I was lost in the raw beauty of the setting.

My trance was interrupted by movement. A small rodent darted across the fallen tree. It paused and stood on its hind legs, sniffing the air. It then leaped onto a standing tree and scurried into the higher branches. Its bushy tail disappeared, rounding to the opposite side of the tree. While I looked for the tiny creature, a bird took flight and glided through the forest. Without thinking, I unlocked the latches and lifted the canopy several inches. *Opal, what are you doing?*

I pulled the canopy down, leaned back in my seat, and took a deep breath. Horrific images from banishment stories rushed into my head. None of them seemed possible in such a serene place. I recalled the discussion with Ares and his reassurance the claims were fanciful and unsubstantiated. He cited his atmospheric data as conclusive evidence the sun wouldn't melt my skin. *Base your actions on logic and reason, Opal, not imagination.*

—

The gauntlet was heavy and awkward at first, but well-balanced. The upper guard fit loosely on my arm. Padding around the trigger rod helped to reduce movement. Gently raising the canopy, I breathed in the cool morning air. I'd never smelled air so sweet. A bird called from high in the trees. It made a short low-pitched whistle followed by a longer higher-pitched refrain. It repeated the call three times then paused. In the distance, a similar call echoed back through the valley. *They're talking to each other.*

Standing on the strut support, I quickly surveyed my bag of supplies. Although not planning to wander far, it seemed reasonable to bring the water. After lowering the canopy, I stepped onto the grassy surface of the glade. The sky glowed brighter, and the forest started to come alive. Another species of bird sang out. Following the calls, I found it perched on a lower branch. With its chest puffed out, it bobbed its little head while making gentle cooing sounds.

I crept toward the trees. The bird cocked its head. It was obviously aware of my presence and monitoring every movement. My right foot landed on a small unexposed branch, snapping it in half. The frightened bird fluttered away in an explosion of feathers, heading deeper into the forest. I froze and searched through the trees. Every muscle in my body tensed, every sense was heightened.

As the report of wings slapping air faded, a new sound became more prominent. It was distant, yet constant and rhythmic. The sound brought memories of ecosystems in the tube display. I closed my eyes and retraced my recent journey around the massive cylinder, stopping at the rain forest segment. *Yes.*

I proceeded into the forest, pausing every three or four steps to listen and scan the horizon. The ground ahead rose gradually to a small ridge. The sound of water became more distinct. Whatever the source, there was an abundant supply. The only other noise came from birds, flittering and chirping in the branches above.

I approached the ridge with the gauntlet extended forward. Crouching low to minimize my profile limited the view. I stretched my neck to peer over the rise, but only saw more tree trunks and branches. The only option was to stand and check the path ahead. A wide, dense clump of bushes stood forty feet away. The sound of water originated behind the mass.

With each step, I mustered a bit more courage and was less intimidated by my surroundings. The power of the weapon added to my sense of security. However, when I pulled aside branches to step through the brush, the gauntlet led the way.

Emerging from the thicket, I saw the water source. It was amazing. In the clearing was a lagoon surrounded by rocks with grass and other vegetation sloping up from the edges. Large stone columns surrounded the banks, like sentries guarding a hidden treasure. On the far side, a waterfall spilled over a ten-foot-high embankment. Cypress trees reached out over the lagoon, their branches reflecting in the ripples.

This is paradise.

I secured the gauntlet in my belt then stepped carefully along the edge of the lagoon, making my way to the waterfall. Looking down through the clear water, I could see every detail of the smooth bottom. Behind a narrow stone column was a layer of flat rocks close to the falls. I tested the formation with my foot then extended my hand under the stream. The cool water splashed over my fingers and palm. After several minutes, temptation overcame sensibility. I closed my hand and gathered a portion of the precious liquid. There was no detectable scent or sign of spoilage. Touching the moisture against my lips, it tasted sweet and pure. I cupped both hands under the stream until they were full and sipped it all down. After drinking my fill, I splashed more over my face and hair, enjoying the wonderful bounty.

A sharp snapping noise interrupted my exuberance. Instinctively, I pressed my body against the stone column. I was slowly pulling the gauntlet from my belt when a second snap caused me to freeze. *Breathe, Opal.* Three minutes passed with no additional noise other than water splashing near my feet. Peering around the column into the thicket, I couldn't see any movement. I waited several seconds then leaned out further.

Near the opposite end of the lagoon stood an enormous stag with large antlers, like the holographic images in the tube. I recalled them being herbivores but didn't know if they were aggressive. It grazed on the short grass and drank from a flowing lagoon tributary. Although being so close was intimidating, it was thrilling to be in the presence of a live specimen.

The creature raised its head and turned toward the thicket. Reacting to some perceived danger, it suddenly lowered its hind legs and bolted. I thought it had slipped on wet grass when it crashed to the ground. Its front legs kicked the air, and the massive antlers raised once before falling still. Watching for the beast to stir, I noticed a feathered shaft protruding from its chest. *Run Opal, now.* Paralyzed by shock, I gripped the gauntlet tightly and watched the thicket.

A section of forward branches shook erratically then separated. A human-like figure stepped into the clearing. It was clothed in what appeared to be animal skins. My heart pounded through my chest. Every brain cell urged me to flee. I considered escape, but it was directly in my path. The gauntlet was no match for its weapon, obviously effective from a distance. Running was not an option; it could drop me like the stag. I was trapped.

I pressed my body tight against the stone and waited. The animal was being dragged away. The sound of rustling leaves and cracking branches slowly faded. Peering around the column, I saw the stag's hind legs disappear through the thicket. A line of blood trailed back to where the creature first fell. An imprint of the enormous body remained, grass stained in red. I was saddened by the poor animal's fate. It was sobering to witness such brutality in this beautiful place. Despite Ares's reassurances to the contrary, bloodthirsty barbarians still roamed the planet.

More than an hour passed. Birds chirped and fluttered in the branches above. The sky grew brighter. *I must get back to the drone.* There was no sound or movement near the lagoon. After filling my container from the falls, I retraced my steps toward the thicket. The gauntlet remained at the ready. Once clear of the brush, I surveyed the path ahead. The disturbed ground and blood trail stopped at the tall trees. Two parallel depressions in the ground headed off into the distance.

The glade came into view. Landing on this end of the opening was a miscalculation. Sun rays were nowhere near the drone. Circling to the front would've required less time on the ground. Making a mental note of the error, a chuckle escaped my throat. *Surely I'll never pass this way again.* I leaned against a thick pine and waited.

—

The canopy was much easier to lift while standing on the support brace. I laid my water next to the center display then pressed the power button. The battery indicator hadn't changed position. A minimum of three hours was needed to complete the charge. *It's going to be a long morning.* I scanned the forest edge once more before jumping to the ground. The landing strut created a small clearing under the drone. It offered a place to rest, creating shade against the coming heat.

I pulled two clumps of grass and turned to toss them away. The hunter was standing near the glade—watching me. The weapon was in his left hand. It was a long arching staff with a cord attached to each end. His clothing was more complex than I originally noticed. The top garment overlapped in the front, secured at the midriff by a red sash. Long sleeves were adorned with tassels. The leg coverings were made from the same material, tassels running the length of the outer seams. His hair was long and dark, held by a band strapped around his forehead. He didn't move.

Staring at the mysterious figure, I considered my options. *Fly away? No. Only minutes of power remain. He could easily catch up to me after another forced landing. Lock myself in the cockpit? The canopy could be breached with a large rock. Even if he didn't attack the machine, there's no food and little water. He need only wait for hunger and thirst to take its toll.*

Only one choice remained. I pulled the gauntlet from my belt and activated the trigger. Bolts of electricity shot from the tapered prongs. It crackled and sparked, emitting an unusual odor. I then stepped away from the drone. If I had to fight, I might need space to maneuver.

A surge of adrenaline raced through my body when the hunter started moving. He trotted at first, heading straight for me. In one motion he reached over his shoulder, pulled a feathered shaft, and attached it to the staff cord. At thirty feet away, he raised the weapon and pulled the cord back. I held the gauntlet out, bracing myself for his attack.

The shaft sailed in my direction. A stream of air swished by my ear. *He missed.* Now sprinting, the hunter dropped the staff and pulled a long knife from his sash. He raised it over his head and lunged at me. I fired the gauntlet and rolled in the grass. The dull sound of bodies colliding reverberated over me. A sickening scream pierced the morning air. A large mass landed with a thud against my back. An animal screeched, kicking and riling against me. The hunter grunted and growled. With eyes closed and head covered, I curled my knees to my chest.

The battle ended. A beast quivered against me, the last bit of life leaving its body. There was a moment of stillness, the hunter's heavy breathing the only sound. I opened my eyes.

Chapter 27

Barbarian

I rolled away and rose to my feet, clutching the gauntlet in front of me. The hunter knelt on the ground, still breathing hard. Blood stained his face and arms. He held the knife in one hand, the other pressed against the dead animal. Our eyes met. He glanced at the gauntlet then back to me. His expression was calm, no indication I might be his next victim. In fact, he'd just saved my life. The beast in front of him was an enormous cat. Its mouth was open, displaying three-inch-long fangs surrounded by jagged teeth. It had been stalking me for a morning meal.

I slowly lowered the gauntlet to my side. The hunter dragged his knife over the grass, cleaning blood from both sides. He slid it into the sash then stood and straightened his clothing. He was shorter than Ares, with a more muscular build. We stared at each other, both taking in the other's appearance. There was a small growth of hair on his chin, but he wasn't much older than me. After several minutes of silence, the mysterious man turned to the drone. He touched the engine cowling while inspecting the top surface and cockpit.

"My name is Opal."

He turned his head without responding. *After so many years, did Out World barbarians retain a language?*

"It's a drone," I said loudly. "It carried me here."

Either he didn't understand my words or chose to ignore them.

"The sun will charge the batteries."

He turned back and lifted the canopy. I watched and waited, assuming he was acting out of primal curiosity. He found my water container and shook it next to his ear. Concerned about my only water supply, I stepped forward and held out my hand.

"That's mine," I said firmly. "Give it to me."

He glanced from my open hand to the container. After surrendering the cylinder, he looked back in the cockpit and pulled out my supply bag.

"Excuse me," I exclaimed, grabbing the bag. He looked surprised when I pulled it away from him. "This belongs to me."

Once again, the hunter turned his attention to the cockpit. He examined it carefully, like conducting a pre-flight inspection. Climbing on the strut support, his head disappeared inside. It was almost humorous, watching this simple barbarian experience such complex technology.

"Are you finished?"

Without acknowledging me, he jumped to the ground and walked away. I thought he was leaving. After reaching the spot where his weapon landed, he picked up the staff and started back. I raised the gauntlet.

"Stop."

His pace slowed, focusing on my raised hand. He held the staff with both hands. Again, his posture was not threatening. *If he wanted to kill you, Opal . . .* I brushed away the thought and lowered the gauntlet. He approached and held the weapon in front of me. I examined it closely and waited, unsure what was expected. He removed a feathered shaft from his sheath and placed the slotted end on the cord. Using two fingers, he pulled the cord back several inches. When it was released, the shaft stuck firmly in the ground.

"It appears very effective," I said.

He pulled the shaft from the ground, placed it back on the cord then extended the weapon to me. Cautiously securing the gauntlet in my belt, I took the staff by the thick, center band. It was light and well-balanced. He watched patiently as I attempted to repeat his demonstration. Releasing the cord, the shaft hit the ground and fell into the grass. There was no reaction from my instructor, no laughter, not even the slightest grunt.

Our eyes met once more. There was a calmness in his gaze. His features were well-defined—strong, yet not too rugged. Females in my class might find him attractive.

"How handsome a barbarian," I quipped.

My mouth fell open when the words escaped out loud. Again, no reaction, no sign of comprehension. *Does he notice the blushing redness on my cheeks?* Several uncomfortable seconds ticked by, then he held out his hands. I returned the weapon and stepped back. Curiously, he detached the cord from the staff, picked up my spent shaft, and returned both to me. I held them and waited. Whatever point he was attempting to communicate, it was entirely lost on me. He continued to stare.

"It won't work," I suggested, shaking my head.

He circled the drone and stepped on the opposite strut support, staring at me over the cockpit. I dropped the weapon and climbed on the drone, using the right strut to pull myself nearer to his height. He tilted the seat forward, exposing the rear space. I leaned my head inward near the battery banks. A frown indicated my growing impatience.

"There's no time to explain how it works."

His expression didn't change. He continued staring, apparently waiting for an alternative response. My frustration continued to build. *This is impossible.* He reached behind the seat and lifted the wiring conduit leading to the right-side battery bank. I looked down and gasped. Half of the connectors were hanging loose. Ares secured the wiring when he changed batteries. Perhaps the turbulence or my radical maneuvers shook them loose.

The hunter climbed down from the strut. I pushed the connectors together then forced the conduit under a support brace, preventing them from further movement. Returning the seat to an upright position, I held my finger over the power button. Several potential outcomes crossed my mind, forcing me to consider the possibilities. Quickly shaking the negative thoughts from my head, I willed the power to return. *Must complete the mission.* I held my breath and pushed the button. The center display blinked once then lit up with a glorious bright glow. Both battery banks indicated nearly 60 percent, all bars in the green.

With newfound enthusiasm, I jumped to the ground. Power consumption was in the range Ares projected; however, there were new variables for the remaining journey. Two mountain ranges needed to be crossed. Wind speeds and turbulence would increase with the rising sun. A full charge would be required to complete my mission and return to the sanctuary. Although feeling more confident about the drone's operating status, it would still be hours before launch.

The hunter dragged the dead cat by its rear legs. He retrieved his weapon and sheathed the feathered shafts. Watching him depart, it suddenly struck me—the weapon, the cord, it was useless without . . .

"You were telling me the cord wasn't attached," I shouted. "The drone—the wires." I sprinted in front of him, and he stopped short. "You're not just a barbarian, are you?"

He stared blankly, no reaction. Perhaps the conduit discovery was random, coincidental. His cord demonstration was elementary at best. *But there's an intelligence in his eyes— awareness.* Whatever faculties were lost after two centuries in the wilderness, there was something behind his gaze.

"No, Opal, I'm not a barbarian. My name is Drake of the Midland Clan. We've been expecting you."

Chapter 28

Philosopher

I froze. *Did he just speak? Was the voice in my head?*

"You—understand me?"

"Yes, Opal."

I watched his lips move to be certain he was speaking, that my sanity remained intact. My mind raced. Bewildered, I backed away and yanked the gauntlet from my belt.

"Where are you from? Are there others?"

"You don't need that, Opal. You're in no danger." He pointed north. "My village begins where the valley ends."

"No—originally. The storms. Where—" I stopped babbling when his first comment finally registered. "What do you mean expecting me?"

"You obviously have questions. We have many for you."

My weapon remained at the ready. "How many are in your village?"

"Over a hundred. Hundreds more of our clan are spread

throughout the midlands. Come to my village, you'll find your answers."

I watched him while absorbing the information. Hundreds, perhaps thousands, of humans live within miles of the sanctuary. *How could so many years go by without contact? Are the nobles aware of their existence? Does Ares know?*

"You didn't answer my question," I insisted. "How could you possibly be expecting me?"

"Your arrival was foretold by our Elder," Drake began. "He said a messenger will come when the last glass mountain blooms." He paused at my expression of uncertainty. "You, Opal, are the messenger."

I searched the ground. As per Ares's instructions, the first segment of my flight circled around level seventeen. He wanted a recorded image of our sanctuary. The exterior surface is covered with photovoltaic cells, creating a glass-like appearance. I envisioned the top-level structures retracting and the wind turbines rising into position—*glass mountain blooms*. I looked at the hunter.

"*Last* glass mountain?"

Activating their turbines meant the first two sanctuaries experienced power failure. Ares explained they're only a supplemental power source, unable to support the entire structure. If the Cores in Eden 1 and Eden 2 reacted as he predicted, human support systems were likely shuttered. There would be no residents left alive.

The revelation didn't change my mission. Although Yanic expected a fresh supply of crystals, my focus was on documenting environmental conditions. The evidence was meant to spark a revolt against ruling nobles. The abundance of resources in this location alone might be enough to move many residents to action. Showing communities of humans living just outside our protective walls might incite all in Life World to join the Seeker Cause.

"How long will it take to reach your village?"

He glanced to the east. "We'll arrive before midday."

Sunlight now covered the top third of the far-end trees. I guessed more than two hours remained before rays contacted the cells. It wasn't worth launching without a full battery bank charge.

"Will the drone be safe here? Are there more hunters in the valley?"

Without responding, Drake approached the drone. He pulled a feathered shaft from his sheath and wedged it upright into the right engine cowling.

"The arrow identifies your machine as my find. It won't be disturbed by other hunters." He glanced around the glade. "Unfortunately, curious animals don't abide by the same code." He grinned with the quip. "Are you ready?"

I pushed my water into my supply bag and looked over the drone once more. To reach the village before midday means a travel time of approximately two hours. If we spent an hour there, the entire journey totaled five hours. It was sufficient time for the batteries to fully charge and enough daylight for a flight over Eden 2. It also meant the opportunity to document one additional destination—the village.

Drake hoisted the dead cat onto his shoulders. Blood from the neck wounds ran down his arm and dripped from his elbow. It was a tragic end to the animal's life. *Thankfully it's not my corpse being hauled away.* Although somewhat civilized, the hunter showed little remorse for taking a life. He might just as easily take mine.

"Are you carrying it all the way to the village?"

He jutted his chin toward the north side of the glade. "Only to my camp."

Without additional comment, he turned and started walking. I followed the path he stamped through the high grass, albeit at a comfortable distance. Despite his load, he maintained a brisk pace. My shorter legs had to move double-time to keep up. I marveled at the wild things around me. Bunches of yellow and purple flowers peeked up through the grass. Small geometric webs, woven between tall reeds, glistened with moisture. Insects leaped away or took flight as we trampled through the glade. It was all so different from the cold, sterile world into which I was born. It was raw—beautiful. The beast bouncing on Drake's shoulders reminded me it was also quite dangerous.

Running several steps, I closed the distance between us. "Was it by chance you found me in the glade?"

"I tracked you from the watering hole," he responded matter-of-factly.

"You knew I was there?"

"Every creature in the forest knew you were there," he shrugged a shoulder, lifting the cat. "Including him."

Anger swelled inside of me. "If you knew I was being stalked, why didn't you warn me?"

"Because, like any startled creature, you would've run." He stopped and turned toward me. "The lion hunts by instinct, it pursues fleeing prey. My bow is useless in the trees, and I couldn't have reached you in time with my knife. The only way to defeat a stronger adversary is to gain an advantage."

Standing in silence, I offered no response. This was his world, not mine. He knew the rules of this wild place, and I didn't. He wasn't speaking down to me, only stating what was obvious to him. These were lessons he and his people learned over generations to survive.

"Then—I should thank you."

"Opal," he started, holding my eyes, "you said I'm very handsome. It's thank you enough." He smiled wide, then laughed as he turned and continued walking.

I gasped with contempt and complete embarrassment. Running to catch him, I felt blood rush to my cheeks. "Of all the—I said *handsome* not *very handsome,* to be clear."

"I stand corrected," he chuckled. "Only handsome then."

I gasped again, trying to think of my next retort. "I also called you a barbarian. Perhaps it was more accurate."

"Perhaps," he replied. "But a handsome one."

With clenched fists and gritted teeth, I suppressed the urge to kick him. He was enjoying my discomfort. It was time to change the subject.

"Why didn't you respond to me? The lion was dead, there was no more danger."

"Maybe not for you," he replied, referring to the gauntlet.

"Had you spoken, our introduction might've been less cumbersome."

"You learn more about a person by listening, not speaking."

"So, you're a hunter and philosopher," I quipped sarcastically.

"I'm many things," he answered. "Today, I learned I'm also handsome."

"Are you ever going to let—" Stopping midsentence, I shouted, "Drake, wait!"

He dropped the lion and crouched to his knees in one quick movement. He scanned the horizon, knife at the ready. I knelt behind him.

"What did you see?" He whispered.

I pointed to where the glade ended. "There. A large beast, next to the trees."

He looked over the grass, then stood. After tucking the knife away, he held out his hand. I hesitated then reached out. The hunter gently pulled me to my feet.

"That beast will carry us to my village. I promise my horse won't try to eat you."

Chapter 29

The Village

Drake held the noseband as I approached his horse. It was large and intimidating, yet beautiful. Her long face and front quarters were brown. The coat blended into a white midsection and hindquarters, with random dark spots where the colors converged. She had straight black hair streaming down one side of her neck with a long matching tail. Her chest and legs were rippled with muscles. Standing with her head raised, she towered over me.

"Don't be afraid, she won't hurt you."

I reached out and stroked the side of her neck. She turned toward me, causing me to pull away. Drake laughed.

"Give me your hand," he said.

I watched his face as he folded my fingers into a fist. His touch was warm. He turned my hand over and held it under the horse's nose. Her nostrils flared and snorted as she absorbed my scent. It was apparent I passed the test when she slowly lowered her head. Drake opened my hand and placed it on top of her nose. He guided my fingers down the soft hair several times. When I took my hand away, she turned and nudged my arm.

"She likes you."

"She's amazing," I half whispered.

"Keep her still while I pack."

I held the noseband and rubbed her face while Drake loaded a thick fur hide and camp supplies over her back. He tied a length of rope around her hindquarters and secured a crude rack on each side. It was constructed of two young trees fashioned into poles, with smaller branches tied between them. It already held the stag he killed at the watering hole. After loading the lion next to it, he covered the dead animals with another hide and tied it down. He made one last search of the camp area then mounted the horse. He pulled a short rope attached to the noseband and leaned toward me, extending his arm.

"You're next," he said.

I grasped his forearm, and he lifted me onto the horse with little effort. The bedroll and supplies secured to the hind quarters pushed me close to him. After settling in, he tugged the lead rope and turned the horse north. We moved with a jolt. I grabbed his sleeves to steady myself. It seemed a long way to the ground, and I wasn't accustomed to the swaying motion of our live transport.

We rode in silence for ten minutes. When we reached the open valley, a light breeze blew through my hair. I breathed in the moist, fragrant air. The rising sun illuminated our surroundings. Birds took flight and small animals darted about. The only sounds were the rack dragging through tall grass and an occasional snort from the horse. Morning clouds dispersed, revealing above the mountain peaks a sky extending into infinity. I was completely out of my element, exposed—vulnerable.

A new feeling grew inside, but it was harder to define. Looking north to where the mountains ended, there was only openness. There were no walls, no barriers, no limitations.

I smiled wide when I realized the significance of the strange emotion. It was the first time in my life I was completely and utterly—free.

As my exhilaration faded, I became aware of Drake's hair draping down over his shoulders. It was dark and silky with a slight curl on the end. A large black and white feather hung from the band around his head and bounced with each motion. The hunter sat with perfect posture, his hips swaying in unison with the horse's movement. My attention then fell on the grass moving below us and a sense of dread came over me. With each step, we moved farther away from the drone, my only means of escape. I was at the mercy of this strange man who had recently killed—twice.

I took a deep breath and reflected on the last hours. *Steady yourself, Opal. If he intended you harm, there was already plenty of opportunity.* Shaking the concerns from my head, I reminded myself we were in Out World, the place sanctuary residents feared more than death itself. Riding behind Drake, I had a sense of safety—comfort. There was also a warmth with my body pressed close to his. I was thankful we faced the same direction, so he didn't see me blushing from the thought.

"Tell me about your village."

"What do you want to know?"

Admittedly, my interest was more in him. However, considering his relentless teasing over my earlier comment, I had to approach the subject delicately.

"Do you have a family?"

"Yes, a large family."

I considered his response. There were obviously differences between our worlds, and at least for the moment, I was only able to conceptualize his. "Are parental units permitted more than one child?"

He didn't respond immediately. It was his turn to decode my vernacular. "I have two brothers and a sister," he replied, more question than answer.

"Are your genetic sequences similar?"

Again, a delayed response. "We have the same father and mother."

I pondered his answer. "So, your mother parent was also your carrier. Did she produce offspring for other parental units?"

He chuckled. "That's not our custom."

Although he was more advanced than originally suspected, I wasn't sure what to expect of his village. *What technology could they possess in such a primitive environment?* "Without laboratories, how are your offspring fertiliz—?" I stopped and held my breath, hoping beyond all hope he hadn't heard the question. *Did I literally just ask about his mating rituals? Please don't answer please don't answer.*

We traveled in silence for several minutes. I finally exhaled, assuming the question hadn't registered. My relief was short-lived. His head tilted down, and his body began to shake. I pushed on his back. "Are you laughing at me?"

"My village begins there," he said, pointing ahead.

I looked over his shoulder as we rounded the foothills where the mountain range ended. Several columns of smoke rose over a hilltop, and in the distance stood more tall trees. We rode up a grass-covered hill and paused near the summit. He turned the horse, allowing us to view the entire landscape below.

At the bottom of the hill was a flowing river with a wide stone bridge arched to the far side. Just right of the bridge stood a large rectangular structure. The base was made of stone. The top half was a flat material which I didn't recognize. Attached to the side of the structure was an enormous spinning wheel partially submerged in the water. It took a moment to determine the flowing river was the wheel's power source.

"What purpose does the wheel serve?"

"It turns stones inside the mill," he said. "Wheat and corn are ground to make bread."

"And what forms the upper walls?"

"Trees taken from the forest." He pointed south of the

village. "There's another mill downstream where they're cut into boards."

Before my next question, he made a clicking sound with his mouth and nudged the horse forward. I moved my head from one side of him to the other, taking in every detail as we crossed the bridge. The rack scratched loudly on the stone surface. I looked in amazement at the clear water rushing below. As we neared the bank, I spotted several fish in the shallows, swaying just below the surface. In the sanctuary, water is scarce and precious, almost worshiped. But here in this supposed wasteland, it's abundant.

We turned in front of the mill and rode to another structure next to the river. It was only one story in height, but more than fifty feet wide. Smoke poured out of two stone columns rising from the rear of the structure. There were several tall racks on the near side with different types and sizes of animal skins draped over them. We stopped near the front entrance and Drake lowered himself from the horse.

"What is this place?"

"The butchery," he responded, untying the rack. "Fish and meat are prepared and preserved for the village." He motioned toward the racks. "Hides are tanned for many uses."

Drake circled the horse to untie the other side. A large man emerged from the front opening. His clothing was also made of animal skins. He wore a dark apron extending from neck to knees and held a long bloodstained knife. Our eyes met; we both stared in silence. Drake released the rack when he spotted the man.

"Alo, Isaac," he shouted.

Isaac continued to stare at me.

"Alo, Drake," he returned.

Drake removed the hide, exposing the stag and lion. Isaac glanced at the animals then looked back at me.

"Good morning," I said.

Isaac staggered forward several steps, inspecting me from

head to toe. My shell sparkled in the morning light. He squinted as if we once met and was trying to recall my name.

"You're not from the clans, are you?" He asked, or stated.

"No. I'm from the sanctuary." His face didn't register understanding. "The glass mountain," I clarified.

"You're the messenger?" he asked in an unbelieving tone.

I looked down at Drake. "So I'm told."

The burly man began to laugh. "You're presenting this child to the Elder?" he questioned Drake. "You believe she will fulfill the prophecy?"

I had no idea which prophecy he was referring to but didn't care for his tone or mockery. I waited for his laughter to subside before speaking.

"I'm no longer a child," I said sternly. "You have no idea what I'm capable of. Perhaps you should restore order to your own burden before casting judgment on me."

His laughter turned to confusion. "Restore order?" he belted. "Burden?"

"Yes," I answered. "Your butchery is burning."

He turned to see smoke billowing from the opening and rushed into the cloud. A primordial howl echoed from within as he dashed about smothering flames. Drake shook his head at me as he climbed onto the horse. We turned toward the village center.

"You make friends quickly," he said.

"If I'm to expect a similar reception from the remainder of your village, you can return me to the drone now."

"Isaac meant no harm."

We rode without speaking for several minutes. I finally broke the silence. "What is this prophecy? Why was Isaac so amused by my presence?"

"All will be revealed, Opal. Please be patient."

Chapter 30

Family

Before I insisted on more details, we stopped in front of a structure made entirely of tree boards. It was two stories high with a raised, covered walkway around three sides. There were several openings on both stories and a doorway entrance in the front. Drake lowered himself from the horse and secured the lead to a post. He turned and held his arms in my direction. I protested, determined to make my own way down. After noticing there was nothing to grasp and concerned about landing face-first on the ground, I reluctantly accepted his help.

The door opened inward, and a pretty female emerged. She wore animal skin clothing covering her chest, midriff, and upper legs. A sash tied around the waist enhanced her delicate form. Long black hair draped over the right shoulder. Her features reminded me of a classmate. On her hip sat a small child swaddled in fur.

She spotted me next to the horse and stopped abruptly. Her

expression first conveyed astonishment, then curiosity as she inspected my shell. She turned to Drake.

"You found the messenger," she said.

Drake bound onto the walkway and took the child. "Opal, this is Miya," he said. "And this small hunter . . ." He thrust the bundle over his head. "This is Max."

"Good morning," I offered.

Miya acknowledged me with a smile and nod of her head. "Will you join us for a meal, Opal?" she asked in a sweet, soft voice.

Drake looked down at me from the walkway. "After we eat, I'll take you to our Elder, Ulysses."

Watching the three of them, a sudden pressure filled my chest. They appeared content and happy. I didn't understand why it bothered me. Drake obviously adored the child, and she seemed—nice.

"Yes, thank you," I replied.

Miya took Max and disappeared into the dwelling. Drake stepped down to unload the horse. He held out my bag, but my mind was absent. I stared into nothingness.

"Your bag, Opal."

His words broke my trance. "She's—beautiful," I mumbled.

He dropped his bedroll and removed the fur cover from the horse. "Miya?" he questioned, glancing at the dwelling. With the cover tucked under one arm, he retrieved his bedroll and bags with the other. "She is beautiful," he acknowledged. "And a good mother."

My chest tightened even more. I was suddenly nauseous. *What is the problem, Opal? This is not your world.*

"My brother did well to join with her," he finished, climbing onto the walkway.

I took two steps, then his words registered. *Brother? They're not . . .* A spontaneous smile crossed my face, and the pressure in my chest lifted. Drake pushed the door inward and allowed me to enter before him. He dropped his things inside. I followed his lead, placing my bag next to his. We entered an adjacent room to find Miya standing near a long table. There were several bowls filled with food and plate settings for three.

"I'll be back," Drake said.

As he walked away, Miya summoned me to a counter. She lifted the handle on an oddly shaped metal apparatus. Pushing the handle inward caused water to flow into an open recess. She handed me a cloth and small yellow block, then demonstrated its purpose with her hands.

"You may wash here," she said.

Miya's happy demeanor reminded me of Star. I thought of our last moments together, her body convulsing on the lift floor, mouth frothing. Ares insisted she was okay but didn't actually see her. He simply relayed the report from Yanic. *How will the noble react when I return without his precious crystals?* Knowing his days were numbered, we would be of no further use. I hoped Ares had a contingency plan. If the riddle about the glass mountain was accurate, nothing was to be gained from Eden 2.

The yellow block slipped from my wet hand, leaving an oily residue. The fragrance was pleasant, like the flowers near the watering hole. I cupped the block in both hands and rubbed them together, using the resulting lather to wash. I used the cloth to dry my hands.

Drake returned just as I finished at the basin. He wore clean clothing and had washed the blood from his body. Motioning for me to sit at the table, he took the adjacent chair. Miya distributed cups of water and sat across from me. Drake took my plate and added food from the bowls. There were whipped eggs, portions of meat, and dense brown bread. After we were served, he broke his bread and dipped it in a viscous golden substance. He obviously enjoyed the combination.

"It's called honey," he said, adding a dollop to my plate.

I repeated his actions, allowing the warm bread and sweet honey to melt in my mouth. An involuntary moan escaped my throat. Both my hosts smiled at me. In Life World, it's considered rude to make such noises while dining. I feared they were insulted. On the contrary, they followed my lead and moaned with delight. We all laughed.

The texture and taste of the eggs was consistent with those in the sanctuary. Poultry is an alternative source of protein, so the majority of eggs are incubated to hatchlings. Occasionally there was a surplus, and residents were allotted a portion for cooking. I sampled the meat before asking about the source. It was dark in color with a coarse texture. With my plate cleared of food, I sipped at the water. Drake was watching me.

"Did you enjoy the meal?" he asked.

"Very much, thank you." I then addressed Miya. "The meat was quite good, is it poultry?"

"Venison," she replied.

Drake noticed my uncertainty. "Deer meat," he clarified. "Like the buck taken at the watering hole."

He watched my expression carefully. It was apparent he expected more of a response. It didn't faze me. The staples of their world were quite enjoyable. It was a perfect opportunity to introduce them to something from my world.

"Will you excuse me?"

I pushed the chair back and retrieved my bag from the front room. It took only a moment to find the sweet cubes. I opened the pouch and offered it to Miya. She picked out one of the tiny treats and examined it closely between her fingers. Drake did the same. I selected my own then demonstrated placing it on my tongue. They looked at each other then followed my example. It was my turn to observe their reactions.

After several seconds, Miya moaned her approval. I watched Drake's face as the cube melted on his tongue. He stared back but didn't speak. A long, awkward silence ensued. Feeling my face flush, I interrupted the impasse.

"You mentioned your brother. Is he also hunting?"

He continued staring at me. "My brothers are at the Lunar

Feast with my father."

"Lunar Feast?"

He leaned forward with his arms on the table, hands clasped together. "When the moon is full, members from the clans come together. The Feast is a time for sharing and trade. Our clan takes bison meat, hides, and boards from the mill. The Northern Clan brings corn and wheat. The Southern Clan brings scraps of steel. Males of eighteen years attend a celebration of manhood. Some are joined together with eligible females."

Miya joined the conversation. "The celebration is where I met Ethan. We were joined at the next moon. In just three years we welcomed Max to the family." She looked at Drake. "Your celebration is in two moons. Perhaps you'll invite Opal."

He looked down at the table. The brave, stoic hunter-philosopher was blushing. I couldn't contain my smirk. It was the perfect opportunity to pounce on him, exact my revenge for his endless quips about the *handsome barbarian* comment. I could easily give him a thrashing his entire family would eventually enjoy, yet I refrained. Perhaps it was enough he was in this futile position, or maybe I wished to spare him the humiliation.

"You don't have much time remaining," he said, rising from his chair. "I'll take you to the Elder now."

I stood and faced Miya. "Thank you for the wonderful meal."

"I hope to see you again, Opal," she responded.

"As do I."

Chapter 31

The Elder

We left the walkway and Drake rolled the hide cover over his horse. He untied the lead, hoisted himself on her back, and held out his arm. After settling into my position, he turned the horse and clicked his mouth. I quickly grew accustomed to the rhythmic motion as we rode and was able to focus my attention on the village.

There were dozens of family dwellings in this segment, all surrounded by well-organized gardens. Females gathered a variety of foods in woven baskets. Young children darted in and out of the plant stalks, laughing and squealing. Occasionally, they stopped and watched as we rode by, likely attracted to my glistening shell. I smiled and waved my hand, causing them to run away. They didn't seem overly frightened, only curious and shy. Some waved back then returned to their games. They all appeared carefree and happy.

"What's the purpose of that structure?" I asked. We

approached a large pavilion near the village center. It was rectangular in shape with multiple stone pillars supporting a triangular roof. The floor was made of flat boards and there were no side walls. It was empty, except for a central platform rising four feet in the center.

"Village meetings," he answered.

"What do you accomplish in the meetings?"

"Important decisions are made."

"What decisions?"

He took his time before responding. "Each spring, our people choose a Council to lead the clan. My father has headed the Council for three seasons. He's a good leader."

It was difficult to put his explanation into context. Other than Life World, I had no system of governance with which to compare. "You choose your nobles?" I asked.

"We don't have nobles," he replied.

"Nobles are the ruling class in our sanctuary. I suppose they're the equivalent to your Council. They're ordained by genetic right, however, not chosen."

He pondered my comparison. "If a noble is a poor leader, how are they replaced?"

"Nobles can't be replaced. They're descended from our Proph—" I stopped midsentence. It was unlikely he would understand or appreciate the system of beliefs forced upon the residents of Life World. A corrupt system we Seekers are determined to destroy. It was tempting to explain everything to Drake, including the reason for my presence and the details of my mission. Ares's words of caution crept into my consciousness.

He said they were expecting a messenger. What message was I to deliver? If the truth is revealed, will they support the Cause or side with nobles? Is it possible Yanic knows of their existence? Is my true purpose to gather reinforcements to save him—save them? Ares emphasized the necessity to remain vigilant and trust no one, but Drake did save my life. Except for one crude butcher, the village has afforded me kind hospitality.

The reality is, I don't know him, or them. The prudent choice was to conceal my true intent for now.

"We exist in very different worlds," I safely concluded.

We rode south of the village to where the forest begins. Following the river downstream, we eventually came upon the second mill. Although there was no activity at the mill, the partially submerged wheel continued to spin freely. Hundreds of tree boards were stacked together in neat bundles. I assumed the workers were attending the Feast.

As we proceeded, the river narrowed, and the rushing water grew louder. It was fascinating to observe the properties of fluid dynamics in this natural setting—with actual fluids. I looked up into the giant trees and watched birds flitter about the branches. They chirped and sang, oblivious to our presence. Several of the bushy-tail rodents pursued each other around a large trunk, stopping occasionally to watch us. Sunlight reflected off the moist green canopy of needles, creating a myriad of shapes and colors.

The tube ecosystems were assembled for our viewing pleasure but lacked certain key dimensions. In spite of a near-infinite capacity for computation, the Core couldn't approach the beauty and majesty of this place. Its designers gave it the ability to think, reason, and even create. It was missing, however, a singular element that cannot be artificially produced. It had no consciousness—it could not feel. Despite its prodigious power, the Core was an unemotional machine.

Drake stopped his horse at the foot of a narrow stone bridge. It had handrails made from boards and was only wide enough for humans to cross. He climbed down and offered his arms. Without protest, I reached for his shoulders.

"I'll wait for you," he said.

Stepping onto the bridge, I scanned the opposite side of the river. Beyond the bank, there were thick bushes and small trees leading to a steep rock formation. The bridge rail was smooth and wet from condensation. The rushing water below was clear and crisp. In the shallows it moved rapidly, creating small whitecaps that snapped when colliding. When I reached the last stone, a clearing in the brush appeared with a slightly worn footpath to one side. Before proceeding, I looked back at Drake. He stood quietly, holding the lead as his horse drank from the river.

The winding footpath led me through the brush and trees. The sound of splashing water faded with each step. After several minutes, I emerged from the foliage and discovered a flat clearing extending to the rock formation. At the base of the formation stood the front of a stone dwelling built into the hillside. Smoke rose from a column on the roof.

"Hello?" I called out.

There was no response. It was a short distance to the dwelling entrance. I crossed the clearing and repeated my salutation in a louder voice. "Hello?" Silence. My impulse was to turn and walk away. I glanced back over my shoulder at the footpath, and the entrance door opened inward.

I stared in astonishment at the figure standing before me. He was certainly human, but his face was worn and wrinkled. His disheveled hair was white and stringy, with bushy eyebrows to match. The skin on his neck and cheeks sagged. Brown patches dotted his face. He wore a simple cloak made from animal hide, secured around the waist by a thin rope. As we examined each other, neither spoke. When our eyes finally met, he managed a slight grin.

"Good morning," he said in a coarse voice.

Drake never mentioned a specific protocol for addressing the Elder. To be polite, I bowed my head. "My name is Opal, from—"

"I am Ulysses," he interrupted, pulling the door open. He pointed his hand, motioning for me to enter. "Please."

I stepped into a warm, dimly lit room that smelled of the glade. A small fire burned in the hearth of a stone column. Two chairs faced the fire, a round table standing between them.

The far corner was separated by a low partition supporting a counter. Steam rose from the neck of an oddly shaped pot. After adjusting to the contrasting light, I saw bundles of cut flowers. It was a pleasant setting.

Stepping to the middle of the room, I noticed a peculiar second door on the back wall. The front entrance door clicked shut behind me. I turned to face the Elder. He moved slowly toward me, studying my face.

"May I offer you tea?"

"Please, thank you," I replied, again being polite.

He motioned toward the chairs. "Won't you be seated?"

I sat with my back straight, hands on my thighs. My host shuffled to the corner area, returning with a flat tray. He poured dark liquid from the steaming pot. I selected a cup as he lowered himself into his chair. He watched me sip the hot tea. It had a light flowery aroma with a hint of honey. After several sips, a warm sensation spread through my abdomen. Whatever the contents, the bitter liquid had a relaxing effect.

We sat in silence, enjoying the warm beverage. After draining his cup, the Elder poured himself another portion and faced me. He looked at my shoulder, then traced down my arm to my legs.

"It's a carbon-based membrane," I offered, "called a shell."

He raised his brow. "I'm quite familiar with the MPS, Opal. It's been many years since I've seen one."

A shiver ran the length of my spine. "How could you—?"

"You've come in search of Eden 2." He paused to watch my expression. "Your wind turbines have been activated, which means your Core detected a failure in the power retention system." He paused again. "You were sent to find help."

His speech had the slow, enunciated cadence of a well-educated person. He held my gaze without blinking. In the past, I'd suspected Ares was capable of reading my mind. He often answered my questions before they were asked, even recited my thoughts before they reached my tongue. In his case, it was likely a keen sense of intuition. This man, however, knew my thoughts—verbatim. *How is this possible?* I immediately assumed a defensive mental posture, turning the conversation to him.

"You foretold of a messenger," I parried, "when the last glass mountain blooms." His grin told me he recognized my tactic. "The turbines were activated just hours ago. How could you possibly know?"

His eyes sparkled, much like Yanic's. "The clans have settled all corners of this region, Opal. Although the territory surrounding each sanctuary remains sacred, the structures are visible from the outer boundaries." He sipped his tea. "As of yet, no one has informed me about your turbines. Your presence alone indicates your facility is in distress."

"Because you had the same experience at Eden 2," I blurted out.

His expression turned cold. "Not exactly." He paused and looked away, possibly summoning a memory. "Tell me Opal, why was a young resident trusted with such an important undertaking?"

"You assume I'm a mere resident?"

"If you were of noble lineage, my dear . . ." He drained the last of his tea. "Your port would have been implanted by now."

I recalled my polite greeting at the door. Bowing my head exposed the back of my neck. The required sign of respect allows nobles to identify residents. Every custom, every action was designed to control us. *That's the last time I'll offer the sign of deference to another human.*

"Perhaps nobles were incapable," I retorted, now perturbed.

His head bobbed, almost sympathetically. "How did you come to be here?" he asked. "You could not have traveled on foot in such a short period of time."

"I flew." My response was too quick, too revealing. I silently chastised myself for succumbing to pride. *Control yourself, Opal.*

He mocked examining my shoulders for wings, finally

drawing his conclusion. "A flying machine," he said, then proceeded to read my mind once more. "A modified drone?" He shook his finger at me. "You were chosen for your stature." Before I lashed out, he completed his thought. "As well as your superior intellect."

Of course, he noticed my spine stiffen with his last comment. Although old, he was sharp and wise. His powers of observation and deduction were remarkable. He used his education and experience to manipulate me, extracting information. However, nothing he learned was truly sensitive. I too was observant, and, despite his advantage, didn't allow him to better me at every stage.

"You were a noble in Eden 2," I stated emphatically.

He was intrigued by my assertion. "Go on."

"Noble offspring are created with edited expiration genes. In defiance of our scriptures, they can live well past their ninetieth year," I quoted Jade.

He leaned forward. "What else?"

"Your power retention system failed, as well. They weren't meant to last five centuries."

His head tilted. "Continue."

"Your turbines were activated but only provided temporary power support. In time, the Core shut down nonessential systems. The sanctuary was cast into darkness. With no food or purified water, residents began to perish. Although last to go, not even nobles would be spared."

His expression intensified. "Yes, Opal," he added, staring through me.

"Many of you managed to evade the Core and escape the sanctuary. The clans are descendants of those survivors."

He lowered his head. "We could have saved more. I waited too long."

Chapter 32

New Genesis

His breathing was the only sound. As he searched the floor, I saw pain in his face. He seemed to be recalling events from long ago, perhaps individuals for whom he cared. I thought of Ares, Jade, and Star. Images of friends and acquaintances in Life World flashed through my mind. Their lives will soon be irrevocably altered. The weight of my burden grew heavier, knowing my actions will determine their fate.

The Elder didn't dispute my summary of events at Eden 2, which meant Ares's prediction was correct. My mission had now expanded. It was no longer enough to gather evidence of an inhabitable environment to start a revolt. The primary strategy to overthrow the nobles was short-sighted. If all support systems were to collapse, we needed to escape the bonds of Life World—forever.

"Tell me, Opal," the Elder started, pulling me from my thoughts. "Who sent you? What are your instructions?"

If I wanted information from him, he naturally expected the same in return. Whatever transpired at Eden 2, it had impacted him profoundly. Despite his noble station, he seemed to express sincere remorse over the outcome. His experience might provide crucial insight for our success. It was time to learn the details.

"My father parent was recruited by the Noble Yanic to construct a remotely controlled drone. The project was sanctioned by the Noble Court to establish contact with Eden 2."

"Your father, is he an engineer?"

"Yes," I responded proudly. "And a respected member of the Professorate."

"This noble . . ." He paused to reflect. "Did he know the drone was capable of transporting a passenger?"

"Yanic was familiar with all design specifications. I wasn't a passenger. Due to limitations of the remote system, the drone required a human pilot."

The Elder nodded. "Your abilities are truly extraordinary, Opal," he said, boosting my ego. "Why contact Eden 2?"

"Lithium-titanate crystals. To repair power retention banks."

"I see," he replied, rubbing his chin. "Did your father parent support this proposal?"

He recognized my hesitance. Part of me wanted to reveal our true objective, but Ares's words of caution once again prevailed. If the exchange were to continue, trust needed to be established on both sides. I wanted to know more; however, our implied quid pro quo conversation was very one-sided to this point.

"How could you have saved more?" I blurted out.

My question caught him off guard. He looked angry, unsettled. He bobbed his head slowly, agreeing to my unspoken terms. "Very well, Opal."

The Elder rose and started toward the back wall, summoning me to follow. He inserted a metal utensil into the second door handle and turned it two clicks to the left. Behind the mysterious door was a large vault. Leaning on the heavy barrier, he caused it to open inward. There was only darkness. He lifted an old lamp from the floor and struck a thin stick. A flame danced under the glass bowl. The light revealed a tunnel carved into the hillside.

"Watch your step," he said, crossing the threshold. After fifteen paces, we came to another metal barrier. It opened into a wide cavernous space. He ignited a second lamp perched on a round table. There were rows of parallel shelving units made from tree boards. They stretched from one wall to the other, spaced four feet apart. Most held thin rectangular objects with words on the edges. Others held boxes of varying sizes.

"What are they?"

"Books," he replied. "Printed words."

The edges were difficult to read in the dim light. Stepping closer, I reached for a thick volume at my height, then held back. He hadn't given me permission to touch anything. They were secured for a reason. The Elder was obviously observing my actions as he granted approval without being asked.

"Go ahead, Opal."

I selected a book labeled *Human Anatomy* and pulled it from the shelf. There were faint words inside the front cover: "Property of Phoenix Public Library System." I turned over several of the thin leaves and found a brief description of vital human organs. Next to the printed words was a crude diagram indicating positioning within the body. I thought it a cumbersome way to learn compared to the three-dimensional aspect of our databases.

"Where did you get these?"

"Explorers in our Eastern Clan have been excavating the remains of a city once occupied by many humans. They generally focus on gathering metal for trade. One expedition uncovered this collection. It was preserved in a facility covered by nearly two centuries of accumulated sand and debris."

"Rather small facility for an entire city."

"On the contrary," he said. "I understand it was quite large.

Unfortunately, the explorers used many books to fuel their fires. One was presented to me as an anecdotal gift at our Lunar Feast gathering. I was able to negotiate the release of what you see here. Many useful devices utilized in the village were derived from them. They also contain a great deal of human history, information long edited from sanctuary databases."

"Another example of noble hypocrisy," I sneered, returning the book. Although interesting artifacts, they brought me no closer to achieving my objective. "How do they relate to the fall of Eden 2?"

"They don't," he admitted. "Opal, lithium-titanate is a chemical compound. It can be synthesized in your laboratories in a matter of hours. As a sanctuary engineer, your father would know this. You're not in search of crystals."

How could he know? Was he forewarned? With the Elder standing between me and the only access, there was no escape from the hollow. Although in a precarious position, my response came more from anger than fear. "No, not crystals," I answered loudly. "We seek the truth."

Neither of us spoke. The flickering lamps cast shadows on his withered face. I feared my outburst put the mission at risk. If his loyalty remained with the ruling class, he might detain me and attempt to alert Yanic. He stared at me for an uncomfortably long time. Much to my relief, his smile returned.

"There's a fire inside of you, Opal. You remind me of a resident I once knew. We shared advanced development classes. Like you, she was strong-willed."

"Did you love her?"

He furrowed his brow, apparently stunned by my question. "Y—Yes," he stammered. "We were young . . . it was forbidden."

"What was her name?"

He didn't answer immediately. A look of pain and sadness returned. The sincere display of emotion was endearing. I never experienced such vulnerability in an adult male. Regardless of his former status, I needed him and his information. It was now or never.

"My mission is to record favorable living conditions outside of the sanctuary," I began. We'll expose our ruling nobles for their centuries of lies and treachery. Our revolt will destroy their reign and free the residents of Life World."

My heart raced. I expected a lecture on why my mission was pointless, why the revolt would fail. None came. Without responding, he turned and shuffled to the opposite wall, sliding a three-foot-wide box to the edge of a lower shelf.

"Place this on the table," he requested.

With some struggle, I lifted the box and pushed it onto the round surface. He stood beside me and placed his hands flat on the lid. He inhaled deeply then released the breath slowly.

"The truth, Opal, is not enough."

"But if residents knew—"

"No," he snapped. "Most will choose not to believe you. For generations, they've been indoctrinated to obey the will of your nobles. The builders designed our societies to exist in this manner. They appropriated and transformed long-standing beliefs to fortify their absolute power. Those desperate, *chosen* souls who first entered the Eden facilities sacrificed all for safety and security. The original residents relinquished all rights by legal contract. This included dominion over their own genomes."

"Then you must tell me. How did you escape Eden 2?"

His focus turned from me to the box. After a long hesitation, he pried the lid open. Using both hands, he lifted a bag containing a round object and held it out for me.

"Open it," he said.

Quickly untying the cinch and stretching the bag open, I immediately recognized the contents. Looking at him for reassurance, he shook his head. I held the object with one hand and pulled the bag away. The serial number behind the visor pivot point started with the number two. The keeper's helmet in the lab started with three. *Eden 2—Eden 3.* The helmets were exact copies. The Elder watched, waiting for me to grasp the significance.

"Biometric scanners recognize features of the helmet," I thought out loud. His raised brow validated my revelation. "They're all the same," I almost shouted. "This will provide unlimited access to all of Life World. It can be used for every lift, laboratory, service corridor, even gateways."

"What do you know about gateways?" he asked, clearly surprised.

Considering what he just offered, there was little use in concealing my recently acquired knowledge. If the Elder was anything but an ally, he wouldn't have placed his trust in me.

"I recently learned my closest friend is a noble. She showed me the gateways."

"This friend. Is she—with you?"

His question hung in the air. There was no way to answer with certainty. During our adventure behind the sanctuary walls, Star and I renewed our lifelong covenant. Even after her secret was revealed, she swore nothing would ever come between us. *We two, forever.* There was no guarantee she was still alive. Court punishment can be swift and severe. How they reprimand their own is unclear.

My response was honest. "I may never see her again."

Recognizing my sorrow, he quickly changed the subject. "The only way to defeat the keepers is to outmaneuver them," he said, pointing to the helmet.

My image reflected in the visor. The keepers had weapons, shields, tactical gear, and unlimited access to every inch of the sanctuary. They were trained, disciplined, and feared. In fifteen years, I never once noticed a sentry lose focus, flinch, or even turn their head—except for the one curious launch observer on Yanic's detail.

"Opal," the Elder called, interrupting my thoughts. "There's one more item."

He held up a gold chain, supporting a four-inch-high triangular medallion. A pattern on the surface created four smaller triangles. *The lines form the "net" of a tetrahedron,* I thought, recalling my Euclidian Geometry. When folded along the edges of the center inverted triangle, it forms a three-dimensional triangular pyramid. The lower corner triangles were fitted with gold inserts. I immediately recognized the designs.

"The first insert, it's the crest for Eden 1," I said.

Below the double helix and large eye, was a fully risen sun. A single, wide ray of light radiated downward—pointing west. The sun on the second insert was also fully risen. One ray pointed up, the other down—east and west. Eden 2. The designs confirmed my suspicion. Each crest held clues to the existence of additional sanctuaries.

"What is it?"

"The reason you're here, Opal. It's what you were sent to collect." He paused. "The key to the Awakening."

"Awakening?"

He closed the box, carefully laying the chain on the lid. He studied the medallion intently for several seconds.

"You seek the truth, Opal?" He turned to me. "Then you shall have it."

I hoped I was ready.

"Our scriptures tell us Prophets built the sanctuaries," he began. "Prophets who received divine guidance to shelter and protect the chosen. In actuality, they were a conglomerate of powerful world leaders and wealthy families known collectively as New Genesis. They were interested only in self-preservation."

"Ares explained the origins of the Eden Project," I said impatiently.

"You were both provided a morsel of information to motivate you into action. Opal, there are six iterations of the Eden Project on the planet. Three sanctuaries were raised on each of the primary land continents, for a total of eighteen."

My look of astonishment caused him to pause. "Eighteen?" I repeated, bewildered.

"The New Genesis elite were determined to preserve their dynasties for future generations. They planned for their heirs to emerge after the storms subsided and establish a new order. An order in which they would control every aspect of human life. Each sanctuary represents a microcosm of that objective. The Awakening is the commencement of the new order."

The tale he wove was remarkably complex. It was incomprehensible, yet seemingly possible. Unsure of the larger implications, I decided to focus on the scope of my mission.

"To be clear," I interrupted, "you escaped Eden 2, which is no longer viable."

"Your eloquent deduction during our first conversation was mostly accurate," he responded.

"And what of Eden 1?"

"Abandoned, covered with foliage. We concluded it was erected too near a water source. The storms transported seeds and spores, reshaping many landscapes. Decades of growth covered the exterior cells, blocking the sun. There were twisted remnants of turbines, indicating the winds were far too strong when they were activated."

"Were there signs of survivors?" I pressed.

"We discovered pockets within the structure where supplies and materials were accumulated. They wouldn't have lasted long."

I pointed to the medallion. "But you found what you needed?"

He blinked slowly. "I knew where to find the chip."

"Are all nobles familiar with this master plan?"

"Like any organized segment of human population Opal, there is an echelon of leadership within the noble class. To protect the elite from dissent within, trustees are selected to preserve the final instructions."

"If those trustees are lost," I added, "clues, like the sanctuary crests, are left behind to guide remaining nobles."

"Correct."

"You were a trustee," I guessed.

He stared quietly. Every new piece of information generated more questions.

"Eden 3 is the last," I thought out loud. "The sanctuaries exist independently but are somehow interconnected."

He watched me pace as I pieced together the larger picture.

Without the ability to communicate, how can any plan be coordinated? I searched my memory. *Ares's atmospheric data was collected from external sensors. The nobles knew conditions have been favorable for decades.* It came to me. "They've been waiting for a specific time," I stated. "A predetermined date."

His subtle grin indicated I was closing in on the answer. He watched and waited, almost willing me to complete the puzzle.

"Tomorrow! The celebration marks 250 years from the beginning of Judgment."

Chapter 33

Illusions

My life revolved around the belief that truth is the foundation of all virtue. What is truth if not an illusion? Like recorded history, it's decided by the masters of the day—used to control the masses. I'd been wholly committed to a faith led by false prophets. It was time to alter the illusion, change reality. Not in spite of my faith, but because The Giver expected nothing less from me.

"Why three sanctuaries in each region?" I asked.

"The developers gathered the greatest collection of experts in the world to plan and build the Eden facilities," he began. "Architects, engineers, geologists, physicians—all of them future residents. Despite their collective intellectual prowess, they had no precedent upon which to establish centuries-long protocols."

"If one sanctuary is compromised, others remain to carry out the final instructions," I concluded.

"Precisely."

"Drake said you were expecting a messenger," I added. "You knew the nobles would attempt contact. The Awakening is upon us."

"You were right about the celebration."

"Our power retention banks are not failing. It's an obscuration conjured by the nobles to justify activation of the wind turbines—to launch the drone."

"You are correct."

Yanic sabotaged the battery banks to elicit a Core response. Every step has been coordinated. Knowing I was a mere pawn in their scheme made me angry. "Why risk sending a resident?" I huffed. "Surely there are nobles capable of completing this errand."

"I would prefer to say you were selected for superior skills, Opal. You have proven yourself worthy. In the minds of nobles, however, your life is not equal in value to theirs. You were selected because you're expendable."

I didn't allow myself to be offended by the comment. "What if the selected resident is part of a conspiracy, bent on revolt? Why take the chance?"

"Yanic is aware of your contrived mission. You said yourself he knew the design specifications. All parts and materials requisitioned for your drone required his approval. He knows about your video sensor. It will all be confiscated upon your return."

I sighed with exasperation. He was right. Ares himself said Yanic would clean up the project, including everyone involved. Our plan centered on presenting the video evidence to all residents. It would be a short-lived revolt if only a hand full of Seekers participated. There was no way to communicate with Ares to develop a contingency plan. The success of the revolt, the Cause, was now up to me.

I pointed to the medallion. "You said it's a key. What exactly does it do?"

The gold chain sparkled in the flaming light. "When the

third chip is inserted in the upper triangle, the medallion will fold into a small pyramid, transforming into an electromagnetic connector. Mated with the proper terminal, it completes a control circuit. An embedded series of commands initiates a chain reaction—the Awakening will begin."

"Yanic wants the device, which means the terminal is located in Eden 3," I guessed.

"All sanctuaries are equipped with terminals. The system requires a functioning power source to complete the launch."

"Launch?"

I searched his face. Our collective futures were literally resting in his hand. Paradoxically, the Awakening returns the planet to humans, yet ensures a world of perpetual servitude under the reign of elite nobles. If it were prevented, however, perhaps the new order would be one of peace and tranquility. A world in which all people were equal, free to pursue desired occupations and join with whomever they love. Where villagers choose leaders to serve, and discard those who are ineffective. A world where children laugh and run and play in castles. Where the dreams of young girls become reality.

I grew suspicious of his intentions. The prospect of completing a fool's errand sent me into a rage. "Why give me the medallion?" I shouted. "Do you expect me to deliver it to Yanic? To my enemy? The Awakening is meant for you, after all—the heirs of New Genesis. Why wouldn't I destroy it? Destroy it all?"

Without speaking, he lowered his head. Looking up slowly, tears rolled down his withered cheeks. "Sable," he said swallowing hard. "Her name was Sable." He wiped his eyes, gasped several small breaths, then exhaled. "From the moment I met her, she spoke of injustice, of change. She was brash and fearless and took whatever she wanted—including me. I quickly fell under her spell, as did most who met her. She belonged to a clandestine organization, a secret society formed by original residents. Sable was their most prolific recruiter."

"Seekers," I blurted out.

"Seekers?" the Elder replied, uncertain. "I don't recall their moniker." He continued his recount. "They planned an uprising against the nobles. Over time, their members infiltrated most sectors of the sanctuary. They secured structural blueprints, including service corridor and lift path diagrams. Makeshift weapons were secretly stockpiled. Their strategy was solid but required the element of surprise. When the time came, they overwhelmed a sentry. Utilizing his helmet, they gained access to secured lifts. Dozens of them made it to level fifteen, within fifty feet of the Core itself. But their plan had been intercepted. A company of heavily armed keepers waited in ambush, riot shields fully energized. The rebels charged the line only to be dispelled by the high voltage barriers. Survivors were interrogated, remaining conspirators arrested."

"Including Sable?" I asked softly.

His somber expression revealed the answer. "They were paraded in front of Assembly, charges read individually. All were sentenced to banishment. She left the stage in shackles. It was the last I saw of her." He sighed. "The following morning, I received a summons to appear before the Noble Court. My mentor was present. I was awarded the *Order of Nobles* citation for unveiling the conspiracy." He stopped again, swallowing hard. "When I was with her—it never occurred to me—I deactivated my drive but neglected to disconnect the Core link. My mentor tracked my every movement, recorded conversations, even when she and I were . . . together." His head fell, his body shook.

"How do we defeat them?" I insisted. "Tell me and I'll bring them all down."

Chapter 34

Return

reached the footpath and looked back at the stone dwelling. The Elder watched from the entrance. Without further gesture, he backed into the shadows and closed the door. He revealed how some of the residents escaped Eden 2, including the final hours before its fall. His story of loss was saddening. Although the battle was long over, there would always remain a hole in his heart. It was both tragic and ironic that a person of such privilege suffered so much. Despite the eternal pain, he found joy in nurturing his clan over many decades. Perhaps what he shared with me would bring the redemption he so desperately desired.

Halfway over the bridge, I spotted Drake sitting at the base of a tree. His arms were folded over his chest, head resting against the trunk. I crept quietly over the remaining span and into the short grass.

"If I was a predator, you'd be my lunch."

My attempt at surprise was less than successful. Instead of jumping, he sat calmly. He pointed his chin toward the horse.

"If you were a threat, she would've warned me."

I approached the horse and patted her neck. She lowered her head, urging me to scratch behind her ears. Drake rose and untied the lead rope. He climbed on her back and extended his arm. My leap was timed perfectly with his pull hoisting me easily into position. He tightened the lead and turned her in the direction from which we came, taking us out of the forest.

"You received gifts from the Elder," he observed. "Was he pleased with your message?"

My grip on the bag tightened in response to his question. I touched the medallion necklace hanging inside of my shell. "We had a productive meeting."

The ride back to the drone was much quicker without the rack in tow. The sun was at its zenith and warmed my face. Despite the weight of my challenges ahead, I enjoyed watching the scenery around me. The mountain ranges displayed mosaics of colors and patterns. Valley grasses swayed in the steady breeze. Birds rose and descended on waves of air. Every passing bed of flowers offered a unique scent. My senses were alive. *It's surreal.*

Part of me wanted to remain in the dream, let others worry about the battles. Perhaps all the sanctuaries in the world were destroyed, and ours was the last. Why not throw the medallion in a deep watering hole and wait for the residents to emerge? My days could be spent in the village, teaching young children mathematics and science. A simple and happy life, free from tyranny and oppression.

"There," Drake said, pointing toward the glade.

Over his shoulder, I saw the drone through the trees. I couldn't determine if there was damage but was relieved it remained. We rode the last several minutes in silence. Drake was on alert, continuously scanning the horizon. Recalling our run-in with the mountain lion reminded me we were in wild and dangerous territory. I moved closer to him.

We reached the landing zone and Drake leaped from the horse, turning to offer his arms. Our dismount procedure was now routine, and he eased me to the ground. While he untied my supply bag, I circled behind the drone and opened an exterior compartment. The space was designed to hold a ten-pound container of lithium-titanate crystals. I scoffed at the irony. *No one on the project actually wanted crystals.* The empty drum now held a keeper's helmet—an important weapon for the Cause.

I inspected the exterior as part of my pre-flight checklist. The undisturbed grass around the landing spot indicated there were no curious visitors during our absence. Seeing no obvious damage, I climbed on the strut support and lifted the canopy. Pressing the power button showed all battery gauges in the green, fully charged.

Drake retrieved his arrow from the cowling, checking both ends of the deadly shaft. After securing the supply bag behind my seat, I jumped from the strut and stood before him.

"Thank you," I said. "For everything."

He searched my eyes. "When you return, Opal," he started, thrusting the arrow forward. "I'll teach you to hunt with the bow."

I smiled. "You intend to make me into a proper barbarian?"

"Yes, a handsome one."

My smile widened; blood rushed to my cheeks. I turned and climbed into the cockpit, securing the harness buckle. Drake closed the canopy and backed away, pulling the horse by the lead rope. After securing the canopy, I scanned my gauges. The center monitor displayed waves of grass, flowers, and a background of enormous trees.

Drake stood motionless, his hair blowing in the breeze. *How do I describe him to Star? We've never talked about males—in that way. It will be a new subject for us if I see her again.* The image of her body convulsing on the lift floor drifted back into my head. My thoughts veered away from the hunter as the rage returned. The next phase of my mission was critical. It was time to focus.

With increased power input, the drone rose to a low hover. The propeller downdraft surrounded me with dust and debris. Climbing slowly out of ground effect, my visibility improved. I nosed over and banked left, taking a wide, circular pattern around the glade. Drake appeared in the monitor as I passed over him. He steadied his horse from the noise and blast of air. The route back to Eden 3 was due west, over the first mountain range. However, there were two segments of Out World I wanted to capture on video before returning—the village and Eden 2.

—

My flight through the valley was smooth. The only interruption was an occasional burst of light in my peripheral vision. The sun reflected off the drone's surface cells. I pulled my interpreters from the case. Although not able to interface, they were capable of blocking bright light. After making a mental note to report the annoying phenomenon to Ares, I chuckled over my concern with the drone's design. This flight, this mission, was meant to be a singular event. If our plan unfolded as intended, there would be no future use for the machine.

I reached the end of the eastern mountain range and climbed to 500 feet. It was midday, and the villagers were out working, children playing. The video sensor would capture structures, planted fields, and animal enclosures. I didn't wish to disturb nor frighten anyone, but evidence of a civilized community with ample food and water sources should convince many residents to join the revolt. The recording was a significant component of the overall strategy and needed to be properly executed.

My first run was over the river for a clear image of the bridge and mill. The nose-down configuration resulted in a minor loss of altitude. Climbing back to 500 feet, I circled north for a run on the dwellings. During my pass, several children waved to the sky. My concern for frightening the young was unfounded. The Elder's vision of a messenger from the glass mountain had been shared with each generation. Many of them saw me riding through the village. The machine was simply an extension of the prediction. It would make for compelling viewing, seeing them greet a stranger in such a friendly manner.

The flight over the village took three minutes. According to the Elder, Eden 2 was less than ten miles away, southeast of the forest. There was enough power to make one pass over the ruins then return to my sanctuary. When the altimeter indicated 1000 feet, a wind turbine appeared on the horizon. I gradually descended back to 500 feet to remain in calmer winds, using the turbine as a visual navigation aid. The lush green fields on the monitor soon faded into sand and rocks.

Approaching Eden 2 from the north, my path took me directly over the broken, still turbines. At first appearance, it looked intact, except for the dull, tarnished hue of the exterior cells. I banked right then made a left-arcing turn for an approach from the south. Lining up for my pass, the damage became evident, precisely where the Elder described. The blast radiated spherically, creating an opening from sixteen to twelve. Fragments of glass and metal were fused together from the heat. Rubble was strewn for hundreds of yards. I slowed to a near hover. Details of the interior came into focus on the monitor. Seventy years of sand and detritus couldn't hide the staggering devastation. It was a shocking and disturbing sight, but it didn't deter my motivation.

I sped away from the abandoned structure and headed due west. Although the terrain was unfamiliar, crossing the mountains from my current position reduced flight time. Eden 3 should be visible after clearing the second range. I selected a target point next to a mountain peak and increased my speed.

The climb to the top ridge was uneventful. Soaring over the first range, the foothills below came into view. The altimeter indicated 3,200 feet above ground. While I admired the valley floor, wind turbulence rocked the drone. I tightened my grip on the controls and concentrated on the instruments. After clearing the second range, Eden 3 appeared on the horizon. I gradually dropped to 500 feet. It would be a short flight, albeit a long night.

The sanctuary glistened in the sunlight; wind turbines rotated in perfect synchronization. It was a ludicrous charade, an absurd hypocrisy. *What if I handed my water vessel to Yanic and claimed success in securing crystals?* I imagined the look of disdain on his face and laughed at the thought. Of course, my reward for the stunt would be detainment and interrogation. I'd be convicted, terminated, and incinerated in the course of a day. The Elder confirmed everything Chet and Flint revealed about the disposal process. He also shared many details about the revolt at Eden 2. Ares and I had much to discuss. *Ares.*

I pulled the bag from behind my seat and retrieved the hand radio. The center monitor showed 12:42 p.m., five hours beyond my expected return time. We calculated forty minutes for the mission but agreed on an additional hour for contingencies. While Ares desired the additional time to record Out World, Yanic was concerned about contacting the appropriate noble at Eden 2. As it turned out, I succeeded in fulfilling both of their covert agendas.

"Ares, Ares. Opal," I said into the microphone. Silence. I laid the radio on my lap and reduced power, approaching the eastern end of the sanctuary. The surface of seventeen was clearly marked, the airlock retracted. My battery banks were just barely green. Including reserve power, there was approximately twelve minutes of flight time remaining. If it became critical, I could set down near the airlock and wait for Ares to respond. I needed to make contact before landing. If Yanic wanted his precious medallion, he needed to meet my conditions.

Chapter 35

Reunion

"Ares, Ares. Opal," I repeated into the radio. The drone hovered over the landing zone at twenty feet. The time was 12:44 p.m.; approximately ten minutes of power remained. The thought crossed my mind that Ares might no longer be there. Perhaps too much time passed, and he assumed the mission failed. A part of me was relieved by the idea. *Plenty of daylight to recharge the drone, return to the village, and—*

"Opal, Opal!" Ares's voice exploded over the speaker.

Lines of dust shot from the surface below. The horizontal air lock cover separated and the change in pressure released a blast of air. With the sun high above, the seam didn't glow like in the morning twilight. When the cover fully receded, the chamber began to rise. I expected Ares to be alone in the control room.

I keyed the radio. "Ares, I have a message for Yanic."

The top of the transparent chamber was now visible. "Opal, let's get you safe inside."

"No, Ares," I said emphatically. "Please contact Yanic now."

As the chamber locked into position, he appeared in the control room window, the radio next to his mouth. Then a second, unfamiliar face appeared.

"Opal," Ares started, "the Noble Yanic no longer oversees the project."

"Tell her to land the craft now," I heard over his radio.

"Yes, Excellency," Ares said, holding the mic key open. It was a different noble. There had obviously been developments during my absence.

"Opal, please land now," Ares instructed.

There was a sense of urgency in his voice. If Yanic was relieved of his responsibilities, Ares was operating under a revised plan. There was no way to communicate under the current circumstances. I had my own plan but needed to improvise—and fast.

"Please tell His Excellency I hold the connector but have one request before landing. If he doesn't understand, suggest he seek guidance from the Court."

The silence told me this noble was not a trustee. He had no idea what I possessed and was awaiting a response. Ares previously mentioned wireless drives were ineffective outside of the sanctuary. If the noble was communicating, it meant the airlock was hardwired to Core links. I quickly put my interpreters on.

Word of my possession obviously reached the right person as the next response was quite cordial. "Opal Five, my name is Noble Panos. How may I be of service?"

"Excellency," I started, feigning respect. "The Noble Yanic swore our team to absolute secrecy; however, I wish to share my accomplishment with my friends."

His response was delayed. "Go on."

"With your permission, Excellency, please have my classmates Tara and Star present for my arrival on sixteen."

A long stretch of silence followed. His friendly introduction meant he was given orders to approve any demand. I had, after all, the nobles' collective futures suspended around my neck. The battery gauges blinked red. This engagement would end in less than ten minutes regardless of the outcome of our negotiations. Panos being unaware of the power limitations was my only leverage. Ares watched me from the window but remained still. I hoped he would follow my lead.

"Opal Five, your classmates have been located and are being escorted to sixteen."

"Thank you, Excellency. Landing sequence initiated."

The rear chamber panel opened. A slight reduction in power brought the drone down to five feet. The green light above the control room window indicated clearance to enter. I maneuvered slowly into position and settled in the center of the airlock ramp. The battery gauges were just above zero.

As the chamber descended, I made final preparations. Decontamination allowed for a few additional minutes. The drive attached to my left hand was now active, neuro-loops settled into position. My gauntlet was out of sight, concealed behind the rear battery cases. Finally, I lifted the gold chain and rested the medallion outside of my shell. The Noble Panos was likely given a crude description of the piece and shouldn't be bothered with details—an oversight on which I was counting.

The decontamination phase ended, and Ares stepped out of the control room. He activated the transport chassis, positioning it under the drone. With a jolt, I was lifted several inches off the ramp. The interior chamber opened, and Ares moved the drone into sixteen. Panos was close behind.

The entire space was now illuminated by overhead lights combined with the flashing red warning signals under the turbines. It was a bit distracting, which played in my favor. I looked toward the maintenance lift just as it opened. Two keepers stepped out, followed by Star and Tara. Everything was moving according to my plan.

I released the locks and Ares lifted the canopy. He put his

hand on my shoulder and looked curiously at my interpreters. "Are you okay?" he asked.

"Yes," I replied in a monotone voice. "The mission was successful."

Panos summoned two keepers and stood by the drone. As soon as I stepped down, he motioned for them to take my bag. "All contraband will be inspected," he said. "I believe you have something for me."

I lifted the gold chain over my head and extended it forward. The medallion swung like a pendulum. Both he and Ares admired the glistening triangle. Panos pulled it from my hand and held it even higher. It was a coveted relic, but he was unaware of its full potential. He looked closely at the shapes, studying the image on the single chip. He raised a brow and looked at me with noted suspicion. I didn't blink.

He turned to Ares. "Retrieve the video sensor drive."

Ares looked puzzled. "The video drive is not—"

"The Noble Yanic was removed from the project," Panos interrupted, "but remains loyal."

Ares circled the drone and climbed on the right strut. His head disappeared into the cockpit as he pulled the sensor drive from the unit. He returned and reluctantly handed it to the first keeper. "Excellency, this project was sanctioned by the Noble Court," he protested.

Panos ignored his comment and turned to the second keeper. "No one approaches the machine until I return." He glanced at me. "Enjoy your reunion. You'll be summoned shortly for a briefing on your—excursion."

"It will be my pleasure, Excellency," I responded, without bowing.

Chapter 36

Loyalty

Panos entered the lift with his detail, leaving two keepers behind. Before it closed, I noticed him studying the medallion. My summons would likely arrive shortly after it reached a trustee. They'd be looking for the Eden 1 chip in the palm of my hand. It was a risk to give them the connector with a single chip, however a plausible expectation considering the limited scope of my mission. They had no way of knowing the status of the first sanctuary.

"Opal!" Star shouted, running toward me.

Without hesitation, Tara bolted from the lift behind her. "Where have you been?" she yelled.

As we embraced, Star lifted me from my feet, spinning me a full rotation. Tara wrapped her arms around our necks. The three of us huddled together, laughing and squealing like children. With our constant movement and distortion from the lights, there was little chance the keepers saw me transfer the drive to Tara's hand. Because it was altered for use on the drone, it could be activated by any user. I hugged her tightly and whispered my message into her ear. She responded immediately and headed toward the lift.

"Thank you for coming, Tara," I said. "Good luck with your assessments."

"I'm so happy you're back, Opal," she replied.

Tara approached the sentry with a special request. He didn't respond. She huffed and donned her interpreters, pretending to interface. Her hand movements were exaggerated. The whole time she complained about being late for an assessment. When her repeated requests went unanswered, she began to rant and threaten him with all manner of punishment. Eventually, the display turned to dramatic crying and stomping like a toddler pitching a fit. With hesitation, the keeper finally acquiesced, and they entered the lift together. Evidently, it wasn't his first encounter with a frantic student late for assessments. It was obviously a meltdown episode he wished to avoid.

Star turned to me, and I took her hands. Feeling the chip in her palm, her expression didn't change. She understood some operation was transpiring and assimilated well into our improvisation. This was her first interaction with Tara, yet even an astute observer might assume they grew up together. She witnessed the drive exchange and continued to play her role. It was an important test of her loyalty, and thus far, she received high marks.

The chip was reassurance of my trust in her. It was a last-minute decision as her presence wasn't guaranteed. My original idea was to give both items to Tara. It was the Elder who suggested Star might be an asset, given her station. During our last moments together, we swore allegiance to each other just before being felled by the gauntlets. My hope was that our covenant was stronger than her obedience to the nobles. The next step was a test of both our wills. "It's wonderful to see you Star," I gushed.

"Opal, I'm so proud of you." She looked over my shoulder. "Professor, tell me you're pleased with her work."

Ares didn't miss a beat. "Her piloting skills are exceptional, Star. Time management needs improvement."

I grabbed Star's wrist and hurried her toward the drone. "You must see the cockpit; it was custom designed for me."

The keeper stepped forward as we approached. Ares quickly intervened. "Opal, Noble Panos left instructions to leave the drone until his return."

I responded to Ares, but my intended audience was the sentry. "Please, Professor. No one will ever see it again. You said it would be stripped for parts after the mission."

Most keepers would stand their ground, never defying the direct orders of a noble. The scuff marks on his helmet suggested this one might be persuaded otherwise. It's the type of damage resulting from recklessness, or perhaps a random stunt. I recognized him from Yanic's detail during the morning launch. He seemed quite interested in the drone. His noble had been removed from the project, and he was likely between assignments.

I stepped forward. "You were admiring the machine this morning. The noble is no longer present."

He didn't move. I tried another tactic, pointing to the engine cowling. "The propulsion system is modeled after the C-54. We used a variable-pitch hub with a hydraulically actuated cam plate. It changes the angle of the propeller blades while in flight."

He turned his head enough to see the rear cowling.

"The modification increased thrust by more than 20 percent," I added. "It was able to clear two mountain ranges at over 3,000 feet, with little effort. Do you want to see the control mechanisms?"

He turned his head toward Ares as if appealing for approval. Ares nodded affirmatively. The keeper pivoted slowly, allowing us to pass. Ares circled to the opposite side and raised the canopy. I lowered the foot brace on the forward strut and demonstrated its use by climbing into the cockpit. Star climbed after me to look inside. I pushed the power button to illuminate the gauges then reached behind the seat, pulling the gauntlet free. Star leaned in and took the weapon, focusing her attention on the display lights.

"Opal, this is amazing," she touted, turning to the keeper. "You must have a look."

She raised her body and leaned back, allowing him to peer inside. I pointed to the center display, identifying the instruments and their functions. While he was distracted, Star shifted the gauntlet behind her back, inserting her left hand. I moved my leg aside and pointed to the lower nose section, describing the view while in flight. He tilted his head for a better look. Star reacted.

It was over quickly; she knew exactly where to strike. Keepers are also equipped with portal implants—a detail I hadn't confirmed until now. Evidently, they're more programmed than trained for their duties. Star later described her instructions on the care and protection of implants, including potential brain damage from direct electrical current. Although earlier model gauntlets produced less voltage than current editions, the result was still catastrophic.

The keeper crumpled to the floor. Star jumped from the strut and hovered over the body, gauntlet at the ready. She breathed hard through her nose, teeth clenched. Ares rushed around to confront her. He moved slowly as he reached for the weapon.

"Star, why don't I take that for now," he said calmly.

She looked at him, her eyes wide with rage—swollen with wetness. Her chin quivered as she lowered her arm. Ares pulled the gauntlet away, placing his hand on her shoulder. Her whole body shook.

"They hurt me!" she shouted, falling into his arms.

I climbed down from the cockpit and embraced her from behind. She shook and sobbed between us. Forcing back tears, memories of my own encounter with the keepers crept into mind. The aftereffects of electric shock are excruciating. There was constant pain while stretching and pulling at limbs to restore movement. It was an experience I wished to never again encounter. *What was her punishment for disobedience? Was it more severe? Perhaps the gauntlet was used on her a second time—or more.*

Her sobbing stopped and she pulled away from Ares. She turned and wrapped her arms around my neck then whispered in my ear. It was too low for Ares to hear but quite adamant.

"Tell me what to do, Opal. I'll follow you."

My embrace tightened around her. "We two—" I whispered. "Forever."

Chapter 37

Seeds of Revolt

Star wiped her face as we separated. Ares watched empathetically, but his patience was obviously waning. It was likely due to the dead keeper at his feet.

"We need to discuss the mission," I said.

"Of course, Opal," he answered, dismissively. "Before we go further, you both understand there's no turning back?" He pointed to the keeper. "There won't be a trial, only banishment—for all of us."

"Then it doesn't matter how many I kill," Star remarked.

Her facial expression turned serious, even cold. Ares nodded to her, acknowledging both her pain and resolve. He waited for my response.

"The nobles mean to perpetuate their treachery throughout the world," I said. "We succeed or die trying."

Ares studied our faces. "Good," he said, returning the gauntlet to Star. "Watch the lift. The other sentry may return with company. Wait for the panel to close before you move on them."

Star glanced at the lifeless body then hurried to the lift. She positioned herself on the side wall with clear sight of the opening. Ares extended a strap from the transport chassis and secured it to the keeper's legs. He handed me the remote.

"When the airlock opens, steer the drone inside," he said.

"Ares, Yanic knew our plan. The power systems are not failing. Please listen to me."

"I'm listening, but we must conceal this body."

He used the manual control in the alcove to open the airlock. I lined the drone up with a center mark on the ramp and directed it forward.

"There was a village of civilized humans, descendants of Eden 2 residents," I nearly shouted. "Their Elder was a former noble who aided in a revolt. The sanctuary was destroyed."

With the drone in position, Ares pulled the body further inside the airlock. I deactivated the remote and joined him in the front. He was holding the dead keeper's helmet.

"Did this noble give you the chain?" he asked, wrestling with the gloves.

"Yes. The medallion is a key of sorts. When mated with a terminal on fifteen, it completes a series of circuits. It initiates a program he called the Awakening."

Ares now worked on the boots, pausing to look up. "And you gave it to Panos?"

"Not exactly. The medallion requires three chips to be activated, one from each of the sanctuaries. Panos has the Eden 2 chip. A trustee within our noble ranks will have the one for Eden 3."

He rolled the body over to remove the tactical uniform. A series of flaps covered the torso seal. Layers of padding made it challenging to manipulate.

"Then it shouldn't concern us," he said. "They'll never get the third chip. They have no way of reaching Eden 1."

"The Eden 1 chip is here."

"Here?" he snapped, rising to his feet. "Opal, where exactly is the chip?"

"Star has it," I replied confidently.

He looked at her then searched the floor. I recognized his brain was operating at full capacity.

"We can use it to negotiate," he suggested, "to demand the video recordings be returned."

"That won't be necessary," I said. "Tara will deliver the recordings to her father parent at any moment."

He paused and squinted. His look of concern turned to elation. "You switched drives on the drone," he asserted correctly. "You gave Tara the video recordings. She wears the seeds of our revolt on her hand, in plain sight, and has a keeper escort." His head bobbed. "How clever a Seeker you've become."

I swelled with pride. Ares was always supportive and took time to recognize my accomplishments. This comment, however, felt like the final rite of passage into the Seeker realm. It legitimized my membership and role in the Cause. There was no greater compliment, especially coming from such a brilliant man whom I admired so greatly.

"There's more," I said. The helmet remained secured in the storage compartment drum. In his haste to deliver the medallion, Panos neglected to have the drone searched.

"Where did you get this?"

"The Elder Ulysses. It's from Eden 2."

He studied the helmet. "The face moldings are almost identical."

"They are identical," I reported. "We know biometric scanners are programmed to recognize the pattern, providing keepers unlimited access to the sanctuary. This one is untraceable."

"Of course," he whispered.

"Ares, Star can provide the locations of all gateways and service corridor paths. We don't need to battle the keepers; we can maneuver around them."

He shook his head. "Opal, I'm quite certain they confiscated whatever credentials she acquired. I told you, first-year apprentices are not authorized that degree of access."

"Evidently noble apprentices are."

He glanced toward the lift. "Star?" His face hardened. "Opal, have you co-opted any more nobles I need you know about?"

Co-opted nobles? His question struck me as odd. Star is my closest friend, and I'd only recently learned her true status. Meeting Ulysses was coincidental. I didn't purposefully . . . The look on Yanic's face prior to launch flashed in my mind. My suspicion about his motives may have been warranted, given his current situation. *But what are his motives?* He was removed from the project for a reason. It might play to our advantage.

"Not yet," I replied.

Chapter 38

Combatant

Ares exchanged helmets with me.

"Put this away," he said, motioning toward the storage space.

We rolled the keeper under the drone. It was enough to conceal the body from a casual glance but would be easily discovered if the chamber was inspected. Keeper squads aren't known for initiative or diligence, a lack we were counting on to buy us time. Ares tightened the forearm band on the second glove. The black uniform was loose fitting but passable. He pulled the Eden 2 helmet over his head. Although the communication integrator wasn't functional, it still provided access to the entire sanctuary. The disguise was essential to our extrication from sixteen. *If he's discovered impersonating a keeper . . .*

We left the airlock and Ares secured the enclosure. After a quick scan of the space, we made our way to the maintenance lift. Star approached, aggressively waving her gauntlet. I stepped between the two of them.

"Star, wait. This is Ares."

With her head tilted and jaw clenched, she looked ready to attack. I stood my ground, hand extended.

"Ares," she repeated.

I pointed to the helmet. "Do you see the number two? It's from another sanctuary. All of their keepers are dead. This disguise will help us defeat our own."

Lowering the weapon, an odd expression crossed her face. "All dead? I would prefer to live in that sanctuary, Opal."

Ares raised the mirrored visor to speak, anxiously watching Star. "Listen carefully. We must return to my lab undetected. From there we'll make our way to three."

"What was the original return strategy?" I asked.

"Yanic's detail was to escort us back when the mission was complete. Panos arrived an hour before your first communication. I haven't had time to consider other options."

"Why three?" Star asked.

He hesitated, exchanging glances between us.

"Ares, Star is one of us. You must trust her."

He reluctantly nodded in agreement. "There's an abandoned storage area on three. It's the rendezvous point for our cell. If Tara delivered the recordings successfully, it will be the main thrust of the revolt."

"Tip of the spear," Star added.

Ares looked at me. If we hadn't known Star, she might have been mistaken for a seasoned combatant, excited by the prospect of battle. Whether motivated by revenge against her tormentors or from the taste of her first kill, she appeared anxious for more. Regardless of her emotional state, we needed her to access the gateways.

"Star, find us a clear route to the lab," I instructed.

With interpreters in place, she manipulated her console. It took only a few moments to identify an option. "We'll take the maintenance lift to eleven. It's Saturday and the atrium will be heavily occupied, easy to blend in. There are multiple gateways on the south side, leading to service corridors."

"It might look suspicious, being accompanied by a keeper," I suggested.

She'd already considered my concern. "It's not uncommon for disorderly students to be removed from the area. Drones should pass by; residents will ignore us."

"She's right," Ares added. "Residents are averse to attention from keepers. They'll go out of their way to avoid contact."

Ares lowered his visor and stepped in front of the lift scanner. The panel opened immediately. After we entered, Star selected our destination then disengaged her drive. The lift sealed shut and we started our descent.

"Disconnect your Core link," I said.

"Why?"

"Do it now," I insisted.

She turned her bezel two clicks to the left. "Okay, I'm off. You do realize reconnecting can take ten seconds or more?"

"Yes, I'm aware. However, your drive can be tracked, even when disengaged. Keepers followed us through the lower levels. That's how they determined our destination after we left the service corridors."

She caught on quickly. "By disconnecting, they can't predict our movement trends. Opal, that's brilliant."

"The tactic wasn't my idea," I admitted. "Suffice it to say, it came at a high price."

We arrived on eleven. Star and I walked briskly through the lift station followed closely by Ares. Their assertions about residents were accurate. Those walking opposite our direction gave us a wide berth and looked away. Others near us found reasons to divert their courses or stop entirely as we passed. Although their actions played to our advantage then, I was concerned how they might respond to an all-out revolt. *We'll find out soon enough.*

Star led us to a grooming facility at the far end of the station.

She and I entered the foyer while Ares took a sentry position outside. Word spread quickly of the keeper's presence and the facilities were soon vacated. We verified both lavatories were clear, then Star reconnected to the Core. I watched in anticipation as she manipulated her console. Ten seconds seems like an eternity when attempting to move about covertly. The familiar glowing line appeared on the foyer wall surface. Ares joined us and we hurried through the gateway. As soon as it closed, Star disconnected her link. The Core might detect our current location, but not our direction of travel. I silently thanked the Elder for his insight.

Star took us down the narrow service corridor in the opposite direction of the lab. She alone mapped our route, so we didn't protest or challenge her. After traveling more than 200 feet, she stopped in front of a six-foot-high air vent.

"We're over the east end of the Great Hall," she reported. "This ventilation shaft descends below eight, into the hall. Once inside, we can walk down to five and proceed to the lab."

"What about sensors?" I asked.

"Only active on Sundays," she replied. "The Hall isn't used otherwise."

"Good work, Star," Ares said. "Let's move."

She touched a control pad. "The vent will only remain open for thirty seconds."

The grate slid upward exposing a cylindrical shaft approximately four feet in diameter. Star reached across and grasped a dimly lit rundle, then pulled her body through the opening. She cleared quickly and we followed behind her. I focused on my grip and foot placement, maintaining visual contact with Star. Although the rundles glowed brighter when pressure was applied, illumination was poor. Below it looked as if we were climbing into nothingness—an endless black abyss.

My forearms tightened, calves burned. The rundles were spaced one foot apart, making it possible to estimate our progress. Unfortunately, a minor slip caused me to lose count.

Despite the pain, I increased my pace to catch up with Star. Just before I asked for a rest break, she looked up at me.

"This is it," she whispered.

She touched a small screen and the grate opened. They were equipped with interior release triggers, likely a safety precaution for technicians. We emerged from the ventilation shaft behind the highest row of seats in the Great Hall next to a staircase. We proceeded quickly down three flights of stairs. Star came to rest inside the easternmost entranceway. She raised her hand to connect her drive.

"Wait," Ares said, taking her wrist.

We watched him in silence. After a moment, he motioned for us to move against the wall. The entranceway suddenly opened. Star pulled the gauntlet from her waist belt. Ares thrust his arm in front of us. I held my breath until I heard a familiar sound—a sweeping porter. The small cleaning device rolled into the Hall on a pre-programmed path. On the opposite side, entranceways opened and closed in sequence as the entire sweeping porter crew entered the facility. They were preparing for Sunday Assembly.

We wasted no time and hurried out of the Great Hall. The timing of the porter was impeccable. By disconnecting her drive, Star left no trace of us on this level. Our best scenario was to reach the rally point without leaving an electronic footprint. It provided needed time to share my information from the Elder. Gaining the element of surprise might expedite our victory and save lives.

Ares stepped in front of the lab scanner. The Eden 2 helmet was accepted immediately, and the outer panel opened. The inner security system also responded positively. Using the helmet reduced the possibility of a security response. We entered the lab and followed him to the drone test room. Again, the helmet was recognized for identification and the reinforced entrance slid open. We followed him inside and hurried to the farthest left storage compartment. He removed a glove and placed his hand on the security screen.

"These locks are not linked," he assured us.

When the compartment opened, he retrieved two metal cases and slid them in our direction. Reaching deep into the space, he also removed a large black bag.

"Use the portable," he said, pointing to the wheeled table.

We removed several spare components and loaded the cases on the lower shelf. Ares closed the compartment, dropped his bag on the top shelf, then covered the table with a tarp. Last, he picked up several tethering shackle bolts and scattered them on the tarp.

"We'll use communal lift stations to avoid interfacing. Wear your interpreters and keep your heads down. If you're stopped, explain you were ordered by the Noble Yanic to deliver salvaged parts to recycling. Opal, take the lead. Star, you have the table. I'll follow as escort. Any questions?"

We shook our heads no.

"Okay," he said, looking us over. "Star, conceal your gauntlet under the tarp. Use it as an absolute last resort. If it's seen in your possession, the keeper response will be immediate and overwhelming."

"Understood," she responded, pushing the weapon between the metal cases.

He pulled his visor into place. "Let's go."

Chapter 39

Tip of the Spear

We made our way through the campus. Only a handful of students meandered about. As before, we were given wide latitude. Not a single passerby made eye contact. When the station was in sight, I identified a lift and selected a direct line to follow. Our pace was steady but not hurried. Although my head was tilted down, I watched ahead for potential obstacles.

At the first intersection, there stood a sentry platform to my right. Our path took us within twenty feet of a keeper. My heart pounded, and perspiration beaded on my forehead. *Remember your training, Opal. The worst thing to do is react.* Any suspicious activity outside our already odd-looking caravan might result in a challenge by the sentry. I focused on the lift and maintained my stride. Three steps more and a surveillance drone appeared from the left corridor. *I've never seen a T-8 on this level.* The nobles had begun preparations. With the connector now in their possession, the Awakening was at hand.

Out of paranoia, they'll likely secure every level and detain any potential threat—real or perceived.

I didn't turn my head as the drone flew over. Ares and Star should have seen it by now. Hopefully, they made no overtures in its direction. We were ten feet from the lift when it opened. I allowed myself to breathe as two residents exited and immediately turned to avoid us. Without delay, I stepped inside and pivoted to the selection screen. Star was on my heels with the portable and pushed it to the far side. Ares entered and immediately turned to face the opening. His presence would discourage others from boarding. I casually selected three. Had we raised any alarm, the sentry would stop the lift and detain us for questioning. It was a test of our deception—a very stressful one.

As the panel sealed, we remained motionless. Lifts are equipped with sensors. Any form of celebration might label us as potential threats, and our participation in the revolt would come to an abrupt end. I thought about the serial number on the helmet. *Do keepers know the difference? Would the Core notice the discrepancy?* To the best of our knowledge, it remained undetected thus far.

We arrived on three. Noise erupted as soon as the lift opened. Beyond the station were several receiving docks where materials arrived for recycling. Dozens of C-54s drifted in and out distributing their payloads onto conveyors. Ground porters rolled by, transporting discarded materials from various collection sites. Everything in Life World is recycled. Worn, broken, or outdated equipment is disassembled, the parts made available for future use. Materials discarded in the morning are found in newly manufactured items delivered the same night. In a completely enclosed environment, there were no other options. This was the reality residents of Life World knew and accepted.

Ares exited the lift and walked toward the docks. Star backed the table out then spun it forward. We were hurrying to catch up with Ares when he abruptly stopped. A T-8 drifted slowly through the outer station corridor, just ten feet above his head. It came to a stop, hovering directly in front of him. He made no sudden movement but swiveled his head slightly to the left. His action turned the identifier code away from the drone. We continued walking in his direction. As we approached, he pivoted left ninety degrees and extended his arm toward us. He raised his hand with elbow bent as if waving us on. We moved past him, toward the number four receiving dock. After we cleared the corridor, the drone resumed its surveillance duties, flying out of sight.

Ares joined us in the dock and removed a hand radio disc from his belt. It resembled the unit we used for communication in the drone. He turned the power on but didn't speak into the microphone. Instead, he compressed the mic button four times rapidly. Eventually, there was a response. It came in the form of static from another user keying their mic. The return code was two dashes, a pause, and then one dash. The cell members were now expecting our arrival. I was excited to meet more Seekers.

We neared the recycling plant center without seeing another resident. On the opposite side of the level were manufacturing facilities. Most parts created in Life World were constructed using three-dimensional printers. The machine size and complexity were determined by the product and composite medium utilized in the layering process. Almost everything required to maintain the sanctuary was designed by the Core. In the manufacturing area, like recycling, residents were only needed to service the equipment.

The concrete floor turned to metal grating. We approached a smelting furnace surrounded by water tanks. They were joined by a network of pipes leading up through level four. The system delivered heated liquid to living quarters. I marveled at the efficiency with which the sanctuary was designed. *The builders knew they were creating their own prison. According to the Elder, they also included means of escape.*

Ares turned right and continued along a narrow grated walkway. Star followed him around the corner. The table wheels made a whining sound on the metal flooring. After several more steps, there was a new noise behind me. I glanced around to see an inventory tracking porter approaching, its collision avoidance beams sweeping the walkway. I ran ahead of Star and touched Ares's shoulder. We guided the table out of the porter's path. Ares let it pass, adjusted his radio, then keyed three rapid clicks.

Just beyond our position, the porter stopped and rotated ninety degrees. The forward beams rose from the floor, illuminating the wall. The conical-shaped beams closed to a single stream, then moved up to a circular protrusion above the walkway. A gateway outline appeared on the wall. As it slid open, the porter turned back forward and moved on. Ares motioned for us to enter the storage unit.

The gateway closed behind us. Ahead, there were luminescent circles in the center of the floor. Much like those in the sub-levels, they provided direction but little light. Ares removed the helmet and turned to face us. He pulled the tarp aside and lifted the bag from the table.

"Bring the cases," he whispered. "Don't speak until you're introduced."

Star secured the gauntlet in her belt. We removed the metal cases and followed Ares. A dim light glowed near the end of the short corridor. The walls were made of thin metal sheets placed over shelving units. The space was no longer used for scrapped material. Perhaps it was contaminated, or damaged beyond repair.

At the end of the corridor, Ares turned left into an alcove. He looked back and waved us in his direction. We hurried and stood in front of a heavily reinforced entranceway. Unlike automated panels, it was supported by large hinges and didn't slide to open. Ares searched the opening, seemingly uncertain of what to do next. After several seconds there was a movement near the ceiling. A video lens retracted, focusing on our faces. I stared at the sensor, wondering who was watching from the other side.

We were hit by a blast of air when the door opened outward. It was an opening to an internal air lock. The hold served as a security block but also prevented odors and DNA particles from escaping the secret location. Keepers sometimes used bio-electronic receptors to track and find wanted residents. The devices analyzed and compared samples to those maintained in Core databases. Records existed on everyone in Life World. There was no defense against a positive identification when a corrupt or subversive act is committed. Guilt or innocence was irrelevant. One's fate was ultimately determined by the Noble Court. *If they wish to dispose of you, they will.*

The man who embraced Ares was introduced as Lake Four, Tara's father parent. His handshake was firm, his gaze intense. Jade mentioned she and Ares attended classes with him, but he looked much older. Perhaps it was the years spent overseeing manufacturing or stress from the Cause. He escorted us into a large open space, segmented by low dividing walls. I couldn't see all their faces but counted twelve performing a variety of tasks. In one corner two females were sharpening metal spikes with abrasive blocks. One saw me and turned around. She laid her tools aside and walked toward us.

"I believe you know Tara," Lake said, resting his hand on her shoulder.

"Hello, Tara," Ares offered.

She had the same intense gaze as her father. "That was a clever way to pass the drive," she said. "Was it your idea?"

"Opal is very decisive under pressure," Star interjected.

Tara glanced at Star, sizing her up. "Except for befriending a noble."

Chapter 40

The Awakening

The room went silent. All turned toward Star. She gripped her gauntlet and fell back one step. Lake raised his hand between the two.

"That's enough!" he shouted, turning to Star. "We've known of your station for years. All young nobles have been identified." He looked at Tara. "If she was loyal to the Court, you wouldn't have left sixteen with that drive."

"Star won't betray us," I added.

"I agree," Ares said. "She's already proven herself."

"I trust her," a deep voice echoed from a dark corner. A tall, imposing figure stepped from the shadows. He approached with a distinctive walk, hands grasped behind his back. As soon as light showed on his face, I recognized Professor Marc. Star ran between us and wrapped her arms around him. He smiled at me.

"After all," he added, "I recruited her."

Tension in the room subsided. After we were introduced to the remaining Seekers, they resumed their tasks. Lake invited us to sit at a large round table. It resembled those in Ares's lab, complete with a holographic projector in the center. I soon learned Professor Marc was the de facto leader of our cell. Silas recruited him shortly after he entered secondary. Lake was one of his first recruits. Ares didn't know Marc was one of us. The Seeker Cause survived because there were degrees of separation between members. If one was discovered and interrogated, only a limited number could be exposed.

As Marc Three spoke, I assembled the pieces in my head. Star was never the best of students, but she was a noble. She knew what her future might hold and was ripe for recruitment. Marc had provided the altered drive she used for assessments. Her results were designed to indicate cyber systems as a match for her skill set. Our professor fully intended to exploit her new position. The revolt was rapidly approaching, and he knew she would be granted access to the maintenance corridors—even as an apprentice.

Star turned and caught me staring at her. Instead of her familiar smile, she held my gaze and offered a reassuring nod. I swelled with pride in her and our friendship. She'd wanted to share her secret with me but remained true to the Cause. When Chet exposed her status, she could've revealed herself as a Seeker. Instead, she endured humiliation and degradation, not to protect herself, but to protect me. After our capture and her excruciating interrogation, she never wavered—never revealed any of us. I know now our bond will never be broken. Star would die for me, and I for her.

Marc summoned everyone for a briefing. As each Seeker approached the table, Lake provided them a refurbished drive. Star received an altered unit but was instructed to retain her original. We donned our interpreters and engaged.

"These drives use encrypted coding," Marc said. "Outside of this shadow space, the Core will detect your presence but not your identity. Your families will be spared any initial response. When we go live, the system will identify us as anomalies—malfunctions. However, when the broadcast is discovered, we'll immediately be tagged as threats. Keeper forces will be sent to intercept and dispose of us."

Lake stepped forward. "We installed navigation files with integrated transponders. You can identify each other's movements, but not those of other cells."

"How do we identify them?" Ares asked.

"Challenge and response codes will be provided one hour before Assembly," Marc answered.

Tara glanced at Star. "I guess we still have trust issues," she half whispered.

"Perhaps you're the one they don't trust," Star replied.

"Enough," Marc said. "Everyone in this room has been vetted. We have one opportunity for success and must work together. Now direct your attention to the display."

A holographic image leaped from the table center. It was a three-dimensional rendering of the sanctuary. Marc used his console to locate the Great Hall and expanded the image. The inverted cone rotated slowly, red dots blinking at each entranceway.

"There are eight sentry stations on each level, two keepers inside the entranceway, one outside. That's seventy-two initial targets." The image zoomed out to include the KPR station. "Keepers are equipped with beacons, which alert their central command to distress. We're counting on multiple beacons being activated from each level when the uprising begins. This will spread their forces, increasing the likelihood our cell breaks through." He held up a sharpened metal spike. "We need to neutralize as many as possible at the onset, but not kill them." He stepped back. "Lake, if you will."

Lake picked up a spike and summoned Ares away from the table. He turned him so his left side faced the group and lifted his arm forward.

"The KPR tactical uniform is designed to protect from direct frontal and rear assaults," he began. "When a gauntlet is extended in attack formation, this area directly under the arm is exposed. The padding is thinner for greater rotation and mobility. This is your strike point."

"Attack teams will work in pairs," Marc added. "One challenging the keeper from the front, the other striking from the side. Don't linger when a target goes down. Move on to the next. We expect residents to collect weapons and join us."

"What about reinforcements?" a male named Flynn asked. His disheveled hair and unshaved face made him appear older than his years. "There'll be panic. What if too few residents join us?"

Ares placed his bag on the table and removed a small metallic orb. He held it up for all to see. "These produce a concussive blast with an effective radius of fifteen feet. Anyone inside the zone will be disoriented for several minutes," he said.

"What about their shields?" Flynn pressed.

"The shields can deflect much of the blast waves. The weapon is most effective when detonated behind a squad," Ares answered. "Keeper tactics are defensive in nature. They respond by massing together in the direction of the greatest threat."

"The reinforcement squads," Lake continued, "will identify fleeing crowds of residents as the focus of their defense. Our teams of two will receive less attention and therefore be more effective."

"Until the T-8s arrive." We all looked at the agitator. I couldn't tell if Flynn was scared or uncommitted, but I did *not* want to be teamed with him.

Ares placed one of the metal boxes next to the bag. He opened the lid and removed an eight-inch-long metal cylinder. One end had a sharp point, the other had three raised fletching vanes. It resembled a shortened version of Drake's arrows.

"The T-8 is constructed with a metallic support frame," Ares started. "When this penetrator is activated, the piercing end is magnetized. It need only be thrown in the direction of the drone and will track to its target."

"We're relying on the melee at Assembly as a distraction," Marc added. "It's unlikely the keepers have a planned response for such a large encounter. The ensuing confusion should provide us the opening we need to reach our primary objective—the Noble Court."

Gasps erupted around the room. The Noble Court was the supreme ruling body of Life World. We were told their genetic lineage descends directly from the Prophets. Our scriptures establish their ordained right to high and holy positions. Threatening the Court is blasphemy, but none of it matters.

"It won't work," I blurted out.

Chapter 41

Altered Strategy

All eyes fell on me. Marc was visibly irritated.

"Opal—" Ares chided.

"Ares, this may be bad timing, but you must know what I discovered. There is no Noble Court." Everyone in the room looked stunned. "The holographs we see at Assembly are augmented reality, images produced by the Core." I looked at Star. "Nobles hold high positions in Life World, however, serve their own master." Her face hardened; she knew my words were true.

Marc slammed a hand on the table. "How could you possibly know this?" he shouted.

"Wait," Ares said, holding his palm toward Marc. He looked at me as he spoke. "She just returned from Out World." More gasps from the crowd. "Go ahead, Opal."

The tension grew heavier. Months, perhaps years, of planning led to this congregation—this day. I was now suggesting it might all be for naught. Precious little time remained, and the plan was about to change. As I inhaled a deep calming breath, the hollow remains of Eden 2 appeared in my mind. The thought of our sanctuary falling to the same fate saddened me. The idea of nobles ruling the planet quickly wiped those emotions away.

"The only way to be free," I said emphatically, "is to destroy the Core."

No one spoke or moved. They all knew the implications. We relied on the Core for every aspect of our lives. Destroying it meant the end of Life World. For the moment, they were unaware any alternative existed.

"Continue," Ares prodded.

"As you'll see in the broadcast, the planet is healed. There are no storms, and clean water is plentiful. Human survivors formed civilized communities and are not the flesh-eating cannibals we imagine. They live in villages, grow food, and hunt animals. Children play and attend school. They establish rules together and choose their leaders."

"Did these civilized humans convince you to destroy our sanctuary?" Flynn asked sarcastically.

"No," I replied loudly. "That suggestion came from their Elder, Ulysses." I looked directly at Marc. "He was a noble in Eden 2." Heads swiveled with confusion. Murmurs rose around the room.

"Silence please," Marc insisted.

"What exactly is Eden 2?" Flynn asked.

Ares spoke up. "Life World is one of three sanctuaries constructed before the great storms. This facility was the third to be occupied." He paused as they absorbed the information. Even Marc appeared perplexed. "Opal was on a Court sanctioned mission to establish contact with the others."

"She's in league with the nobles?" Tara quipped with noted suspicion.

Flynn sized Ares up. "How do you know about other sanctuaries?"

"Flynn, stand down," Marc asserted. "We all have questions."

Lake stepped forward. "Ares and I cooperated on the design and construction of a large-scale research drone. We were under the guidance of the Noble Yanic. He provided the information."

"Before his recent removal," Ares continued, "Yanic served as Court liaison for the project. The drone was meant to establish contact with Eden 2. I was given access to external atmospheric files. The data indicated Out World can support human life. Opal has returned with indisputable evidence of those facts."

"Lake informed me of a data gathering project," Marc inserted. "He also presented the broadcast concept as a tool to incite a resident revolt. He never mentioned sanctuaries or that the drone contained a human passenger."

"Pilot," I corrected him.

Marc glared at me, but Ares intervened. "The distance and mountainous terrain prohibited remote control of the drone. The only alternative was manual flight."

A young female standing next to Tara spoke for the first time. "You flew a drone? Over mountains?"

Before I could respond, Marc cleared his throat. He continued staring at me, but his expression grew softer. "You can discuss your adventure with Grace at a later time." He looked around the table. "Obviously Opal has important information to share. I suggest we hear her out."

"Seventy years in the past, rebels in Eden 2 staged a revolt. Their plans, however, were intercepted and they were stopped. Most of their members were tried and terminated."

"You mean banished," Marc offered.

"No," I replied. "There is no banishment. Not there, not here. Anyone considered a threat to a Core is terminated, their bodies incinerated." I pointed to Star. "Nobles exist to carry out orders from a machine. The KPR enforce those orders."

"Tell them about twelve," Star suggested.

The entire room hung on my every word. Even Flynn listened attentively. "Residents who reach the age of Transition don't spend their final year in luxurious quarters. Many are preserved cryogenically, their organs harvested to lengthen the life span of surrogate processors."

"Surrogate process—" Lake muttered.

"Surrogate processors," Star enunciated, moving closer to the table. She turned her head, exposing her port. "If selected, mature nobles are given the privilege of providing the Core additional random-access memory—by direct interface." She straightened her collar and looked at Tara. "We share the same enemy."

"What about Eden 2?" Ares asked.

"Destroyed. Much of the structure remains, but it's uninhabitable. The survivors formed clans and are spread throughout this territory. They live off the land and trade in peace with other survivors."

"You mentioned three sanctuaries," Marc added.

I answered for Ares. "The Elder told me Eden 1 was also destroyed, likely damaged by storms decades before."

"And you believed this—Elder?" Marc asked.

The group looked to me in anticipation. At the time of my transformation to Seeker, I too had questions, doubts, and uncertainties. My faith fell to Ares and Jade whom I had known my entire life. Although we shared an allegiance to the Cause, many in the room had never met before that day. If one of them were relaying this tale to me, I, too, would be skeptical. Their lives were about to change beyond anything they'd imagined. They needed to believe there was a future for them, for their families—for humanity.

I looked in their faces and continued. "A rebel named Sable led the initial revolt at Eden 2. The Noble Ulysses was in love with her. He was betrayed by his mentor, and she was exposed. She was terminated with the other conspirators. Ulysses was enraged and secretly swore his revenge, but didn't act immediately. Because of his mentor's influence, he was elevated to a high noble station called a trustee. He gained access to closely held information about the sanctuary and the Eden Projects."

"Projects?" Marc inquired about the plurality.

My audience barely breathed. "Before the great storms, an elite world organization called New Genesis constructed six Eden Projects throughout the world." Eyes widened, mouths fell open. "The elitists recruited top scientists and skilled laborers to maintain each facility and serve them in exchange for safety. They appropriated ancient religions and created unbreakable laws designed to perpetuate their reign over the subjects. Those perverted laws became our scriptures, the subjects are now called residents, the elite—nobles." No one moved, so I continued. "The creed says our descendants will emerge after 500 years to inherit the planet. A small echelon of high nobles believe they were chosen to lead those descendants. They intend to rule the planet when the time arrives. But, the true emergence is marked by the Sestercentennial, 250 years."

Marc exchanged glances with Ares, then Lake. "That celebration begins at Assembly tomorrow," he exclaimed.

"Except it's not just a celebration," I added. "It's called the Awakening, the beginning of a new order. What the nobles don't realize is the chain of events they set in motion will also enslave them. When initiated, a series of launch vehicles near each sanctuary will deliver satellites to geostationary orbits surrounding the planet. They'll establish communication links, joining the remaining Cores as one. The collective processing power will be immeasurable. Humans—all humans, will exist only to serve one omnipotent Master Core."

Chapter 42

New Asset

Marc searched our faces. Whispers surrounded me. I noticed Star and Tara watching each other. To my surprise, both nodded. They now understood our mission was no longer about residents and nobles. We were fighting for freedom, perhaps the very existence of our species.

"You said those you encountered were from Eden 2," Marc finally spoke. "How did they manage to escape?"

"They destroyed their Core," I began. "Many lives were lost because residents refused to follow Ulysses's instructions. Those who did made their way out of the sanctuary through existing subterranean tunnels."

"Did he tell you the location of the tunnels?" Ares asked.

"They begin in the northwest corner of sub-level four, terminating in a rocket silo near the outer surface. The silo lies north of the sanctuary. He said the tunnels were constructed to hold fuel lines for the orbital rocket and estimated their length at 300 feet."

"Northwest corner puts them in the air separation plant," Flynn interjected.

Several of us looked at him. His occupation was in the bowels of the sanctuary. Most dreaded the thought of such an existence. If nobles held the highest station in Life World, sub-level four workers held the lowest. They treated wastewater and sewage, and they maintained air purification systems. The only things beneath them are petroleum and water storage reservoirs. He looked back with a recriminating stare, knowing he was being judged. It explained a great deal about his demeanor.

"Opal, did Ulysses tell you how they destroyed their Core?" Ares asked.

"Not exactly," I replied. "He mentioned liquid nitrogen and said you would understand. What does it mean?"

Ares leaned forward, fists clenched on the table. "Right, right," he murmured.

"What are you thinking?" Lake asked.

Ares straightened his back, making mental calculations as he spoke. "Flynn, do porters leave the air separation plant with any regularity?"

"Every night at 6:10 p.m.," Flynn responded.

"6:10?" Marc inquired.

"Not a minute after," Flynn answered. "Right between shift changes. The night crew starts at 6:15."

"For security," Ares added. "Fewer residents means less risk."

"Risk of what?" Marc asked.

Ares didn't respond. His right arm now crossed his body, supporting his left elbow. He rubbed his chin in silence. We waited in anticipation. After a minute, he raised his brow. The imperceptible grin, which only I noticed, meant he found his answer.

"Geostationary orbits are more than 20,000 miles above the planet's surface," he began. "The only rockets that were capable of placing satellites at that range utilized liquid-propelled engines. Liquid hydrogen was typically the fuel, liquid oxygen the oxidizer. The tunnels hold vacuum lines to feed the rocket tanks."

Most of us were lost. It wasn't clear how a rocket impacted our plan. Ares recognized our collective uncertainty.

"Liquid oxygen can't be stored for long periods due to evaporation. It must be produced shortly before a launch, using liquid nitrogen as a cooling agent." More blank stares. He continued. "Quantum computing platforms, like the Core, can only operate in extremely cold environments. At the time the sanctuaries were constructed, liquid nitrogen was the most commonly used cooling source for those platforms. It's produced through the fractional distillation of liquid air. Even in a vacuum, nitrogen in that state experiences loss due to evaporation." He turned to Flynn. "The porter leaving the plant at 6:10 p.m. is replenishing the Core cooling system."

Marc shook his head. "The porter must pass through several checkpoints. I don't believe we can gain access to the Core through its path."

"We don't have to gain access to the Core to destroy it," Ares responded. "Liquid nitrogen boils immediately upon contact with warmer substances. When rapidly vaporized in a vacuum, the force it releases can be catastrophic. The Core cooling system is likely designed with a storage reservoir, which is replenished each night. We need only introduce a contaminant into the reservoir." Ares turned to me. "Ulysses gave you the answer."

"Flynn, do you have access to the nitrogen distillery?" Marc asked.

"No," he answered. "But we have someone who does."

"Can you get to them tonight?" Ares inquired.

Flynn shook his head. "Tell me what needs to be done."

The meeting continued for another hour. Marc covered every detail of the new plan. Each cell member was assigned a specific task, with no redundancies. If any of us were captured, we would be sacrificed. Our numbers were too few to risk rescue attempts. Although every Seeker in the room was highly motivated, I was uncertain about the other cells. There was no direct communication, no way to coordinate our efforts. If they didn't perform, we might be quickly overwhelmed. The Cause would be dead, and we along with it.

I watched Ares's face as the final preparations were discussed. There was a determined intensity in his gaze. He was highly intelligent and had a remarkable ability for reason and deduction. There was another side of him, however, a strength and fortitude I only witnessed in one other person—Drake.

Drake. I reflected on my brief encounter with the hunter. He was young yet wise, strong yet gentle, and yes, quite handsome. An opinion of which he'd surely remind me if I were to see him again. *What was his remark after killing the lion? "The only way to defeat a stronger adversary is to gain an advantage."* Did we have a true advantage? The plan seemed solid, but something was missing. Glancing at the eager faces around me, my attention fell on Star. I thought of the chip secured in her belt. *The medallion must be in the hands of the trustee by now. They would know—* "Yanic!" I blurted out.

"What is it, Opal?" Ares asked, concerned.

"He's the trustee," I replied. "Just like Ulysses."

"You mentioned the title before," Marc said. "What exactly is a trustee?"

"A trustee is part of the high noble echelon, a historian of sorts," I said. "Each generation is hand-selected by their predecessor. They alone have access to the directives left by New Genesis."

"Including construction documents and atmospheric data files," Ares added.

"If there's no true Court . . . our project was sanctioned by the Core," I concluded.

The others looked on as we traded comments. Ares then addressed the group. "The Noble Yanic approached me to lead the drone project several months ago. I was permitted to enlist Lake for parts manufacture. The idea of broadcasting a video to initiate the revolt was conceived then. Yanic oversaw the project until just before Opal returned from her mission. We suspect he's being detained."

"If his orders were from the Core, why is he being detained?" Marc asked.

I responded. "According to Ulysses, the trustee knows every aspect of the Awakening, including how to prevent it."

"If there was any suspicion of Yanic's motives," Ares interjected, "the Core would take defensive actions." He looked at Marc. "If the Core doubts his loyalty, he may prove to be an asset."

"How do we find him?" Marc asked.

Star stepped forward. "I can help."

Chapter 43

Dawn of Freedom

The remainder of the night was spent debating and planning alternative courses of action. My information changed everything. New priorities were established, assignments altered. We were all mentally exhausted. After finishing an evening meal of cold fish and baguettes, Marc ordered us to rest. I remained seated at the round table, head on my arms. Sleep eluded me. The faint whispers and constant shuffling around me suggested I wasn't alone.

Although trying to focus on my assigned tasks, it was difficult to stop the onslaught of images racing through my mind. One moment, Star and I were in the atrium castle, planning our curriculum for new students. The next, I was on Drake's horse with my arms wrapped around his waist. A stream of faces appeared in succession: classmates, professors, Jade, Yanic, Kane, Chet, Ulysses. Even strangers appeared, residents passing in corridors or following me around the tube.

A recurring image both frightened and angered me. It was the menacing likeness of a keeper's helmet. At first, my reflection appeared in the visor. Then the visor lifted, revealing my own face, eyes wild with fear. My mouth moved, screaming the same warning over and over, but there was no sound. The screaming stopped, and my mouth closed. Blood poured from my head, covering my face. When I reached for the helmet, something grabbed my arm, pulling me away. The helmet started spinning, I was falling farther and farther . . .

"Opal—Opal."

I woke with a gasp, jerking my head up. My hands shook on the table in front of me. My breathing was shallow and rapid. Ares stood next to me.

"Opal," he repeated. "Are you okay?"

I took a deep breath then exhaled. I squeezed my hands together, then stretched my fingers in and out. The shaking subsided, my breathing slowed.

"You were dreaming," he whispered reassuringly.

"Yes," I managed.

Rubbing my temples to clear the fog, I glanced around the room. Others were stirring, securing weapons, checking drives. A screen on the far wall displayed 5:23 a.m. We agreed on five-minute intervals for team departures. Flynn had already gone to meet his contact on sub-level four. His assignment was critical to our success. I wasn't fully convinced of his commitment.

Ares and Lake were scheduled out first at 5:45 a.m. They expected to draw little attention with a keeper disguise. The helmet assured them access to the power transformation plant on level one. Yanic and Ares had surveyed the electric grid and battery banks when the project was first proposed. Shortly after, Yanic likely sabotaged the storage unit. Due to the critical nature of the plant, all communication lines are hardwired to Core links. Lake would upload the edited video into one of the plant's data transfer channels using a high-efficiency compression coding module. He copied a standard communication module from a technician's 3D print order, ensuring it mated perfectly with the motherboards. The broadcast was to begin at precisely 8:02 a.m. after Assembly trumpets had sounded.

Although the Core would detect the transmission, it wouldn't be able to isolate the channel without disrupting system commands to the plant. By the time cyber techs located the module, the broadcast would be complete. The final word residents would hear on the six-minute recording is *freedom*. It was the signal for Seekers to strike—for the revolt to begin.

Ares put his hand on my shoulder. "Don't deviate from your orders," he said quietly. "When your task is complete, go directly to the tunnels. We'll find you—out there."

My orders were clear and, for all intents, quite simple. At the onset of the uprising, Star would infiltrate the keeper center databases to determine where Yanic was being held. We'd use her access to find and free him. Ares convinced Marc that Yanic must have some plan to disrupt the Awakening. Once he was released, our role in the revolt would be done—simple.

"You'll enjoy it," I said. "Out there."

"Of course, we will." He released my shoulder and started toward the entrance. After two steps, he turned back. "Opal." He paused. "Use your mind. It's your greatest asset." Before I responded, he pulled the helmet on and followed Lake into the airlock. The screen displayed 5:45 a.m.

Teams of two departed every five minutes. Star and I were scheduled to leave at 6:15 a.m. Once clear of the security hold, our connection to the shadow space personal area network would be lost. We needed her original drive for navigation to the Great Hall. I was concerned about the heightened security and worried she was marked for arrest. If the body was discovered on sixteen, Panos would have us all labeled as fugitives. It was a risk, but we had no other option. Activating the altered drives too soon might raise an alarm.

The time was 6:13 a.m. I adjusted the objects in my belt. Each cell member was issued a metal spike. Ares also provided me a penetrator missile. Although Star and I weren't part of the offensive wave, he suggested the weapon might be of use during escape.

Star looked at me with an intense gaze. She was focused and confident. I used to rely on her carefree smile for reassurance but now found solace in her fortitude. Whether motivated out of devotion to the Cause or desire for revenge, nothing was going to stop her. We were relying on her to perform.

"Ready?" she asked.

"Ready."

We exited the hold after a short decontamination cycle. It took a moment to adjust to the darkness in the metal-lined hall. The gateway outline glowed dimly ahead of us. Motion sensors monitored the exterior walkway for additional security. We waited for a final sweep before being released. I was surprisingly calm and took the time to admire the intricate weave in Star's chignon hairstyle. The thought of my own unkempt appearance made me grin. Then I wondered how I'd looked to Drake. *My hair must have been a mangled mess after the lion attack.*

My thoughts returned to our assignment as the gateway opened. Star moved quickly over the metal grate, retracing our path to the lift station.

"Hold," she said, stopping abruptly.

We slid into a side recess to activate her drive. She plotted our course and waved me on. At the primary corridor, she turned right. After twenty paces, we stopped near a bundle of pipes. Star entered commands on her console, and a gateway opened in front of us. We used service corridors for the remainder of our trek to the Hall.

Except for having to avoid two service techs, our journey was uneventful. We exited through a grooming facility on seven and joined a group of residents making their way to Assembly. Star deactivated her drive and disconnected the link. If she was being tracked, it would become evident soon. Two keepers were standing sentry at the entrance.

We funneled into the Hall and took separate routes to our assigned areas. Much to my surprise, Jade was already seated. She had reported Ares's absence before the ceremony. The only acceptable excuses for missing Assembly were essential work assignments or bodily injury. She likely used a Seeker connection in the hospital to falsify his medical treatment. A keeper would verify the claim after ceremonies ended. I stepped through to my seat.

"Praise be to The Giver," I whispered.

She responded without looking. "To the virtue of truth."

The challenge and response codes were authenticated. It was our first meeting since my return, but she showed no emotion. *Whether geneticist, professor, or revolutionary, she's always the consummate professional.* I scanned the crowd after activating the modified drive. Lake said it was common for multiple drives to malfunction on Sunday. With cell members spread throughout the Hall, there was little chance of discovering the altered units. I still held my breath until the trumpets sounded.

When the lights dimmed, the familiar glow of interpreters dotted the hall. The floating doorway materialized on center stage. Court members emerged one by one. Before the last was seated, the ceremony was interrupted. Lake's voice boomed over the audio system while segments of my recorded mission appeared in front of our collective eyes.

"Residents of Life World, the images before you were recorded less than twenty-four hours in the past. Your Noble Court does not wish you to know the truth. Our planet is healed. Out World is inhabitable. You can escape the bondages of Life World and live as free humans."

The crowd was eerily quiet as the footage continued. It was stunning, seeing the horned creatures Drake called *bison* grazing near the foothills. Gasps erupted around me as the drone crested the first mountain range and dove toward the glade. The video froze, and my heart skipped a beat. On stage, the nobles' holographic images flickered. The Core was attempting to disrupt the broadcast. Murmurs began to rise, then quickly ceased as the video resumed. Lake had known exactly where to insert the module. To stop the broadcast, the Core would have had to interrupt its own power supply. It was a small victory.

"The grass and trees before you have grown over the once decimated landscape. Surviving clans of humans have formed civilized societies and live in peace."

Lake may have been a talented programmer, but he was even more skilled at video editing. The image of Drake at the glade's edge transitioned seamlessly to us standing face to face. It was the exact moment he spoke his first words. My expression on the video was one of giddy surprise—part shock, part exhilaration. There was no footage of the mountain lion.

"Water is plentiful in Out World. Crops are grown on large parcels of land. An abundance of animals roam the plains and are hunted for food."

My flight over the village captured many clan members. They worked on construction projects, tended animals, and harvested gardens. Children played and waved happily at the drone. Home structures circled the central lake, wisps of smoke rising from their stone columns. It was peaceful and beautiful. Residents around me were enjoying the spectacle until the image of Eden 2 appeared.

"Life World is one of many sanctuaries. Structures built by powerful elitists before the great storms. The residents of our neighboring sanctuary learned the truth and rose up against their noble oppressors. They fought for their families. They fought for their lives. They fought for FREEDOM."

Chapter 44

Revolt

The signal had been given. Seekers throughout the Hall leaped into action. Screams rang out in the darkness as battles ensued. The entranceway behind me burst open as cell members attacked keepers and broke through security holds. Residents near the scuffles rose to their feet. Most didn't move at first, appearing uncertain of what to do. Others tried to escape the Hall in near panic. Those in the center rows couldn't move immediately and were shouting orders to their families. The lights came up, displaying the masses moving about in all directions. It was near pandemonium.

Star made her way toward me. She jumped onto a row of seats and ran behind the line of standing residents. When she reached my section, we headed to the opposite stairway. I turned to find Jade gone. She was attached to a different cell and had her own instructions. Just as we reached the end of the aisle and started up the stairs, a familiar voice rang out from the stage below.

"Residents of Life World, rise up against your oppressors!" Jade shouted. "Fight for your freedom. Life World is finished. Resist the nobles or they'll destroy you."

We slowed behind a dense crowd pushing through the entranceway. I turned again to find Jade, but she was gone. Faded holographs of nobles drifted across the stage. The Assembly ceremony was prerecorded, and the Core had neglected to stop the proceedings. It was proof there was no Noble Court. Hopefully, all the residents recognized the facade.

Star pulled me by the arm through a gap in the line. I looked down in time to avoid a dead keeper. He lay face down and a pool of blood surrounded his underarm. The back of his neck was also charred from a gauntlet strike. If Seekers followed the attack strategy, it meant he was executed after the first wave came through, and at least some residents were joining the fight.

We made it out of the Hall and ran toward the grooming area. Through the crowds, I saw a squad of keepers in the corridor to our left. They carried riot shields and were positioned in a defensive formation. Shouts rang out as a group of thirty or more residents charged the squad. They were led by a young male holding a recovered gauntlet. *It's Kane.* A resident following close behind him lobbed a small object over the squad. The concussion orb exploded, dropping most of the keeper line. *Seekers are with him.* The marauding band fell on the squad, pummeling them with kicks and punches. They collected gauntlets and shields, then terminated every keeper before continuing down the corridor. I wanted to shout at Kane to let him know how well the drone performed, but he was gone.

Star opened the gateway, and we paused inside to catch our breath. She worked her console in search of Yanic, becoming visibly frustrated.

"This makes no sense," she thought out loud.

"What is it?"

"A directive mentions your noble, but . . ."

"But what? Did you find his location?"

"He has been detained by order of the Court, however, not in the detention center. He's being held on twelve."

"Star, we need to move fast. He's being prepared for—"

"Cryogenic storage," she finished. "Stand by."

After several swipes of her fingers, she pointed east. We sprinted down the corridor for almost a hundred feet. She finally stopped and bent over, gasping for air. I encouraged her to keep moving but was ignored. She entered several commands on the console. A service lift opened, and we stepped inside. We leaned against the back wall, both breathing heavily.

The lift opened on twelve. It was a restricted area where few were permitted. Panos had obviously not discovered the dead keeper on sixteen because Star's credentials were still accepted. We stepped out of the lift and viewed our surroundings. At an early age, we learned level twelve was a virtual paradise for those transitioning to The Giver. The last year of a resident's life was said to be spent in luxury. Food and water were supposed to be plentiful, and all were waited upon like royalty. I recalled watching the tinted windows from the atrium, imagining the happy faces staring back at me.

I scanned the storage enclosures lining the perimeter. Each glass cubicle was thirty feet wide, extended from floor to ceiling, and had a single entranceway at the center. There were no Transitioners enjoying their last year in luxury. Instead, rows of stainless steel cylinders, stacked five high, lined the back wall of each cubicle. Large tanks labeled LIQUID NITROGEN stood at the foot of each stack. Feeder lines to the cylinders maintained the cryogenically frozen state of the internees. It was just as Chet described. I was appalled, disgusted, and angry.

"State your purpose," a voice snarled from our left.

A technician in a white lab coat stepped from a glass cubicle. Star raised her gauntlet and moved toward him.

"Where is Yanic?" she yelled.

He raised his hands, palms outward. "Wait, who are you?"

"Star!" I shouted. "We're running out of time."

She stepped forward and pushed the prongs into the base of his throat. "I'll ask you once more. If you don't answer correctly, I'll fry your brain. Where—is—Yanic?"

"The Noble Yanic," I added.

"Bay four," he quivered, pointing behind Star.

"Show me," she ordered.

He kept his hands in the air and shuffled by her, toward the cubicle. She followed close behind and prodded him with the gauntlet every few steps. I felt bad for the technician who was only performing his job. A single cough and Star would fulfill her promise, ending his days via an extraordinarily painful death. After opening bay four, we all stepped inside the glass enclosure. He carefully reached for the first layer of cylinders, entering a numerical code on a control pad. A hissing sound broke the silence as the pressurized tube released its contents.

The cylinder bottom opened. A steel slab supporting an elliptical-shaped capsule was slowly ejected. I stepped forward and looked through the acrylic square over the occupant's face. His eyes were closed and his mouth slightly ajar, like he was flash-frozen.

"This is Yanic," I reported.

Star pushed the prongs into the technician's neck. "Open it," she insisted.

"I, I can't," he stammered. "There must be orders from . . ."

She lowered the prongs to his chest and squeezed the trigger. His body contorted as it collapsed to the floor. Although the jolt didn't kill him, he would awaken to a full day of pain and discomfort. Star had warned him, but he gave the wrong response. Her expression didn't change when she looked back at me.

"Stand aside," she said.

An electronic pad on the capsule indicated interior temperature and pressure. There was a third, larger number showing the value of 9 percent. As we inspected the components, the larger number suddenly blinked to 10 percent. The freezing process had recently begun. We looked at each other, then at the technician sprawled on the floor. Star shook her head, pointing the gauntlet at the pad. I turned away in anticipation of the explosion. Sparks flew in all directions. She dropped the gauntlet and grabbed her wrist as a backlash of electricity jolted through her arm.

The capsule lid split open. A liquid-vapor mist poured out of the seams, rolling down the support slab. The normally colorless vapor glowed blue from the interior lights. Star pushed the lid open and waved her hand over Yanic's head, clearing the mist. His face was pale and lifeless. *We're too late. Now how do we stop the Awakening?* I turned away.

Chapter 45

Conflict

"**O**pal," Star said.

"Give me a moment," I replied, cupping my hands over my nose and mouth.

"Opal," she said louder.

I dropped my hands and turned abruptly, finding Yanic sitting up in the open capsule. He looked disoriented, and he was shivering in the mist. Glancing slowly between the two of us, he blinked several times, trying to focus. He squinted hard until a small grin crossed his face.

"Opal Five," he said in a coarse voice. "So good to see you."

Star depressed a foot pedal, lowering the slab support to the floor. We helped Yanic out of the capsule onto his wobbling legs. His pale body showed little contrast against the singular white undergarment. He appeared much thinner without his cape. Noticing my gawking, the now humble noble pointed across the aisle.

"My things," he whispered.

We assisted him to the technician's booth. A simple hand wave opened an unsecured opaque panel. He stepped inside and sat on an armless chair, waiting for us to leave. We moved back into the aisle.

"What are we supposed to do now?" Star asked. "He doesn't look strong enough to walk, let alone stop this Wakening."

"Awakening," I corrected.

"Really, Opal?"

"Sorry," I replied. "You're right, he can't do this alone. Star, I know we have orders, but he's going to need our help."

She scoffed. "Did you really expect me to run to the tunnels when things are just getting interesting?"

Her face then turned hard, austere. Her thirst for revenge hadn't been quenched. She could've easily killed the technician, firing the gauntlet against his throat and fulfilling her promise. He wasn't a noble, however—not her enemy. He was simply a resident in the wrong location at an unfortunate moment. *Star's not bloodthirsty, she has a specific target in mind. Giver help them when they finally cross paths.*

Yanic stepped out of the booth. The transformation was astonishing considering the short period of time since his resurrection. Color was returning to his face. The cape padding made his shoulders appear broad again. Standing straight and steady, he appeared taller than before. Star turned squarely toward him. Although our task was to secure his release, she was obviously uncomfortable in his presence. He sensed her trepidation.

"I owe you my gratitude," he said, slightly bowing his head.

"You showed your gratitude when we returned from the lower levels," she quipped.

His eyes glimmered as he addressed her. "I did not have you apprehended, Star Five." He turned to me with the same hypnotic gaze. "The actions of my ambitious colleague put our mission at risk. We nearly lost Opal to his sadistic appetite."

"So, it was you who intervened," I stated. "You told Ares she wouldn't be harmed."

Star grasped the gauntlet on her belt. "You could've stopped him?" she shrieked.

"I did stop him!" he shouted in return. "You were to be terminated after . . ." He paused, catching himself.

I glanced at Star who quickly turned her head away. It took a moment to understand what wasn't being said. Star was not only subjected to gauntlet strikes during her interrogation; she had been abused. Yanic called the noble sadistic. *What did she endure to protect me?* I finally understood the depth of her rage. An intense anger swelled inside of me. Despite the physical and mental torture, she never revealed her connection to the Seekers. *I swear to The Giver, regardless the outcome of this revolt, I'll personally track down her tormentor. What she does with him after that is not my concern.*

After a short period of silence, Yanic turned to me. "Opal, did you procure the connector?"

"Of course," I replied. "It was given to me by a former noble from Eden 2." He raised his brow in anticipation. "Panos commandeered everything upon my return."

His jaw clenched. "Panos has the connector?"

"Not all of it," Star added, turning to face us.

Pulling the chip from her belt, she held it high for him to see. He rushed toward her with his hand extended. She closed her fist.

"This belongs to Opal." She scowled.

"It's okay, Star. Give him the chip."

Glaring intensely, she slowly opened her hand, almost daring him to make a wrong move. Yanic gently removed it from her palm. He examined the relic between his thumb and index finger.

"Eden 1," he whispered.

"Are you the trustee?"

He looked at me inquisitively. I guess I knew more than he

suspected me to.

"Yes, Opal. However, there are two of us in this sanctuary. Rest assured my counterpart has examined the connector. She'll be looking for this—and for you."

"Which is why her drive isn't linked to the Core," Star blurted out.

He turned to her. "But your drive is active," he observed. "They're aware of your relationship. They'll find you together."

She smirked. "I'm guessing they're preoccupied at the moment."

He tilted his head toward me. "Opal, what have you done?"

"You approved the installation of a video sensor in the drone," I began. "It recorded every aspect of my flight. There's no point describing what was witnessed because you already know." He squinted as I continued. "Panos believes he intercepted the recordings, but the drive in his possession belongs to me. The broadcast started in Assembly just after the trumpets sounded. The revolt has begun."

Yanic tightened his grip on the chip, shaking his hand up and down as he pondered the situation.

"The Noble Ulysses told me about the true emergence," I added. "Do you intend to prevent the Awakening?"

"No, Opal," he replied, without looking at me. "Preventing it is not enough. The launch must be initiated to preserve our future."

"Initiate the launch?" I repeated loudly. "Ulysses said the launch is the first stage of the Awakening. He was also a trustee; he knows the sequence."

"Then why risk giving you the connector, Opal?" He faced me. "Your noble has ulterior motives."

"Indeed he does," I replied sternly. "He seeks revenge for the love taken from him."

Yanic shook his head. "No, Opal," he said. "He sent you to carry out his final directive. You underestimate their resolve. The elite believe they can harness the Core's power. Your revolt will be short-lived, and all those involved, terminated. The Awakening will commence, and you made it possible."

Chapter 46

Ambush

My hands clenched into fists involuntarily. The thought of being manipulated by the Elder and responsible for the Awakening made me furious. I wanted to hurt the nobles, take Yanic's throat, and squeeze the life out of him. Every muscle in my body strained with tension. I was about to scream when I remembered Ulysses's words. *"Remain stalwart, Opal. You have but one chance for success."* Releasing my fingers, I inhaled a deep breath then slowly released the pressure.

The Elder had warned me not to succumb to deceit. *"They'll attempt to bend your thoughts, cast doubt on the truth."* Yanic's sparkling eyes resembled two kaleidoscopes. Hundreds of tiny specs orbited his pupils, glowing then fading, altering shapes and sizes. *Are they even real? Human?* At that moment I suspected we were being watched through them, but not by Yanic. It was then that a sensor moved over the technician's booth.

"Star—!"

Before I finished my warning, the main entrance split open. Keepers rushed in and filled the aisle. A whole squad surrounded us, shields pulsating with power. Two of them bore down on Star, who quickly dropped her gauntlet. Although prepared for battle, she wasn't a fool. Yanic stood his ground, unfazed by the disturbance. I expected him to shout orders at the leader, but he remained still, looking over my shoulder.

"Zora," he announced.

The Noble Zora stood six feet tall. She had an intense gaze and hard features, making her look more warrior than noble. Her skin was darker than Star's, and her short-cropped hair accentuated her fierce appearance. I had dispensed with greeting protocols for the ruling class and didn't bow my head. She ignored my presence as she approached Yanic.

"The chip," she demanded.

"You can't take the—" was all I managed before her backhand connected with the side of my head. Spinning to the floor on my knees and elbows, my face was instantly numb. A bright light obscured my vision as I tried to focus on the keeper's black boots in front of me.

"Opal!" reverberated from across the circle. Star shouted my name, but her voice was muffled by the ringing in my ears. Touching my face, I felt the numbness give way to pain. Moisture trickled from my ear; blood coated my fingers. I searched the floor while my internal debate ensued. *Stay on my knees, or rise in defiance?* I didn't relish more of Zora's wrath.

A hand suddenly gripped my left arm and yanked me into a standing position. Zora put her face close to mine.

"Where is the chip?"

"I—don't have it," I stammered, my head still swimming.

She raised her free arm, fist curled. I pulled my head away, trying to avoid the next blow.

"Wait!" Yanic shouted.

Zora lowered her arm and turned to him. "The chip, now,"

she replied, in a more forceful voice.

I looked up at her face through my haze. Her lips were pursed together. Her brow furrowed tightly. She was either putting on a display for Yanic, to impress upon him the seriousness of her demand, or she was prepared to tear off his limbs. Either way, he didn't protest. He stepped forward with his hand extended. I gasped as the chip fell into her palm.

Zora released her grip on me. My arm prickled as blood flowed back into the temporarily paralyzed appendage. Finally able to focus, I noticed Star glancing around. She was obviously looking for an opportunity to make a move—to strike. Willing her to look my way, our eyes met. I shook my head with an imperceptible *no,* speaking to her as if she could receive my thoughts telepathically. *Not now.*

The message was received. She exhaled and her shoulders relaxed, only enough for me to notice. Similar to when we played in the atrium castle, we were able to communicate in a way logic couldn't explain. Perhaps we shared some bond created through our genetic engineering. Jade said there were immeasurable possibilities that had not yet been explored. Our scientists eliminated diseases and afflictions in their attempts to create a superior line of humans, but I don't think they know how many permutations they had created.

"Bring them," Zora commanded, interrupting my digressive thoughts.

Without hesitation, the keepers pushed the three of us together. They fell into a box-like formation, surrounding us on four sides. Yanic moved ahead, and we walked behind him shoulder to shoulder. As we started to march, a movement caught my attention. The technician lying next to Yanic's would-be cryogenic coffin stirred. I didn't envy the suffering he would soon endure—the aching head, cramped muscles, and burning sensation on every inch of his skin. Star also glanced in his direction. She turned forward without expression.

We exited the storage area and turned in the opposite

direction from which Star and I first approached. It was difficult to see ahead of the formation, but there was a service lift at the end of the corridor. The squad halted in front of the lift. A sentry opened the panels and Zora stepped inside next to the control screen. The three of us were jostled in and pushed to the opposite rear corner. We were followed by four members of the squad. Yanic was being treated more like a prisoner and less like a noble. There was an obvious conflict between the two trustees. Zora was making her position clear.

I expected to be shuttled to the detention center for interrogation. My hands began shaking at the thought of another round of electric shock. Although I was trying to focus on the revolt, I knew we were in no position to make a difference now. The panel closed and the lift started to rise. We were not heading to the detention center. I tried to get Star's attention but could barely move due to the large keeper in front of me. Turning my head to the right, she appeared in my peripheral vision. She remained still, staring into nothingness.

Frustrated by my inability to communicate with Star, I looked down, only to notice a strange movement. The keeper in front of me was twisting his left fist back and forth. It appeared he had a problem with his glove until I noticed a deliberate rhythm to his motion. Three twists, then two, then one—repeat. *Was it a code? A signal? Was it meant for me?* Taking a risk, I gently cleared my throat, acknowledging the gesture. He stopped the twisting and slowly opened his hand, releasing a small object. It landed on the lift floor with a barely perceptible clink. The silver object looked vaguely familiar. Searching my memory, I quietly gasped. It was a noble port cover.

His hand turned so the palm faced backward. He then extended three fingers. The lift slowed as we approached our destination. One finger curled under, leaving two extended. It was a countdown. Curling the second finger, he moved his right hand into the gauntlet on his thigh. The keeper on his right made the same motions. The lift opened and Zora hurried out.

As the two lead keepers stepped forward, Chet and Flint drew their weapons.

The crackling sound of gauntlets firing echoed through the lift. The smell of ozone and burned flesh filled the enclosure. The Seekers hurdled their victims and rushed Zora. She turned and threw her open cape into the path of her pursuers. Star brushed past me, racing to retrieve a gauntlet from a fallen keeper. Just as I cleared the lift, an explosion erupted down the corridor Zora had taken.

"Opal, wait." A weak voice beckoned from behind.

Yanic stumbled over the bodies, almost falling to his knees. I ran to his side and helped him recover his balance.

"Let's move," Star yelled, following Zora's path.

"No," Yanic gasped. "Not in that direction."

Star hurried back and took Yanic by the arm. "But she has the chip."

"You won't catch her," he insisted. "She led them into a trap." He pointed to a narrow corridor entranceway to our left. "We'll go through there."

"Where are we?" I asked.

"Fifteen," he answered. "That corridor leads to the Core sanctum."

Chapter 47

The Core

"The Core?" Star looked at me, brow raised.

"What more can we do?" I asked. "They have the medallion and all the chips. The connector is complete."

"The Core will be heavily guarded," Star observed. "All squads will be alerted to our status. I'm quite certain we're no longer on the ally list."

Yanic took three steps then turned back toward us. "Leave your weapons," he instructed.

"You can't be serious?" Star shouted.

We both hesitated, staring blankly at one another. Although I suspected Yanic's motives, we had few options. If we entered the sanctum with weapons drawn, the guards' defensive response would be swift and certain. Whatever plan Yanic concocted, we had no choice but to follow along. Star shook her head then reluctantly lowered the gauntlet. After placing my dart and metal spike next to her weapon, we joined Yanic at the entrance. He made one final inspection to ensure we were unarmed.

"Stay behind me," he said. "Do not speak, make no sudden movement, and do exactly as I say. Do you understand?"

We both acknowledged with a single nod.

He addressed Star directly. "The Noble Panos will likely be there; you must constrain yourself." He looked at me. "Opal, not everything is as it appears. You need to trust me."

I trusted a select few people, and Yanic wasn't one of them. I was struck by his comment that not everything is as it appears. It was the same advice Ulysses shared before we departed his vault. It wasn't impossible that they were in league together. Many parallels existed between the two nobles, but they had no way to communicate. *They couldn't have coordinated these events. Could they?*

Although we were operating with no specific plan of action, Yanic was leading us to our primary target. If an opportunity arose to destroy or damage the Core, I needed to act quickly. Searching my mind for possibilities, it occurred to me there was no background noise. Battles loomed beneath us on every level. Residents were fighting and dying for freedom. The revolt was at its peak, but fifteen was quiet—almost peaceful. *Focus, Opal. Use your mind, your greatest asset.*

Yanic approached the entrance. A biometric scanner traced his face. Surprisingly, the panel opened. Thirty minutes in the past he was being processed for cryogenic storage. Now the most secure zone in Life World welcomed him without hesitation. *Has the system malfunctioned? Or is the feud between trustees a private battle?* Either way, the Core would have known of his sentence. Even Star was able to locate him through her limited clearance level—*curious.*

After a short walk through the narrow corridor, we came to another secured entranceway. Behind the reinforced panel was an air lock like the hidden space on three. Entering, we each submitted to a full body laser scan before the decontamination phase. The additional step was likely meant to prevent unwanted weapons or contraband from entering the area. I expected to hear a siren, alarm, or some other indication of our intrusion, but we proceeded to the next checkpoint without incident.

As we approached an intersecting corridor, I looked down both directions. There was no movement, no keepers, no security—just some barely perceptible T-8s hovering in the distance. Their beacon lights blinked a familiar pattern but otherwise didn't move. I glanced at Star, and she shrugged her shoulders. From an early age, we learned the Core sanctum was an impenetrable fortification. No resident ever accessed the zone. Given the vital role it played in the functions and operation of Life World, we never questioned the necessity of such isolation. The machine was the responsibility of nobles. All discussions ended there.

Just before clearing the intersection, a movement down the left wing caught my attention. A large porter entered a docking station. *Delivery. Was Flynn able to intercept the cooling system unit?* Assuming he was, we were walking toward a rather large explosive device. If the vessel contents were introduced into the reservoir, we'd be vaporized by the blast. The end of my life could be imminent, but I wasn't frightened. On the contrary, the thought of bringing an end to this Core—to the Awakening— was quite satisfying. Ulysses would rejoice at the sound of the explosion. Ares and Jade would be proud of me.

A single keeper stood sentry in front of a large round entranceway. He was adorned entirely in white, including his helmet. He appeared—sterile. I'd never seen this version of the uniform. He was obviously a member of a special unit assigned to protect the Core. There was likely a full garrison of them in the sanctum.

Yanic approached the lone sentry and stood at attention, arms at his side. The keeper stepped forward, pointing a handheld scanner at Yanic's face. As the laser traced his features, the machine made a single chirping sound. With his credentials verified, our noble summoned us forward. Star and I were subjected to the biometric evaluation, with the same results. Without further delay, the sentry entered a numeric code on a portable keypad. A circular panel rolled into a side pocket. The tunnel-like corridor pulsated with blue light.

We followed Yanic closely. The parabolic effect created by the arched walls magnified the sound of every step. As an additional security measure, it would make intrusion without detection nearly impossible. I was astonished at our progress thus far as if we'd been invited into the enemy's lair. After one more biometric scan, the final obstacle rolled open, and we passed into the Core sanctum. White uniformed keepers were positioned at each of the half-dozen entrance tunnels. They didn't move, nor react. Yanic turned right and led us along a curved outer platform toward a grated stairway.

I shivered, adjusting to the lower temperature within. Everything in view was white, translucent, or stainless steel. Recessed lighting made the entire space glow with a blue aura. The cool color added to the frigid sensation. Marveling at the surrounding spectacle, I quickly forgot about the cold. Below us and in the center of the round sanctum, was an enormous silver sphere—the Core. It was encased in a series of thick, acrylic ramparts and encircled by a flat apron. Between each solid barrier were interlocking wiring portals connecting the Core to input and output gates—electronic pathways to Life World. Breakers protected the machine from electric surges, and, I assumed, cyberattacks.

At the base of the left support pillars was an oval stainless steel tank, nearly half the size of the Core. It was positioned between two ramparts and had an adjacent feeder magazine stacked with oblong vessels. Based on Flynn's description of the liquid nitrogen containers, it had to be the cooling system reservoir. I looked for any distinguishing marks on the vessels, trying to determine if any had been intercepted. Nothing was immediately evident.

As we descended the stairs, a series of metal slabs came into view. They were previously shielded by the apron. Each supported a capsule resembling the one from which we liberated Yanic. There was a noticeable difference from those in the cryogenic storage facility. The entire top half was completely transparent. There were twelve total, spaced approximately six feet apart. They radiated outward from the Core, resembling a full sun. As we approached the nearest slab, I gasped in shock. Nothing could've prepared me for the horror lying within.

Each capsule held a shriveled, aging noble draped in white undergarments. Secured by a series of straps, they had multiple wires and tubes protruding from their limbs. Blinking monitoring devices displayed body temperatures and vital signs. They seemed to be nourished by the regulated flow of fluids and intravenous feeding. Under the front of each slab hung a bundle of micro-cables leading into an interface gate. *These poor souls are surrogate processors, just as Chet described. Their brains are linked directly to the Core through their cranial ports— more machine than human.*

Yanic stopped near the foot of a capsule. Turning my head away from the disturbing sight, I spotted Zora in the sanctum. She was leaning over an auxiliary terminal, her interpreters reflecting digital characters. Panos stood close behind her. Neither looked in our direction. Although their presence made it difficult to see clearly, I recognized the triangular pyramid connector hovering over the terminal plane. It was Ulysses's key. The three sanctuary chips had obviously been inserted. Final activation started the launch sequence, so the Awakening was now inevitable. *Why are they waiting?*

I was startled by a sudden movement in front of us. The foot of the slab lowered while the head was raised. After fifteen seconds, the capsule was almost perpendicular. We were just a few feet below the surrogate noble under the transparent cover. It was a grotesque display. The body was emaciated. Surgery scars crossed the chest and abdomen. Bones protruded through thin layers of cracking skin. His matted gray hair hung loosely over his shoulders, and his fingernails were absurdly long and curled under. He was alive, but not well cared for. It was an obscene, offensive way to treat a human being—a fate certainly worse than death. I was nearly over the shock of the appalling sight when it spoke.

"Yanic," the living corpse hissed through an amplified external speaker.

"Yes, Most Worshipful One," Yanic responded, bowing his head.

Star and I looked at each other. We had the same expression of surprise and disgust as the surrogate's lips opened and closed. We looked back in time to see the crusted-over eyes peel open.

"Opal Five," it continued, causing my skin to crawl. I didn't respond immediately until Yanic nudged my arm. We weren't speaking to the encased noble, we were communicating directly with the Core.

Chapter 48

Unjust Reward

"**M**ost Worshipful One," I responded mimicking Yanic. Although determined to never again bow to a noble, I heeded instructions and acquiesced. A long pause ensued. The surrogate's eyes bounced rapidly, apparently trying to focus. It may have been days since they were last used by the accompanying brain. As we waited in silence, Chet and Flint's description of the nobles they collected for incineration came to mind. They referred to them as *depleted.* Looking at the skeletal figure addressing us, I found the description apt, if not kind.

The surrogate drew long, raspy breaths before speaking. His thin chest swelled as air was forced into the lungs. His eyes continued darting about like they were some new attachments being tested. *Does he know he's still alive? Does the brain register his prior existence?* I despised the ruling class and all they represented, but I pitied this poor human.

"Star Five, fledgling noble," he exhaled from his throat.

She took one step forward but didn't bow.

The lungs expanded; his chin jutted forward. "You have betrayed us."

Star looked to me with an angry scowl. She pulled her shoulders back in defiance before responding. Oddly, she addressed the sphere instead of the surrogate. "You betrayed me!" she shouted.

Before we could intervene, Star turned and bolted toward the terminal. Her piercing, bloodcurdling shriek echoed throughout the sanctum as she ran at Panos with her arms extended.

"Seize her," the surrogate commanded.

Zora thrust a leg in Star's path. In one movement, the warrior-noble grabbed an extended arm and flipped her a full revolution onto the floor. She twisted the arm around, pressing her foot firmly against my friend's throat. Star flailed her legs but couldn't escape the hold. She finally stopped resisting and gripped Zora's ankle, gasping for air.

"Bring her to me," the voice wheezed.

Zora rolled her body over and twisted the right arm behind her back. Star groaned loudly as she was lifted into a standing position. She continued to struggle, and Zora pushed Star's arm higher, causing her to wince in pain. I watched helplessly as she was shoved before the surrogate and forced to her knees.

"Demonstrate for Opal Five how traitors are disciplined."

Zora drew her gauntlet and pushed the prongs onto the base of Star's skull.

"No!" I screamed, lunging for Zora.

Yanic wrapped his arms around me, pulling me off my feet. I squirmed and kicked, but his grip tightened. Star stared at the floor. She blinked slowly, as if anticipating death—accepting her fate. Zora looked up at the surrogate, awaiting his order. I turned my head away.

"You can spare her life, Opal Five," the surrogate hissed.

I turned back slowly. Star was upright on her knees, staring at me. The gauntlet was still pressed against the port in her spine. She shook her head no. Yanic loosened his hold on me.

"H-how?" I muttered.

"Tell her Yanic."

Yanic lowered my feet to the floor. He spun me around to face him, gripping my shoulders firmly. "The connector has been altered, Opal," he said. "Your lovelorn noble inserted a multifactor authentication protocol."

I shook my head. "You're the trustee. What does it have to do with me?"

He smiled nervously, but I could see the desperation in his pursed lips and twitching eye. It was obvious what they wanted. The advantage was now leveraged in my favor. Without the Elder's code, the connector was useless; the launch couldn't be initiated. At first, I controlled my emotions. Staring at Yanic, however, I had an epiphany. Both his eyes began to twitch when he saw my expression change to rage.

"You were never sentenced to cryogenic storage," I stated, pulling free from his grip.

The shriveled surrogate remained silent. Zora glanced at Yanic. He didn't speak.

"The revolt had begun, you suspected we had the remaining chip," I continued. Star looked confused. "We were meant to find him," I told her. "They were tracking your drive the entire time." Yanic wasn't out to destroy the Core. He was one of the Elites. The Awakening was supposed to ensure his rise to power.

"Well done, Yanic." I sneered at him, disrespect intended. "Your subtle comments in Ares's lab, the odd expression before my flight, even your sudden removal from the project—all meant to cast doubt on your loyalty." I was even more furious at the thought of being a pawn in his game. "You manipulated us, drew us in. Your elaborate charade in the cryo-storage unit was the grand finale, to secure my trust and complete your plan."

He looked down at me contemptuously. "I'm so glad you approve," he said with noted sarcasm. "Now, there's the matter of an alphanumeric code."

I ignored his demand. "You would never knowingly put yourself in harm's way."

The answer came to me. "He was being monitored the entire time," I thought out loud. "Just as we were being tracked. It was no coincidence we arrived at the right moment to rescue him. It was staged." I looked at Star. "They knew our plan. There's a traitor in our ranks." Yanic waited, anticipating my next deduction.

"Flynn," I said, assuming my suspicions about the bitter sub-level worker were correct. He didn't react to the name. In my mind, I searched the faces in the secret meeting. *Who knew every aspect of the plan? Who was able to communicate with the outside? Not Ares, not Lake, not . . .* "Professor Marc," I said, more statement than question. Yanic lifted his chin, an obvious tell. Star's expression changed to absolute horror.

"No," she cried. "I don't believe it."

Yanic glanced at Zora. "Praise be to The Giver," he quipped.

She smirked, looking down her nose at me with a confident arrogance. "To the virtue of truth," she replied, completing the confidential response. She pushed Star's head down with the gauntlet. "The code now," she demanded.

"No, Opal," Star shouted at the floor. "They'll terminate us anyway."

I watched Zora's face. She would fire the weapon and take Star's life without hesitation, but not without orders. I had what they needed. It was time to use my leverage.

"Release her," I said turning to Yanic. "Let her go and you'll have your code."

He scowled at me. There could be no greater insult to a noble than a common resident holding an advantage over them.

"Opal, no," Star repeated. "Don't let them win. Not for me."

Yanic turned to the surrogate. Oxygen filled its lungs.

"Release the traitor."

Yanic nodded at Zora. Her fierce expression returned, and she bared down on the gauntlet. He shook his head no. She pulled the gauntlet away in a high exaggerated arc and screamed with apparent disappointment. Without further gesture, she sheathed the weapon and walked calmly toward the terminal.

Star rose from the floor, holding her injured arm. She walked toward me and shook her head, indicating disapproval. Pausing in front of Yanic, she turned her head toward Panos. As if sensing her gaze, he lifted his head from the terminal. His expression transformed from confidence to fear as she glared at him with dagger-like eyes. When Zora arrived by his side, he raised a brow and pursed his lips with a pompous smirk.

I watched Star climb the stairs, retracing our path to the entranceway. As soon as the panel closed behind her, Yanic spoke.

"Your loyalty is admirable, Opal," he said, somewhat sincerely. "Now, demonstrate your integrity and give me the code."

"What's to stop you from detaining her in the corridor?" I asked, stalling for more time.

Yanic sighed with frustration, looking again to the surrogate. The now-familiar sound of inflating lungs resonated behind me.

"Observe, Opal Five."

A life-size holographic image appeared on the opposite side of the sanctum. Star was being escorted by a white-unit keeper through the narrow corridor we first entered. The Core was projecting real-time sensor images as she made her way to the lift. The keeper bodies had been removed, and there was no sign of an altercation. After she entered the lift, her escort programmed a destination. He stepped back, assuming a sentry position. Star stared out at him as the panels closed. She was safe.

"The code," Yanic insisted. "Now."

My mind raced as I walked slowly toward the terminal. Without a weapon, there was no way to damage the Core. No amount of anger or adrenaline could help me physically overcome Zora's combat skills. Drake's words drifted through my head. *"The only way to defeat a stronger adversary is to gain an advantage."* The only advantage in my possession was the code. I tried another stalling tactic.

"Yanic mentioned he and Zora are the only trustees," I said to Panos. "Are you a member of the elite?" He looked up, suddenly aware he was being addressed. His head pivoted from Zora to Yanic. "They alone have access to the directives left by New Genesis," I continued. "You are aware of the final decrees, correct?"

"Silence her," the surrogate hissed, not drawing in enough oxygen to shout.

"That's quite enough, Opal," Yanic roared. "Recite the code, now."

"What code?" I yelled over my shoulder, moving closer to the terminal. "Only the elite will rise to power, Panos. Surely you're one of them." He squinted at me. I was getting to him.

"The code!" Yanic shouted.

A young female screamed behind me. I turned to see another holographic projection filling the lower segment of the sanctum. There was a keeper squad advancing on a crowd of residents. They used their shields to electrocute fleeing children.

"She defies you Yanic." The volume was raised on the capsule speaker. "Perhaps a greater sacrifice will persuade her."

I watched in horror as innocent residents were trampled. Suddenly a silver orb flew over the crowd, landing behind the squad. Sound from the blast echoed through the sanctum, but there was no shock wave. A veil of smoke momentarily blurred the scene. As the view cleared, there was a group of Seekers gathering weapons. *It's Kane.* He was shouting orders like a true leader. I smiled defiantly. His head then whipped around as a T-8 entered the corridor, followed by a second squad. Kane thrust his gauntlet at a charging keeper. Without warning, the drone fell from mid-air. At first, I thought it was downed by a magnetic dart until it exploded just a few feet from the floor.

There was little smoke from the explosion. The T-8 was

filled with a nitroglycerin charge instead of the potassium nitrate, carbon, and sulfur mixture used to make the orbs. The results were devastating. Everyone was terminated—Seekers, residents, even the keeper squad. The bodies were mutilated. The Core detonated the drone near the center of the battle. Kane was gone.

The image disappeared. I felt numb, waiting for Yanic to again demand the code. It was one thing to offer my life for the Cause. It was something quite different being responsible for the death of others. Although able to save one friend, the trade-off was the loss of thirty. If I capitulated, the Awakening would commence, ultimately enslaving all humans. *Is it better to be terminated, or serve in perpetuity with no hope for freedom? Who am I to decide the fate of seven thousand residents? Would they not want to live, even in slavery?*

A new image materialized. Another group was filing out of a lift. I recognized the intersecting corridors on fifteen. The last to emerge was Jade. She was commanding her cell. They were advancing on the sanctum. One of the Seekers held up a captured helmet, which provided them access to the narrow corridor. They carried enough weaponry to overpower the white-unit sentries. My heart raced as they approached the entrance. I then saw the T-8 approaching them from behind.

"Alpha one nine one nine two zero Oscar!" The T-8 maneuvered slowly toward them. "Stop the drone," I pleaded. "Alpha one nine one nine two zero Oscar is the code." The drone stopped. Yanic turned to the surrogate.

"No correlative anomalies detected. The code is random. Proceed."

Yanic hurried to the terminal as Zora entered the final alphanumeric symbols. Light burst from the pulsating connector, illuminating their faces. When I turned back to the holograph, the drone remained in position. Jade's cell hadn't breached the panel to the narrow corridor. The Core was preventing their progress. I turned again toward the terminal.

The hovering connector started to spin, projecting rays of light that danced on every surface of the sanctum. Yanic rushed back to the surrogate capsule.

"Most Worshipful One," he managed, between heaving breaths. "The launch sequence is initiated."

"Your mission is complete, Opal Five."

"You have your Awakening," I shouted, pointing to the image. "Release them, release everyone. Use your precious nobles to serve you. You have no need for us."

"You chose your pawn wisely, Yanic. Her loyalty clouds her resolve."

Yanic bowed deeply, accepting his accolades. I scoffed at his back. His only accomplishment was a lifetime of servitude for himself and his kind. The most disturbing reality, which I had failed to prevent, was the entire human race being sentenced to the same fate. *If The Giver is just, he'll reward the arrogant noble with an eternity of suffering.*

"Opal Five," the Core hissed at me. "As reward for your perseverance, I concede to your demands."

My first reaction was elation. I imagined taking Jade and Ares to the village, introducing them to Drake, and starting a new life. My reflections were quickly shattered when Yanic turned toward the holograph with a look of triumphant satisfaction. I watched as the T-8 sped forward and dropped from its flight path. It happened so quickly words didn't escape my mouth. They never saw it coming. The explosion dropped the entire cell. The last I saw of Jade, she was standing behind the group encouraging their work. The Core indeed released them. Released them from servitude, from enslavement—from life.

Chapter 49

Exodus

"Jade!" I screamed, falling to my knees. The image disappeared. I stared at the now-empty space with my mouth open. All of them were gone. They'll quickly be removed, their bodies incinerated like refuse. The Court—the Core—will charge them as corrupt insurgents, enemies of Life World. All records of their existence will be erased, replacements selected to resume their occupations. *This is my reality, my world.*

When I joined the Cause, Jade issued a stern warning: "*The path of a Seeker can be perilous and wrought with pain. If you're to join us, you'll need to be strong. No more time for tears.*" I had no tears, only pain manifested as pressure in my chest. My heart swelled to the point of exploding. I thought of Ares, Star, and all those in my cell. The Core wouldn't stop until it crushed the revolt and destroyed every facet of the Cause. It wouldn't discriminate between insurgent and resident, adult and child. All barriers in its path would be eliminated: Seekers, nobles, keepers, any human who threatened its ultimate goal of absolute power over the world.

"Fueling has begun; all systems are operational," Zora announced from the terminal. "Launch will commence in thirty-nine minutes."

"Go, Opal Five," the surrogate hissed. "You have exhausted your utility."

I looked up at the pitiful being—mouthpiece of the Core. Yanic stepped forward and pointed toward the staircase.

"Leave now, Opal," he insisted.

"Do you realize what you've done?" I yelled, almost delirious. "All humans will serve a Master Core." I stood and faced the terminal. "You will all serve a machine."

Zora raised her chin defiantly. Panos watched her as if looking for reassurance.

"New Genesis planned for your elite to form a new order. Not a qubit brained, ball of liquid nitrogen."

Silence. Only Panos looked concerned as if he wasn't part of the inner circle. The unsuspecting enforcer may have been a pawn, like me.

"Go now," Yanic repeated through gritted teeth.

Ares had trained me to be observant. Yanic presented strange cues from the moment we met. There was something odd about the noble and his furtive mannerisms. Even now, his head was tilted slightly, a single brow raised. The expression was undetectable by the others. *Perhaps his motives aren't entirely aligned with theirs.* Despite my suspicions, he was doing nothing to disrupt the current operation. I stood thirty feet from the Core but had no way of causing damage. Attempting to interfere with the launch meant brutal retaliation from Zora. My only hope now was escape. I headed for the stairway.

Stepping onto the upper platform, I took one last hopeful glance at the cooling system reservoir. As if on command, the magazine shifted, loading an oblong vessel into the tank refueling coupler. The top vessel rotated 180 degrees. At the entranceway, a sentry turned and opened the circular panel. I kept my head down and watched his hands for movement. There was no interaction as he led me out of the sanctum.

I continued my purposefully dramatic walk of shame, knowing the Core was surveilling every step. Despite the feeling of complete exposure, I held my emotions in check, determined not to reveal my thoughts. We entered the final narrow corridor. The keeper maintained his stride, but I fell behind. *What's behind the panel? Torn bodies? Death? Jade?*

I felt my heart racing and struggled to avoid hyperventilation. My escort reached the entranceway and turned back. His head tilted, perhaps surprised at the distance between us. He snapped into a sentry pose, waiting for me to continue. I mustered my courage and hurried to the end of the corridor. *There's no guarantee of my release. He may have been instructed to dispose of me.* I stopped several feet away from him, arms by my side.

Several seconds elapsed. Orders were likely being broadcast into his helmet receiver. I had no weapon, no defense. *Think, Opal. What can you do to stop him?* He turned suddenly. Instead of reaching for his gauntlet, he faced the control pad and waited to be scanned. The panel slid open. He turned back, remaining directly in my path. A shadow flashed behind him. The crack of a gauntlet echoed through the corridor. My escort dropped to his knees, then fell face down within inches of my feet.

"Take the helmet!" Star shouted.

I didn't ask questions. Unsnapping the collar support freed the white helmet. There was a massive, scorched hole at the top of the keeper's spine. His face was grotesquely contorted. The foul odor of scorched flesh filled the space. Star had chosen the highest power setting. She had no interest in causing injury and wouldn't hesitate to kill them all.

"Opal, let's move."

I stepped into the main corridor. It was pristine, no bodies, no blood, no sign of an explosion. *It couldn't have been cleaned in such a short time.* Yanic's comment before we entered the sanctum returned to mind. *"Not everything is as it appears."*

Ulysses had described the Noble Court as mere holographic images, created by the Core. *"Residents won't willingly succumb to the demands of a machine,"* he said. *"They will, however, follow without question those humans perceived to be their superiors."*

The Core addressed me as Opal Five. A simple sort function of my data file revealed everyone I knew. A face, a body, a familiar person can be superimposed into a battle facade. My spirits soared. *Jade may be alive.*

"Star, the images in the sanctum weren't real. They were simulations, generated using stored data."

"What images? Opal, let's go."

I ran at full speed behind Star. *If Seekers defeated keeper squads on the lower levels, and enough residents joined the fray—we might be winning.* My temporary elation was curtailed. *The launch. The countdown has begun.* My lungs ached from the exertion. I had no idea where we were headed.

"Star, wait."

I sprinted to catch her. She finally stopped in front of a service lift, bending to catch her breath.

"The helmet," she said between gulps of air.

I passed it to her from my bent position. She held it in front of the scanner. We stumbled inside the oversized lift and leaned against the walls. Once again, she used the helmet to program our destination.

"What are you doing?" I gasped. "Why did you return?"

"You were willing to sacrifice everything to save me, Opal." She paused to share one of her bright smiles. "No way I was leaving you behind."

I shook my head in disbelief and was about to chastise her when the lift stopped. As soon as it opened, her plan became clear. Looking out at the empty space and flashing lights on sixteen, I tried to calculate the amount of thrust required to carry both of us on the drone. There was enough power left for four, maybe five minutes of flight time. That included a single pilot, not an added passenger. Finally catching my breath, I stepped onto the concrete floor and looked toward the air lock chamber.

"We two," she said, as the panel closed.

"Star wait—" It was too late. "Forever," I yelled, catching one last glimpse of her face.

—

Nothing had been disturbed in the alcove. Panos was focused on the launch. He'd neglected to order the area searched. The manual control pad for the air lock was operational; a simple access code opened the acrylic barrier. The drone was still secured to the transport chassis. I entered the chamber control room and closed the barrier, sealing myself in the air lock.

The secondary screen in the control room displayed elementary diagrams. *Was this designed for apprentice technicians?* It took only seconds to prepare for the ascent. The dimly lit communications module reminded me of my earlier discovery—the airlock is hardwired to Core links. *Through this terminal, I can communicate with all in Life World.* There was no time to search for individual locations. My only option was to utilize the services of a third party.

"May, are you there?" I said to the screen.

"Good day, Opal Five. You did not utilize your sleeping pod last night."

"May, there's no time to explain. Are you able to access emergency channels?"

I requested she notify residents to evacuate all levels above ten. According to Ulysses, the blast in Eden 2 was dampened by the thicker floor construction at that level. Many killed in his revolt attempted to avoid the fighting by fleeing to higher levels. He still carries the guilt of those lives lost.

The ceiling above separated as the chamber rose. I initiated a sequence countdown and needed only to release the drone. The body lay right where we left him. With the entire keeper force engaged in the uprising, he obviously wasn't missed. For a moment I pitied the unfortunate conscript who was only fulfilling orders. Star showed no mercy when she terminated him. *Why have sympathy for his kind? If Star had missed her mark, it might be my body on the floor. Keepers aren't programmed with emotions. They shed no tears for residents.*

I secured my harness and locked the canopy into position. It took ten seconds for the chamber to open after settling flush with the external surface. To preserve batteries, I waited until the drone was clear to maneuver before powering up. The turbines twisted in the bright sky. It was beyond midday; the sun was high. I hoped the intense rays would add additional charge. Total flight time was crucial to get as far away from the sanctuary as possible. *Did anyone make it out? Will I see my family again?*

The chamber locked into position, and the rear panels opened. I quickly visualized my starting sequence and initial maneuvers. Satisfied with the checklist, I pushed the power button. Nothing, no response. *No. It can't be. There's no other option.* I took a deep breath and pushed once more. *Giver, please.* The charge indicators blinked to life, bars barely visible on the scale. I exhaled with relief, then pulled on the throttle handle. The drone lifted to a wobbling hover. My exuberance caused me to overcorrect the controls. One more calming breath and it stabilized. I backed cleanly out of the chamber.

Climbing just enough to clear the outer structure, I accelerated forward. As soon as the sanctuary base appeared below, I banked left and nosed down. If the silo was where Ulysses described, residents should be emerging to the north. I dropped down close to the surface, in the event power was exhausted. The video sensor was inoperable, so I had to maneuver by sight alone. The clear acrylic allowed me, skimming along ten feet above ground level, to avoid large brush formations and other obstacles.

Just when I spotted a group of residents moving east, the engines quit. My flight controls stiffened. The sound of propellers striking air quickly wound down. With no way to slow forward momentum, I gripped the control handles and braced for impact. There was a moment of silence when the propellers stopped completely. The drone veered left. Without warning, the front cowling collided with a massive rock formation. The impact ripped the engine from the frame and sent me spinning into the desert floor. I lost all orientation. Landing upright, the final jolt knocked the breath out of me. Darkness came quickly.

The pounding startled me awake. I opened my eyes and gasped for air. There were arms and faces pressed against the canopy. My first impulse was to defend myself from attack. I reached for the gauntlet, which was no longer there. My arms flailed in panic until a familiar voice called my name.

"Opal, can you hear me?" Lake repeated. "Turn the locks."

My faculties gradually returned. I released my harness and leaned forward, grasping the right lock handle. It took all my strength to free the latch. Leaning back to take a breath, a sharp pain shot through my leg. The lower nose cone was buried in sand. Acacia branches penetrated the right section. My calf was impaled by a thin stalk. Shifting my foot caused the muscle to flex, aggravating the wound and releasing streams of blood. Gritting my teeth, I leaned to my left and turned the opposite lock. As soon as it was free, the canopy burst open, and Lake pulled on my arms.

"Stop!" I screamed, cringing in pain.

Lake released my arms and leaned inside the cockpit. After surveying my predicament, he began shouting orders at others around him. The drone started rocking as the top half of the nose was pulled from the frame. Lake worked his way in through the front and cut the stalk from the main tree branch. I was lifted from the cockpit and lowered to the ground. A resident physician injected a micro-ampoule near the wound.

"The neurolytic block will provide relief," she offered.

After making a small incision around the stalk, it was pulled straight out. Fortunately, the penetration wasn't deep and did little damage to the muscle. She cleaned away the blood, sprayed an antiseptic into the opening, then covered it with a gel substance. The wound closed. Nanoparticles began repairing the tear in my shell.

"Can you stand?" Lake asked, holding out his hand.

"Where is Ares?" I gasped. "Have you seen Jade?"

"Ares and I were separated at the tunnel entrance. He went back to direct the flow of residents." He shook his head. "I haven't seen Jade."

He pulled me to my feet. The anesthetic allowed me to put pressure on both legs. His grip tightened when I stumbled. It took a moment to find my balance.

"What about Tara?" I asked, knowing his daughter was in heavy fighting.

His sullen expression gave the answer. We all accepted risks when committing to the Cause. The fact that he and I were alive was nothing less than miraculous. It didn't make her sacrifice any less painful.

"How many—" I coughed. "How many escaped?"

"Come, see for yourself."

He took my elbow and led me up a small incline, providing a greater view of the surrounding area. When we reached the top I gasped and leaned against him, nearly overcome with emotion. Moving like a rhythmic wave across the desert floor were hundreds, if not thousands, of tan and gray shells. Originating at the silo, an exodus of residents hurried to the east, away from the sanctuary. They were alive and free.

I tried to calculate the elapsed time from my release. Only minutes remained before the launch. If the tunnel was an outlet for the rocket exhaust, all who remained within will be burned alive. My elation for those who escaped was overshadowed by the horror awaiting those in transit. *What have I done?*

Chapter 50

Vengeance

I watched helplessly from the distance as a loud siren echoed across the desert. The last residents to leave the silo were now racing away from the noise. After several minutes, the siren stopped. The only sound, a gentle breeze blowing across my ears. For a moment I thought—hoped—the launch had failed, that the code was useless. My wish was dashed as a circle of massive steel plates rose from the ground, surrounding the silo. The blast barriers were designed to deflect exhaust upward, protecting the sanctuary from heat and debris. The last group of residents made it beyond the barriers and were running to catch the others.

The rocket engines ignited, causing the ground to vibrate. At over two hundred yards from the site, the noise was still deafening. Smoke and flames shot upward from exhaust ports inside the barriers. I felt some relief, knowing the tunnel was sealed before ignition. Although safe from the flames, anyone remaining in the sanctuary would have to find other means of escape.

A massive ball of smoke and dust billowed outward. The ground shook violently as the rocket rose through the cloud center. Flames extended thirty feet out of the thrust nozzles. Everyone watched the projectile streak toward the sky. The cloud of dust rolled over the crowds. Lake and I stood silent, tilting our heads back as it climbed.

"All is lost," he said, turning to me. "The Awakening—nothing can stop it now."

"It's my fault," I whimpered. "I'm so sorry."

My eyes welled with tears. My sorrow wasn't for me, but all humans. The world would soon be enslaved by a machine with virtually limitless power. Those who resisted would be terminated, others bred like the bison in Drake's village—service animals. Our race was sure to be lost through extinction as new machines filled our roles. It was the beginning of the end for whatever remains of humanity. *How can a merciful Giver allow evil to prevail?* My brain was tired, numb, ready for it all to end. I wanted to lie down and be taken by the sweet peacefulness of sleep.

Then the rocket exploded.

We watched the sky in disbelief, verifying what we already suspected. The smooth exhaust trail scattered into multiple ribbons as the rocket disintegrated. A low murmur spread through the crowd below. The flight path took the projectile west of our location, so there was no danger of falling wreckage. Voices grew louder in the sea of confused and frightened residents. They didn't understand the significance of the spectacle above them.

Overcome with giddiness and delight, my torso shook with laughter. It was so loud and hard, crowds near us turned to watch. My midsection ached from my contorting diaphragm. Still laughing hysterically, I fell to my knees then rolled in the sand. I turned to find Lake peering down at me, his expression indicating concern for my sanity.

"New Genesis—has failed!" I shouted. "Two and half centuries of planning lost to a defective rocket." My squealing and laughter continued.

Lake's attention was drawn to something in the distance. "Our troubles may not be over, Opal," he said. "A storm is approaching."

I climbed to my feet. "Storm? Where?"

He pointed north, where the mountain range converges with the desert floor. A large billowing cloud was approaching. Smoke from the launch dissipated in the breeze, and the rolling mass was now visible. The crowds began moving in our direction, away from the threat. I watched the distant disturbance as residents filed by our position. Their movement was pointless. There were no structures for protection. Boulders near the lower mountainside might provide cover, but the storm would be over before they reached the range. *The cloud is not strengthening or rising.* It drifted west, pushed by winds flowing down the mountain slope. The sky above was clear, blue, and calm.

"It's not a storm," I said. "Look."

Lake followed my arm, pointing toward the horizon. It took him a moment to recognize the first rider on horseback.

"Are they from your village?"

"There's far too many to be from one village," I said. "No, he didn't just bring his village, he brought them all."

"Who, Opal?"

I answered Lake while focusing on the lead rider. "Drake. He brought the clans. They left their Feast to witness the prophecy."

"They mean you no harm," I shouted to residents now running toward the mountains. "They're friendly. They're here to help."

Five riders slowed as they approached the trailing crowd. I recognized Drake's horse from the pattern on its chest. The one next to him appeared to have no rider. Residents parted, clearing a path as the group moved forward. The initial panic subsided, and the crowds now looked on curiously. The horse next to Drake turned, and I could see it pulled a two-wheeled chariot. Poles were secured to the horse's flanks. A driver held long reins attached to a bit. I didn't know the driver but recognized the passenger—Ulysses.

Drake spotted me on the mound and waved his hand. I was unable to subdue the smile stretched across my face nor stop my arm from waving vigorously back at him.

"Alo, Opal!" he shouted over the hum of voices.

"Alo, Drake!" I yelled back.

Groups of residents, who were sprinting away just moments before, gathered around us. Perhaps they recognized me from the broadcast or were relieved the barbarians weren't devouring their families. Drake jumped from his horse and sprinted up the ten-foot rise. Lake stepped between us, shielding me from the would-be attacker. I pulled his arm back.

"Not to worry, Lake. He's not as dangerous as he looks."

Drake stopped short and squared his shoulders with Lake. They took measure of one another. Drake then slowly extended his right arm.

"I'm Drake of the Midland Clan," he offered.

Lake reached out and grasped his wrist. He glanced at me then back to the long-haired hunter draped in animal skins.

"I'm Lake," he replied, omitting his genetic line indicator.

"Thank you for looking after Opal," Drake added.

Lake turned to me. "Look after Opal?" he asked, chuckling. He scanned the hundreds of residents watching our interaction. "Look after Opal?" he repeated louder. Lake raised his arms and opened them wide, motioning toward the onlookers. "She is responsible for all of this! I assure you Drake from the Midland Clan, it was Opal who looked after us."

Drake held his hand out to me. I couldn't hold back my grin, or the silly gasps of laughter. Placing my hand on his palm, a sudden warmth came over me. For the moment, I forgot thousands of eyes were upon us. A tremendous weight was removed from my shoulders. With his strong hand wrapped around mine, I was safe. Happy.

—

Our moment was interrupted by another massive explosion. A roar spread through the crowd as the sanctuary was blown apart. Debris flew horizontally to the north and south. The deafening noise was followed by a shock wave, knocking many to the ground. Horses screamed and reared wildly. Drake pulled me to the ground, using his body to shield mine.

After several minutes, I lifted my head. There was a great deal of smoke and dust, but no flames. Two wind turbines buckled and collapsed in a twisted heap. Large portions of the outer structure tore away and careened down the sloping exterior. There was a barrage of smaller explosions in the distance as large fragments of metal and concrete struck the desert floor. Residents around us wailed. Any hopes of returning to Life World were gone, forever.

Drake helped me to my feet and inspected my body for injuries. Although there was no physical damage, he recognized the fear and anxiety in my eyes. Of the thousands of survivors, Ares and Jade had not yet appeared. I dropped back to my knees. *The Core is gone. We won the battle, but at what price?* Drake knelt beside me, placing his arm around my shoulders. He understood my grief. The Elder mentioned Drake's fascination with the past and the fall of Eden 2. He knew about those who were lost and the sadness that haunted Ulysses.

Ulysses. Prophecy. Messenger. The answer hit me all at once. I was the messenger, but I took nothing to the village. No, the message I delivered was to Panos, to the nobles of Eden 3. Ulysses called the connector a key, and indeed it was. It unlocked a sequence designed to prevent the Awakening. I sprang to my feet and raced down to the chariot. The driver steadied his horse. Ulysses had just returned to his feet.

"It was you," I shouted. "The rocket—but how?"

The Elder leaned on his cane. "Did you secure the chip as I instructed?" he asked, watching me carefully.

"Yes, exactly as you described. I gave it to Star after landing. A second trustee named Zora used Yanic to trap us during the uprising. She took it back."

He raised his chin. "Their launch window was closing. Your delaying actions caused them to panic. The trustees neglected to analyze the chip." He looked skyward. "Had they followed proper protocol, they might have discovered the modified lines of code." A mischievous grin crossed his face. "The final launch stage was coupled with a self-destruct command."

In the distance, a wind turbine succumbed to damage and tumbled down the exterior surface. We watched as it crashed through the lower cells. Eden 3—our sanctuary, our home— will never again be inhabited by humans. *The remaining Cores can no longer be united. We'll contact the other sanctuaries and stage new revolts to end noble tyranny.* There would be sacrifices in the struggle, but residents throughout the world could once again be free. I turned back to the Elder.

"She'd be proud of you."

My comment caught him by surprise. He closed his eyes as a tear rolled down his cheek. His head swayed back and forth as he recalled memories of Sable. My heart ached watching this wise and venerable old man break down. *Is there a love so powerful? How does one hold on for so long? Will his vengeance ease the pain?*

Chapter 51

Rescue

Horse-drawn wagons arrived by the dozens. Five hundred clanspeople responded to the needs of our masses. Large tents were erected, and residents were provided with food, water, and shelter. Those requiring medical attention received treatment from our physicians and clan healers. Occasional skirmishes broke out when nobles were discovered. Many shed their cloaks and attempted to blend with the crowds. Clan leaders had well-established rules to address crimes, so unruly residents were detained in holding areas and angry mobs were held at bay. Despite confusion and uncertainty, there was relative calm among the thousands of displaced souls who abandoned their home just hours before.

Drake led me to a tent where several people were gathered. We wove through a crowd to the opening. Nine men and women sat in a semicircle. A fully cloaked noble stood before them.

"This is our Village Council," Drake whispered. "They

represent us in the Congress." He pointed to a man in the center chair. "My father, Cyril, was recently elected to lead the clans."

The noble addressed the Council. He claimed to have been assaulted by several residents for no apparent reason and was demanding protection.

"What is this meeting?" I asked. "Why hasn't the noble been detained?"

"Under clan law, he is afforded a trial."

"A trial?" I repeated too loudly. "They've enslaved us for two centuries. Why is a trial needed?"

"Opal, the laws established by our Congress are meant for all. He has the right to be heard and present witnesses."

"Witnesses?" I scoffed. "The nobles will line up and attest to one another's character. You're suggesting they can be exonerated of their tyranny should a compelling case be presented?"

"Ulysses was a powerful noble. If we were standing in the shadows of Eden 2, would you want his story to be told and a fair trial granted?"

He watched my expression. When Chet exposed Star as a noble, he made his feelings clear. Had I not been there to intervene, she might have never returned. Contempt for the ruling class runs deep among residents. There'll be plenty of witnesses willing to testify against them. *If Star materializes from the ruins, will she be felled upon by resentful survivors?* Despite protections afforded under clan law, I needed to find her before some cavalier resident took matters into their own hands.

—

The dust had settled around the sanctuary, and Cyril instructed his sons to organize a search party. Drake assured me their objective was to find survivors in the ruins.

"I'm coming with you," I insisted.

Drake's older brother Ethan led the party. "She'll slow us

down," he retorted.

"On the contrary," Lake said, stepping forward. "You'll need a guide with knowledge of the sanctuary to expedite your search."

Cyril looked at my bruised face, compliments of Zora. "You've been through much already, young Opal." Apparently, he was briefed on my recent exploits. "You may not like what you discover in there."

"If my family is alive, I'll find them." My resolve was absolute.

He studied my face. "Very well."

We left on horseback. Wagons loaded with food, tools, and medical supplies accompanied our group. The last time we rode together, I assumed it was my last journey with Drake. It was now apparent our lives would somehow be intertwined. The thought brought a grin to my otherwise solemn mood.

It took less than an hour for our caravan to reach the sanctuary. I was shocked by the devastation. We maintained a fifty-foot distance from the base to avoid falling debris. Twisted metal and shattered photovoltaic cells hung from the gaping hole starting near level ten. The blast destroyed support columns, leaving large slabs of concrete stacked diagonally where the Core once stood. *There's no way anyone on the upper levels survived the explosion.* The quiet stillness was eerie.

We rounded the southeast corner of the structure, and Ethan stopped his horse. He held his arm up, signaling all to stop. I looked around Drake's shoulder at the piles of concrete and metal. The segment of wind turbine that fell now jutted out of the structure, having penetrated the lower exterior. It created a large opening but blocked direct access to the lower levels. Drake dismounted the horse then helped me to the ground. The others joined us.

"Leif, bring pry bars and torches," Ethan instructed his younger brother. "Drake, ready a draft team to remove the wreckage. This will be our entry point."

Ethan, Leif, and two others set off toward the sanctuary. Drake and another rider attached four large horses to a central horizontal pole using an elaborate set of harnesses. Thick, oval-shaped collars fit neatly around the horses' necks. The draft animals were larger in stature and had enormous hooves, thick legs, and broad, muscular chests. They were obviously engineered for brute strength as opposed to the grace and speed of our horse.

Drake steered the team using multiple sets of reins. A long thick rope lay twisted over the backs of the rear pair. The docile and cooperative nature of the animals was amazing. Drake handled them sternly but without abuse. The whole scene was amusing. *Certainly not the Out World replete with bloodthirsty, flesh-eating creatures as described in primary.* The fear-inducing narrative was perpetuated as we aged. Resident dissent was controlled by the threat of banishment—a fate purported to be worse than death itself.

I watched Ethan climb onto a pile of rubble under the twisted turbine then pull Leif up by his arm. He disappeared momentarily into the damaged hollow. Leif tossed a metal bar into the opening then turned to face us. He made several hand gestures, prompting Drake to move the team closer. After reaching the pile, Drake turned the team away from the structure and beckoned me over.

"Take the reins and keep them still."

The massive lead pair towered over me. "Are you serious?"

"If they move, tighten your grip."

The second rider followed him to the rear pair. They dragged the large rope over to Leif. The brother gathered several yards, twisting it into a coil. He spun around using momentum to hurl the rope into the opening.

The horses shifted at the movement, and I pulled the reigns, expecting to be lifted off my feet. Ethan appeared out of the hollow with the rope tied to his waist. He climbed the damaged turbine with relative ease stopping above the midpoint to secure the rope. Leif held a fist in the air.

"Hold the team," Drake directed.

The brothers worked well together. They analyzed and solved problems with incredible efficiency. Their system of gestures and hand signals allowed them to communicate silently and at great distances. If they hunted together, their unfortunate prey stood little chance of escape. I envied their close relationship.

Ethan, Leif, and the other clansmen returned from the rubble. Drake took the reins holding the lead horses.

"Well done, Opal."

He clicked his mouth and the team moved forward. The exposed turbine segment was approximately forty feet in height. Ethan obviously made similar calculations measuring the rope being laid behind. He whistled for Drake to stop, then made several loops over a bar perpendicular to the center pole. He whistled again and the team moved taking up the slack. When the rope was taught, Drake snapped the reigns and the horses bared down at the resistance. The neck collars tightened as they lowered their heads and dug hooves into soil. Every muscle in their massive bodies bulged at the strain.

The sound of twisting metal and cracking cells echoed from the opening. The turbine leaned, then recoiled. With an exerted pull by the team, it finally gave way and crashed down over the rubble. Ethan ran forward and pulled the rope knot, freeing the horses. Drake drove them away from the rising dust; their heads were held high.

Another rider took the reins and led them away. Drake picked up torches made of branches and twine then motioned for me to follow him. Ethan and Leif were surveying the opening. The fallen turbine had crushed through many lower cells, clearing a path to the interior. Ethan pointed to a flattened turbine blade bridging the damaged framework.

"We'll cross here," he said. "Move purposefully and watch for jagged edges. Opal, when we're inside, you'll provide direction."

I acknowledged his instructions. Leif knelt and struck two pieces of metal together over the torch ends. Sparks bounced onto the braided twine. After several strikes, a flame engulfed the tight balls of oil-soaked grass. He handed a torch to Ethan and kept the other. Drake climbed onto the wide blade and extended his hand.

"You're next."

He grasped my wrist and lifted me effortlessly. I stood and peered into the dark abyss. *Only hours ago, I escaped with my life.* Looking into the torn and twisted remnants, a sense of foreboding sent a shiver down my spine. I wasn't afraid of climbing through the damaged structure. My concern was over Cyril's comment. *What will we discover inside? Did the Core retaliate and unleash the T-8 arsenal? Our mission may be more recovery than rescue.*

Ethan entered first, illuminating the opening with his torch. Drake and I followed with Leif close behind. The walls of the sanctuary were much thicker than I suspected. They were constructed with parallel girders spaced nearly twelve feet apart. The outer solar cells rested on layers of overlapping steel plates. A series of conduits penetrated the plates where cell module wires converged. *The network of conduits feeds the primary electric grid. It's just as Star described. The space between girders and the grated corridors allows technicians to repair internal defects.* What I'd failed to notice during my excursion with Star were the vertical ladders connecting the levels.

"Watch your step," Drake said pointing to a jagged shaft. He jumped down next to Ethan. They helped me to the floor, and we waited for Leif to join us.

"Do you know this space?" Ethan asked.

"The sanctuary has sixteen internal levels and five sub-levels," I replied, searching the walls for identifying features. "This must be level one."

"Where do people gather?" Drake asked.

I shook my head. "The Assembly Hall is on five, but there's

no plan for this sort of catastrophe."

Ethan turned, his torch revealing an endless row of tall gray boxes. "We'll start with the Hall," he said. "Can you lead us there?"

"Lithium-titanate banks," I thought out loud.

Drake looked down the row. "What purpose do they serve?"

"Battery banks for energy storage. Ironically, the reason for my mission."

The entire space was dedicated to solar power transformation—the heart of our electric grid. With no Core to provide commands, the entire system shut down. Without electricity Life World no longer functioned.

We were alarmed by a clanking noise to our right. All three brothers turned to face the threat, lowered in defensive postures. I didn't realize their weapons were drawn until a knife reflected torchlight. They stood frozen, focused, and ready.

A familiar humming sound broke the silence. In the darkness, a fan of red lasers appeared near the floor, tracking the corridor's center line. The brothers stowed their weapons and watched curiously as the sweeping porter rolled by, oblivious to our presence. The machine was following a pre-programmed path. *Well, little fellow, I guess you'll live until your batteries are drained.* The thought gave me an idea.

"We'll follow it to the central lift station," I said. "From there we can get to the Hall."

Ethan took the lead, staying close to the sweeper. It paused occasionally when dust or small particles were detected. The vacuum whirred then wound down as it moved on.

The porter wove through the maze of corridors stopping at the lift station entranceway. Its program allowed time for the panels to open. Fortunately, they were already retracted. With the cleaning route complete, it veered toward the recharging bay. *That door will never open.* The machine would continuously transmit commands until drained. There it would remain, a dead remnant of a once vibrant and extraordinary world.

"The lifts are of no use," Drake observed.

"We'll use service corridors to work our way up," I said pointing into the darkness. "We need to go there."

Drake stayed close as we made our way to the grooming facility. He was being very protective considering we hadn't seen a single human. It was unlikely they all made their way through to the silo. Marc assumed many would retreat to living quarters when the fighting began. If so, they may have collided with ongoing battles and faced keeper squads or exploding T8s. I pushed the notion from my mind. We needed to find survivors, and fast.

The grooming facility was open, like the lift station entranceway. I presumed the panels were secured by electromagnetic locking mechanisms. Without electric current, they defaulted to an open state. If the theory held true for the elusive gateways, our journey should be much easier.

Ethan stepped into the foyer with his torch extended. It took a moment for my eyes to adjust. The gateway on the far wall was open. I hurried around the older brother intent on leading them to the service corridor. Just when I passed the male lavatory, a figure lunged out of the darkness. A keeper wrapped his arm around my throat, the rigid uniform padding pressed against my face. I squealed in pain as he applied pressure to my jaw, still tender from Zora's strike.

"Opal!" Drake shouted drawing his knife.

My attacker didn't show a weapon. He dragged me back pressing himself into the corner. I pulled at his arm gasping for air. Leif rushed into the foyer. The second torch lit up the space. Ethan circled toward the gateway. Drake crouched low, the blade of his knife pointing down. The keeper tightened his grip, cutting off my air supply.

I was nearing unconsciousness when a second keeper emerged from the opposite lavatory. My eyes widened but no sound escaped my mouth. In my oxygen-starved state, everything moved in slow motion. Drake rolled to his right and thrust his arm backward. He plunged the knife into the second keeper's abdomen. Ethan stomped his leg and waved the torch at my attacker. The keeper flinched at the movement momentarily releasing his grip. I gasped a short breath before he reapplied his hold. The distraction drew his attention away from Leif. I caught only a glimpse of his hatchet blade as it tumbled over my head and found its target.

The arm around my neck fell limp. Drake grabbed my waist and pulled me away. The keeper slumped into the corner. I held onto Drake, taking deep breaths as the brothers searched the lavatories.

"All clear," Ethan said, emerging behind us.

"Clear," Leif added.

He then stepped on his victim's chest and wrenched the hatchet free. It was a perfect strike, the blade piercing at the visor pivot point. Had it impacted an inch in either direction, the helmet's curvature might have deflected the weapon. Blood pooled around the lifeless body. Drake held me up by my shoulders.

"Are you hurt?"

"I'll be okay," I coughed.

He held my chin, examining the now aggravated bruise.

"I'm sure it looks worse than it feels," I reassured him.

He glanced at the corpse below him. "Stay next to me," he suggested.

I agreed. His tone wasn't demanding nor condescending. He wanted only to protect me. Although able to push fear aside, I was no match against the brute strength of a keeper. My reckless behavior placed us all in danger; exuberance clouded my judgment. Drake stared at me. There was a strong connection with him—a kind of certainty. *Does he feel the same?*

Chapter 52

Burden of Fate

Ethan leaned through the gateway and checked both directions. Drake held my arm as we stepped over the lifeless body. Leif backed out last, watching the foyer entrance for movement from behind. I entered the corridor and pointed north.

"That way," I said, my voice still hoarse. "To the central lift station."

Ethan acknowledged and moved quickly over the metal grating. I nearly sprinted to keep pace. Leif paused to check the south direction before hurrying to catch us. We traveled the nearly fifty yards in less than two minutes. Ethan found an opening near the central station and waited for us to reach him. When we arrived, he allowed a short rest. It was obviously for my benefit, being the only one breathing heavily. Despite my fatigue, I didn't want to delay longer than necessary. Pacing the grating, I discovered our objective just fifteen feet beyond the gateway.

The lower segment of the ladder was enclosed by a metal partition. Although it was obvious to me now, I never looked above eye level while exploring with Star.

"Over here," I announced.

The partition was secured with a locking device. Leif stepped forward with a metal pry bar. He inserted the flat end between the wall and bolt, then leaned his body against the handle. The lock gave with a loud popping sound. We pulled the partition open, and Ethan looked inside.

"The torches will slow our ascent," he said. "But we'll have difficulty judging progress in the darkness."

The ladder started two feet from the floor. "Count the rundles," I suggested. "They're spaced one foot apart. Each level is twenty feet, separated by five feet of flooring and support. Ninety-eight feet puts us at five."

"Good." Ethan flailed his torch to extinguish the flame then slid the handle into a sash loop. "Opal will follow me, then Drake. Leif, give them light to get started then join us."

Wasting no time, he mounted the ladder and started his climb. From my experience in the air vent, I knew to pace myself. *Push with the legs instead of pulling with the arms.* Cramping during the ascent might result in a fall. I stepped onto the first rundle and gripped another at shoulder level. There was no turning back.

I focused on my count and took long deep breaths during the climb. The darkness was absolute, the only sound, shuffling of leather clothing. I reached the forty-ninth rundle and stopped to rest. We were only half the distance to five, and my legs ached. Drake touched my ankle with his hand.

"Leif, hold," he whispered below. "Opal, are you okay?"

"Just need a short break."

I held the last of several deep breaths, forcing oxygen into my bloodstream. Ethan was well ahead, his movement no longer audible. He warned us to stay close. I was holding up our progress.

"Resuming now."

"Don't rush," Drake replied. "Focus on your grip."

I nodded in agreement then smirked as my hand touched the next rundle. Drake was unable to see a few inches in front of him, let alone notice my bobbing head. Reinvigorated by the break, my pace quickened. The even spacing between rundles provided a rhythmic motion during the ascent. *Push, grasp. Push, grasp.* After the break, I counted down from fifty. The exercise motivated me to keep moving.

Just as my hand touched rundle ten, a loud popping sound echoed from above. Ethan broke the lock on five then reignited his torch, providing light for the remaining climb. He helped me onto the grated walkway. Drake was close behind, followed by Leif. It took a moment to adjust to the light.

We found the gateway. I stayed close to Drake as we made our way to the lift station. Unlike on level one, both residents and keepers were present. Thirty or more torn bodies lay scattered around the lifts. The walls behind them were pocked with gaping holes and protruding bits of metal—evidence of a T8 explosion.

The Core was indiscriminate when interceding in battles. Perhaps the complete disregard for human life was psychological warfare meant to discourage uprisings. It might explain why the revolt was two and a half centuries in the making. Ares and Jade warned me the Seeker path was wrought with danger but never mentioned the slaughter of innocent residents.

"Which way to the Hall?" Ethan asked. He was on high alert, speaking without turning his head.

"Center corridor. One hundred feet ahead."

We moved quickly, staying close together. More bodies lined the corridor. This level of the Great Hall saw many of the largest battles. My chest tightened at the sight. It wasn't the blood or contorted faces that bothered me. *My actions played a role in every death.* When Jade and Ares invited me to join the Cause, I understood the risks. I accepted my fate but didn't consider how my decisions might impact others. *This is the burden Ulysses carries.*

The Hall entranceway was closed. Ethan inspected the opening and then raised an opened hand in our direction, instructing us to remain still. Holding the torch away, he pushed his ear against a panel. After several seconds he returned to our position.

"There's movement," he whispered. "It's occupied."

"What do you suggest?" I asked.

"Pry it open," Leif offered, holding out his bar.

"No, brother," Drake responded. "We'll lose the element of surprise."

"We don't know their numbers; they might be hostile," Ethan added.

Looking at the floor, I noticed streaks of blood leading up to and under the entranceway. "They're not hostile," I concluded.

"How can you be sure?" Drake asked.

I pointed to the streaks of blood. "Keepers wouldn't drag their wounded into the Hall. They're programmed to return to a central station." Leif held the metal bar in front of him. "Can I use that?" He looked to Ethan, then pushed it toward me.

We crept toward the Hall. The constantly vigilant brothers surrounded me, weapons at the ready. At the entranceway, I raised the bar and began tapping, metal to metal. The series of dots and dashes spelled out the name Ares. My father parent taught me the antiquated communication system. We had great fun at Jade's expense, assuming she never caught on.

I repeated the series three times then paused. Ethan shook his head, indicating no response. I was raising the bar for another attempt when there was a loud clanking noise behind the panel. Drake pulled me away, stepping in my place. The panel slid open less than a foot. We couldn't see anything in the darkness. Ethan pushed his torch forward, illuminating the alcove. I held my breath until a voice called from within.

"Opal?"

Gasping at the sound of her voice, I couldn't respond. The panel was pulled open. Drake stepped aside as she walked into the light.

"Jade?" My voice cracked. "Is it—really you?"

My mother parent hurried past the brothers and flung her arms around me. She squeezed tightly, causing me to grimace in pain. After holding me for half a minute, she took my shoulders and inspected my face and neck.

"You're injured."

"It's not bad," I assured her, searching her eyes. "Ares?"

She nodded rapidly. "Inside, caring for others."

Knowing both my parents were alive brought immediate relief. My comfort then quickly faded. I peered around Jade into the darkness. She had anticipated my question.

"Star is with her mother parent."

"What about . . . ?"

Her expression turned somber. There was no need for words. I lowered my head. Star was one of us, but we never spoke about our parents. She obviously knew Ares's position but never asked about Jade. It wasn't the Seeker way. If her father parent joined the revolt, then he died for the Cause—for freedom. If not, he was an innocent victim, and Star would forever blame herself for his death.

"Come with me," Jade said taking my hand.

Leading me into the Hall, she scrutinized my oddly dressed escorts. They followed in silence. We wove our way through the alcove and stopped where rows of seating began. It was quiet with only an occasional cough or moan. The torches behind us provided sparse lighting. Several males peered over the alcove walls, weapons at the ready. Jade unclipped a globe lamp from her belt and held it above her head.

Near the center stage, another lamp was activated. The light cascaded down over a small group of residents. A third lamp shown on the right, revealing more residents. Two more were activated in the seating area to our left. Soon, the lower Hall was aglow in a blue haze. Families huddled together in tight groups. I was concerned by the number of survivors staring in my direction. Maybe two thousand made it out before the launch, but so many remained inside. I hesitated to ask, perhaps not wanting to know the true outcome.

Lamps began to glow in the upper seating sections. Level five alone holds two thousand. The fact that it was nearly filled to capacity brought hope. Lights continued to appear on six and seven. Residents were scattered about and not well-organized, but they were alive.

"How many were lost?"

She didn't look at me. "Hundreds. Most of the keepers were terminated. The T-8s took their toll."

I gasped at the number.

Jade turned to me. "Opal, don't. Your actions set us free."

My head spun. "What about nobles?"

"The majority retreated to the safety and comfort of fourteen. They died when the Core exploded. Some escaped through the tunnels, others walk among us. We'll find them."

Chapter 53

Survivors

Ares knelt with open arms. Overwhelmed with emotion, I collapsed into his embrace. I was saddened by the loss of life yet relieved by the number of survivors. The whole experience was mentally and physically exhausting. I wanted to remain in his arms, and let others finish the task at hand. One week in the past, my focus was on a comprehensive skills test designed to determine my destiny. Now my future path was entirely uncertain.

For the first time in my life, I had no direction—no goals. The complete lack of structure might have crippled me with anxiety. Instead, it was liberating. *What is this sensation?* It was difficult to define. There were few memories with which to compare it. I then recalled riding through the valley with Drake, the sights, smells, and boundless sky. It was all-encompassing and empowering. I was finally experiencing . . . freedom.

"I thought we were finally rid of you," a familiar voice rang out.

Ares released me from his embrace. I ran to Star and wrapped my arms around her.

"Sorry about your father," I whispered.

She pulled away. "He saved many."

"Was he—with us?" I asked, ignoring Seeker protocol.

"Of course," she replied proudly.

Her loss was terrible. Shouldering the responsibility for his death would make it infinitely worse. I wanted to say more, to reassure her his passing was not in vain. We both endured much and would never be the same. My friend was intelligent, beautiful, and loyal but no longer innocent. Although she was stronger, part of her brightness had faded. She now had an edge to her, an underlying tension like a coiled viper prepared to strike.

"You've taken another beating," she said, inspecting my bruises with her lamp.

Before I responded, her attention was drawn behind me. Her expression changed from alarm to disbelief, then curiosity. I turned to see Drake approaching.

A smile exposed my excitement. "Drake, come meet my dearest friend. This is Star."

"Alo, Star," he offered, extending his hand.

"Hello—Drake," she muttered, staring at him intently. There was an awkward moment of silence. "You're very . . ."

"Handsome?" he finished for her. "Yes. Opal has told me many times."

Star squeaked a laugh. Completely unprepared for his response, I was immobilized by shock. My mouth dropped open, but no words came. She tilted her head at me, eyes wide. It was an unspoken accusation.

"I said it once," I huffed defensively. "You refused to speak to me, let alone acknowledge understanding." I turned to Star. "Our first meeting wasn't entirely pleasant. He acted like a barbarian."

"But a handsome one," Drake added.

My pulse raced and blood rushed to my cheeks. Star noticed my embarrassment and pursued the jabbing.

"Opal, do you find all barbarians handsome, or just this one?"

Her tormenting was unbelievable, especially in front of Drake. I dared not look at him again.

"Stop," I demanded through gritted teeth.

Although the exchange was highly uncomfortable for me, it made Star laugh. It was a consolation and distraction from the enormity of our current situation, if only for the moment.

"Drake," Ethan called from the alcove.

The three of us made our way to a group surrounding the brothers. Ares, Jade, and others were in discussion with them. The circle of residents cleared a path as we approached.

"We're organizing an evacuation," Ares said. "Opal, you'll join us on stage for the announcements. Residents know your face; it will help maintain calm."

Ethan turned to Drake. "We'll take thirty armed volunteers," he added. "They'll be positioned along the route to guide and protect the others."

"What about the injured?" I asked. "They can't make the climb."

"We're attending to them, and most are stable," Jade replied. "We'll evacuate the uninjured first."

Ares continued, "Ethan described the damage to the sanctuary. We can't be certain of structural integrity. We need to move as many as possible, and quickly."

I scanned the circle of faces nodding in agreement. Life World was no more. They realized escape was the only solution, lest the sanctuary become their tomb. The perceived fear of Out World was far outweighed by their current reality. One encouraging factor was my escorts. The oddly dressed yet well-spoken brothers served as great ambassadors to a misunderstood world. In time, we would all evolve to their level of sophistication.

"Silence please," Jade announced from the stage. "Silence." The acoustical design carried her voice throughout the Hall. After a few minutes, conversations ceased. Thirty or so residents surrounded the rise, their lamps illuminating our position. *How interesting. Just seven hours in the past, Jade stood in the same spot urging residents to join the revolt.* They listened then, they followed, and many died. Now she was back, asking them all to abandon their home.

"The Core is gone," she stated, pausing for effect. "Nobles no longer reign over your lives. You are free."

A murmur slowly spread through the crowds. Waves of applause soon followed, erupting into shouts of triumph. The collective cheers echoed through the Hall. The sound was deafening, yet wonderful. Jade and Ares waved their arms repeatedly to bring order. Slowly the celebrations waned. Jade put her arm around my shoulder.

"This is Opal, our fearless explorer who piloted her drone into the world beyond our walls."

She paused again as more cheers rang out. Most recognized me from the video feed. *Did she say fearless?*

"Her unselfish bravery serves as an example for us all."

Jade grabbed my hand and raised my arm. I waved as the applause continued. I'd never witnessed such fervor before. Surrounding me was a society in need of change, opportunity, and hope. My assumption that only Seekers recognized the oppression under which we lived was wholly abated. The images from my flight not only revealed a hospitable planet, they underscored years of lies perpetuated by the ruling class. The residents of Life World were ready to start over.

Chapter 54

New World

Leif led the first group of ten guides, each equipped with a gauntlet or shield and globe lamp. Drake took the second group, Ethan the last. The guides were positioned at fifty-foot intervals. Their lamps served as beacons, marking the return route from which we entered. After a ten-minute delay, I led a line of twenty residents along the glowing path. Star and her mother parent accompanied me. Jade and Ares remained in the Hall to organize subsequent groups for evacuation. The injured were to be removed last with assistance from family members or volunteers. Many residents nearing their fiftieth year stepped forward to help. Perhaps they considered themselves expendable. Even if they made it to the new world, their time would be short-lived.

Just as we reached the central lift station, a guide yelled out a warning. We turned to see a pair of keepers emerging from an adjacent corridor. Star drew her weapon and rushed to assist. A second guide positioned near the grooming foyer joined them. I signaled for our group to stop. We waited in silence, anticipating the sounds of a scuffle or firing gauntlets.

Star soon returned and motioned for us to come forward. I stepped out of the corridor to find the keepers standing quietly with our guides. They surrendered all weapons and removed their helmets. It was a disturbing sight. Like the sentry on sixteen, their skin was pale, heads completely void of hair. They weren't aggressive nor intimidating and watched anxiously as we approached.

"They abandoned their post," the first guide remarked. "A T-8 destroyed the remainder of their squad."

The pair looked bewildered, lost. With no communication link to the Core, their programming was useless. They received no directives nor guidance and were returned to their purely human form. Unfortunately, their genetic codes were arranged to maximize physical strength, not intellectual prowess. In this state, they were simple, childlike, and probably frightened. I felt a pang of remorse for the two terminated earlier by the brothers. They were likely in hiding, reacting to our threatening presence.

"They'll join my group," I stated. "We can position them at the ladders to assist with the injured. Star, please look after them."

She motioned for them to fall in line. They healed at her side like trained virtu-pets. She grinned and raised her brow, seeming to enjoy the power. The guides returned to their positions just as the next group joined us from the Hall.

Our precession of residents descended the ladder. On each level, guides were positioned in the service corridors to provide light and assist those in need of rest. After reaching the central lift station on one, we made the fifty-yard trek to the southern station. I gathered my group and quickly briefed them for the final stage. Star remained by my side, her head on a swivel. She was anxious, guarded, ready for anything. I felt safe having her there.

Drake greeted us at the base of the twisted turbine. Large metal boxes were stacked together creating a makeshift stairwell. One by one, residents made their way through the damaged wall into their new world. As per my suggestion, each donned their interpreters, shading their eyes from the bright sunlight. They were greeted by men and women from the clans who were eager to help. Leif rode back to the camp and returned with more wagons filled with supplies.

Star and I waited for the last of our group to depart before climbing the stairwell. Drake followed close behind. He left several guides to assist the new waves of residents arriving with regularity. Outside of the sanctuary, evacuees were loaded onto wagons for transport to the camp. Before long there was a constantly moving caravan stretching between the two sites. We remained at the opening to direct and reassure emerging residents. Most remained silent and stared blankly at the surrounding desert landscape. They were leaving the safety and security of the only home they knew. Their reward would be a new life, a new freedom—a new world.

Chapter 55

Resettlement

The evacuation of Eden 3 took two days. The majority of surviving residents had gathered in the Great Hall and followed our guides to safety. Search parties made several return trips to pull stragglers from hiding places. Twenty or so keepers were discovered wandering about aimlessly. In time, they would regain some memory and return to a semi-normal existence. None, however, escaped brain damage from the constant stream of electric current through their ports.

More help arrived from the five clans. They brought large quantities of food and supplies to the camp. Equally as important, they brought law and order. Weapons were confiscated from all combatants. The scars of battle were fresh in the minds of many who lost friends or family to the savagery, and helpless keepers fell victim to angry mobs, thirsty for revenge. Agitators were separated from the crowds and held for Judgment by a Tribunal Court. The clans had long established rules against assault on humans. Given the circumstances and testimony from other residents, most perpetrators were sentenced to temporary confinement.

Several nobles attempted to establish themselves as a governing body. They coerced many weary residents to follow them, citing their divine right proclaimed by the scriptures. One of those nobles was Panos. As usual, he was protected by the ever-present Zora. Her stature and fierce expression were enough to strike fear in residents and clanspeople alike. I never learned how they escaped the explosion on fifteen.

The two of them led a march of nobles and several dozen residents to demand autonomy from tribal law. Panos climbed aboard a wagon to begin his speech. Zora stood between him and the crowds. Unfortunately, they neglected to monitor the hospital tents behind them. He belted out his opening comments in a high-pitched, condescending tone. The crowd swelled and he was forced to respond to jeers and insults. Just as he began to recite scriptures to support his demands, a loud crack rang out from behind him. Zora turned in time to catch his lifeless body before it tumbled from the wagon. Cheers rang out from the crowds. Star dropped the gauntlet and disappeared through the tents.

My friend later faced a Tribunal where she was forced to publicly recall her torture and abuse at the hands of Panos. Ultimately, she was exonerated as Zora gleefully substantiated her claims. The sentiment was not lost on Seekers who held Star in high regard. The tales of her bravery and skills in combat made her somewhat of a hero. Three days after the trial, Zora was found dead in her bed. The cause of death was strangulation. There were no witnesses. Star was on a hunting trip with fellow Seekers at the time, or so we were told.

Cyril convened the Congress to determine the fate of our displaced residents. It was decided to divide them among the five clans based on the ratio of village populations. The Northern Clan was the largest and occupied the most land. It was rich in agriculture and could easily support a larger share. Most residents who worked in poultry production gravitated to the north. The clan also agreed to accept keepers, whose strength made them well-suited for field work.

Many residents were assigned to clans based on individual skills. Lake took his entire crew from manufacturing to the Southern Clan where metal recovery and fabrication made up a great deal of their trade. Nobles were evenly distributed to avoid an accumulation of power-hungry elitists. Although they held the same rights and privileges as everyone, they were often looked upon with suspicion and disdain. Not surprisingly, my family was invited to join the Midland Clan. Several members of the professorate followed. Star and her mother parent were included.

Before we departed from the camp, teams returned to the sanctuary. They retrieved much of the remaining poultry and fish from the holding tanks. The food was needed to support the masses on their journeys home. Some would travel for a week or more to reach their destinations. Our trip lasted three days, slowed only by the terrain and speed of the wagons. We stopped frequently for those on foot to rest and relieve themselves. Except for a small rainstorm that drenched the lot of us, the journey was uneventful.

Chapter 56

Utopia

I celebrated my fifteenth year of creation as a guest in Drake's home. When we arrived in the village, residents were temporarily assigned to local houses. It was crowded at first, with entire families occupying single rooms. Camp tents were erected in surrounding areas, providing additional shelter. The Council formed a committee to plan and develop an expansion of the village. Residents were put to work logging the local forests, and the sawmill ran around the clock. Although many trees were taken for boards, only a portion were removed from each forest stand, and new saplings were planted in their place. The loggers had to continuously travel farther distances due to established conservation rules. Clan leaders were determined not to repeat mistakes made by previous generations.

Ares formed a close relationship with Ulysses. He spent a great deal of time at the Elder's cabin reading books recovered from the lost cities. In time he would join Lake of the Southern

Clan on research expeditions into the Phoenix Valley. He always returned with more books and historic artifacts for the vault. On his most recent visit, he found an entire series on the history of aviation. Evidently, I was not the first human to take flight.

Life had improved in the three months since we abandoned the sanctuary. During the last full moon, I was invited to the Feast. Drake celebrated his manhood the month before and asked that we be joined together. He was embarrassed to learn I hadn't reached the age of consent. Although we wouldn't be officially joined for another year, we were scarcely apart.

His days were filled instructing young villagers to hunt. They spent hours in the forest identifying animal tracks, discovering trails in the brush, and mimicking bird calls. They returned to take up bows and practice shooting at bailed-grass targets. Star was his best pupil. She mastered the weapons quickly and grew impatient with the pace of his lessons. On the morning his class was to depart for the first group hunt, she disappeared. They came upon her deep in the forest standing over a large black bear. Blood stained her hands and face. She had performed her own blooding ritual for the kill. Her reputation instantly rose from skilled combatant to legendary hunter.

My experiences were less dramatic. There were large numbers of young students, and the village needed someone to organize the growth. Jade accepted the position of principal educator for an expanded primary development program. She invited me to join her as an apprentice teacher. I quickly discovered being an educator takes more than simply acquiring knowledge. Understanding how young people learn and adapting a curriculum to meet their needs required an entirely new skill set. Although it meant embarking on yet another new course of personal development, I enjoyed every moment. My lifelong dream of joining the professorate finally materialized, albeit with a younger student population.

For the remainder of residents, life evolved into a series of new routines. Many found solace working in the logging and livestock trades. Others started cottage industries: filling requests for clothing, footwear, and wooden utensils. Every member of the village was expected to contribute to the greater good, but self-sufficiency was also expected. Families tended gardens, growing vegetables, and herbs. A market was established to exchange abundant crops for other goods and services. Neighbors shared responsibilities minding children and animals. Occasional disputes arose but were managed by the Council who ruled with fairness and equality. With very few exceptions, our days were spent in harmony.

I often thought back to my former life in the sanctuary. I missed sparring with May in the mornings, stalling to stretch and snooze in the comfort of my pod. Village bread was good but didn't quite replace the flaky crusts and soft centers of our baguettes. Fresh honey was delicious, but my mouth still watered at the thought of sweet cubes. Although we saw each other every day, I missed Star's radiant smile and cheerful laughter.

Each day I took a moment to remember those lost in the revolt. Kane was so full of pride and optimism. He wouldn't have been surprised how well the drone performed. We learned that an injured Tara charged a squad of keepers, detonating a concussion orb in her hand. Her sacrifice cleared a path to the weapons depot, turning the tide of the battle. Chet and Flint finally made their way out of the sub-levels, only to be ambushed by Zora. Their ingenuity in infiltrating the keeper ranks and disrupting her plan likely extended delay of the launch. Flynn was captured attempting to destroy an air separation pipeline at the beginning of the uprising. Though he didn't survive the interrogation, his attack had been a diversion. While occupied with Flynn, no one noticed the altered vessel being inserted into the delivery porter. The oblong nitrogen tank with a shamrock etched on one end was delivered to the Core cooling reservoir ten minutes later.

The most intriguing person was the inscrutable Yanic. At times he seemed sympathetic to the Cause, but his actions were often contradictory. He was skilled at manipulation and often played both sides of the conflict. He had me convinced that Marc betrayed us by revealing the challenge and response codes. Many believe he helped bring about the end of the Core. Lake even suggested the noble was Flynn's secret contact. Yanic played his role superbly and without apology. We heard that someone fitting his description resided with the Eastern Clan. I have a strange feeling our paths will cross again someday.

Not all of these brave souls were Seekers, but all played a part in our victory. As did the thousands of residents who rose up against the nobles, against the Core—against tyranny. Many lost their lives; many more were injured. What they gave can never be repaid or replaced. We can only honor them by living the remainder of our lives to the fullest, preserving the freedom they bequeathed to us. Though most of our residents will expire at age fifty, their natural-born offspring will populate a healed planet. Their legacy will be a new world community built on equality and justice, free from oppression.

Epilogue

Our clans have lived in harmony for years. The population is growing. Many villagers and former residents have settled new territories where land and resources are plentiful. Colonies of survivors have been discovered through the expansion, which has increased trade. Fortunately, most understand the necessity of preserving earth's bounty for future generations and agreed to strict sustainability policies. Drake's father has been instrumental in creating treaties that benefit all.

Explorers in the Eastern Clan recovered a well-preserved vehicle motor from a destroyed city. Although it didn't work, it raised concerns among Council members. Ulysses spoke at a hearing, suggesting we have returned to a pioneering age without the luxury nor burden of technology. He insisted the inventions of the past would be reproduced at our peril. In response, the Clan Congress passed laws limiting the development of machines to those powered by sun, wind, water, human, or beast.

Our planet is mostly healed. We're recovering from the destruction brought on by centuries of waste and misuse. We've been given a second chance and a new opportunity to build a free society. Our people practice their beliefs and participate in rituals without restriction or interference. We choose our leaders by election, and they adhere to station time limits. Peace and prosperity exist throughout the land.

But there's a new storm rising. We've learned that former nobles have gained control of the Eastern Clan Council. Their delegates continuously challenge congressional laws and are threatening the stability of regional trade. Our ambassadors are concerned that they're co-opting outlying colonies into creating tariffs with other clans. There are rumors that some of those colonies have begun arming themselves. Cyril is working to resolve the disputes through negotiation and diplomacy. If he fails, we fear it may lead to conflict. A group of us have begun meeting in the midland valley forest to discuss a response. Our once secret organization may be the only hope for restoring order. We fought tyranny once—and won. We'll not sit by and watch the freedom we earned be destroyed.

Seekers will rise again.

About the Author

Ron Lewis enjoys a variety of books, especially those of action and adventure, appreciating an author's ability to grab the imagination and pull one into a story.

He has spent over 20 years in college administration and rediscovered his own passion for research and writing while working on his master's degree.

After completing graduate school, he dusted off old files and finished a movie screenplay started many years ago. Longing for a new challenge, he embarked on the journey of writing his first full-length novel.

Ron lives on the Treasure Coast of Florida with his wife, daughter, and Shih-Poo puppy named Archie. In their spare time, the family enjoys travel, unique dining experiences, and the occasional Segway tour.

https://www.facebook.com/ron.lewis.3152130

https://www.linkedin.com/in/ron-lewis-ms-ed-69445a233/

www.ingramcontent.com/pod-product-compliance
Lightning Source LLC
Chambersburg PA
CBHW050756190726
48285CB00005B/1680